GIVE FIRE!

*A Commander Lord
Charles Oakshott novel*

ROBERT CHALLONER

$\underline{C}$

CENTURY PUBLISHING
LONDON

First published in Great Britain in 1986 by
Century Hutchinson Ltd.
Brookmount House, 62-65 Chandos Place,
Covent Garden, London WC2N 4NW

ISBN 0 7126 0888 5

Printed in Great Britain by
Anchor Brendon Ltd, Tiptree, Essex

For the crew of the old
Jenny Darling

His Majesty's sloop-of-war 'DAISY' 18 guns

The ship is a Square-rigged Three-master. Here are the names of the sails and masts that provide her motive power:

1 Fore royal sail
2 Fore topgallant sail
3 Fore topsail
4 Foresail
5 Spritsails

6 Main royal sail
7 Main topgallant sail
8 Main topsail
9 Mainsail
10 Mizzen royal sail

11 Mizzen topgallant sail
12 Mizzen topsail
13 Mizzen sail
14 Fore topgallant mast
15 Fore topmast

16 Foremast
17 Main topgallant mast
18 Main topmast
19 Mainmast
20 Mizzen mast, with its topmast & topgallant mast

Facts and Figures about the ship
18 – 16 pounder cannons. 130 officers and men in the crew.

Dimensions: Length at gundeck, 110 feet.
　　　　　　　Breadth: 28 feet.
　　　　　　　Depth: 9 feet.
　　　　　　　385 tons burden.

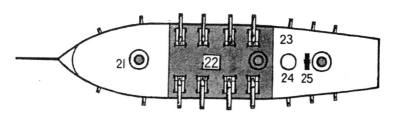

Decks: 21. Forecastle (fo'c's'le). 22. Gun deck (extends under
　　　　fo'c's'le and quarterdeck). 23. Quarterdeck. 24. Capstan.
　　　　25. Wheel.

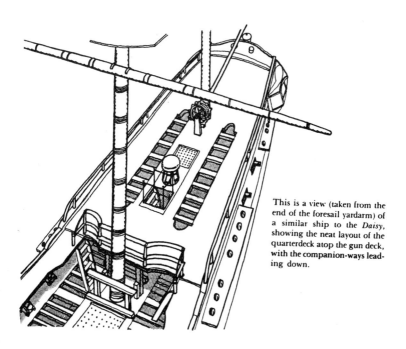

This is a view (taken from the end of the foresail yardarm) of a similar ship to the *Daisy*, showing the neat layout of the quarterdeck atop the gun deck, with the companion-ways leading down.

Part One
TO NAPLES

One

The rising star of Napoleon Bonaparte, an obscure captain of artillery, promoted to brigadier general at the age of twenty-four for his part in the taking of Toulon,* soared even higher when he led an army of ill-fed, ill-equipped, ragged, ill-shod and mostly mutinous French to the conquest of northern Italy four years later. Bonaparte, the darling of Revolutionary France, could not put a foot wrong – it seemed.

In May of 1798, sailing upon sealed orders from the Admiralty, Charles Oakshott's command, the sloop-of-war *Daisy*, eighteen guns, was proceeding southwards through the Bay of Biscay, close-hauled against a brisk south-westerly wind. It was mid-afternoon, six bells had just been sounded. The tall, powerfully-built figure of the sloop's captain stalked the leeward side of his quarterdeck: six strides for'ard, six strides aft, that was all the *Daisy* offered him in the way of exercise – and the regimen of hard tack and ship's biscuit washed down with small beer that he had taken aboard for luncheon took some walking down; for Oakshott, though the epitome of physical and mental health was, nevertheless, a martyr to a mild dyspepsia.

'Permission to lay over on the starboard tack, sir?' This from Rufus, first lieutenant and officer of the afternoon watch.

'Carry on, Mr Rufus.'

*Charles Oakshott's part in the siege of Toulon, and his curious encounter with Captain Bonaparte, is told in *Run Out the Guns* (Century, 1984).

11

'Aye, aye, sir.'

The duty watch, ushered out on deck, and helped on their way by half-playful thwacks of bosun's mates' starters (for the *Daisy*, though a tight ship, was not harshly disciplined, nor needed to be), saw to their lines as, with a flutter of spilled sails almost immediately filled out and straining again, the sloop bent grandly over to incline slightly towards the grey-blue smudge of distant coastline that was France.

The manoeuvre was well and unfussily done. Rufus, Oakshott opined to himself, was not the best Number One in the Navy by a long chalk, but he was well above average. Having served in *Daisy* for a twelvemonth, he had put in a formal request to be considered for a junior command, which Oakshott had had no hesitation in endorsing. There had been no response from on high; the application was like as not already mouldering in some pigeon-hole in Whitehall.

Six paces for'ard, six back ...

And then there was the letter from home, thought Oakshott. It burnt a hole in his coat-tail pocket, as it had done since it was brought aboard with the last postal delivery before they had warped out of Portsmouth a week previously. Anything connected with his family, with the delicate relationships that kept his entire future in a constant state of hazard, was a seed of anxiety that burned deeply into his peace of mind. And this latest missive – read and re-read at close intervals daily – was a fair example.

Six paces aft again ...

'*Sails on the port bow – fine!*' From the main topgallant lookout.

Oakshott was up on the mizzen chains in a trice and shading his eyes against the low afternoon sun. On the next wavecrest he thought he saw a glint of whiteness.

The next cry from the masthead fleshed out the first, exiguous intelligence: '*Three two-deckers! Same course as us! Can't see their colours yet!*'

Forgotten his nagging family worries, forgotten all else with the surge of fierce delight as Oakshott made the standard response to any encounter with unidentified vessels in enemy waters:

'*Beat to quarters!*'

12

The rattle of kettledrums, shrieks of bosuns' pipes, and the pattering of bare feet on holystoned deck were swiftly followed by the creak of cordage, the rumble of heavy wheels as the eighteen 16-pounder cannons that were all of the *Daisy*'s reason for being were dragged nearer the centre-line to allow for loading.

Rufus approached his commander; touched the rim of his hat. 'Ready for action, sir.'

Oakshott replaced his half-hunter in his fob pocket. 'Seventy-five seconds. Not bad, Number One.'

'Thank you, sir.'

Both their glances went to the southward, then to the figure high up on the mainmast.

No sound but the creaking of cordage, the faint sigh of straining spars, the hiss of white water under the stem. Minutes passed.

And then: '*Masthead – deck! They're Froggies!*'

'*All guns load!*'

'Search your piece! – Put home your powder! – Put home your wad! – Regard your shot! – Put home your shot! – Put home your wad! – Prick your piece!' – the cries of the gun-captains blended one with the other in a flat blare of sound so that only the ear of faith could distinguish the commands – scarcely necessary to men who could perform the evolution of loading a 16-pounder with propellant, waddings and ball in their sleep – that would make the *Daisy* like a swift wasp with eighteen deadly stings.

'All guns loaded, sir. Pricked, but not primed.'

'Very good.' Oakshott raised his telescope. The enemy's sails were well within view by now, and the lookout had made a fair assessment of their course. Two-deckers, indeed, yes. Seventy-four guns all. Probably out of Brest and heading for – where? For the Gironde? Or aiming to brave the British cruisers and, shooting the Straits under cover of night and a fair wind, to head for Toulon or Marseilles? It was his business to find out.

'Maintain the present course, Number One,' he said. 'We'll close with them and read off their names – for the record.'

'Aye, aye, sir.'

Oakshott was aware of someone standing by his side, someone who had crept up, soft-footed. Soft-footed indeed, it was his passenger – and he was literally *en pantoufle*, having no doubt come straight from his bunk in the quarter cabin, aroused from the laudanum-induced torpor in which he had been sunk for most of the time out of Portsmouth, save to rise and be seasick, or to push food unenthusiastically round his plate, or to play – and win – an exceedingly skilful series of chess games with the *Daisy*'s captain.

'More of the enemy, Oakshott?' ventured the passenger.

'Yes, the Frogs are decidedly up to something,' replied Oakshott. 'This makes six line-of-battle ships we've met up with in the Bay and all moving south. But to where, and for what reason?'

'Have you no notion?' asked the other enigmatically.

'Have you, Gisborne?' demanded Oakshott, and met the gaze of his passenger's curiously pale eyes, which, white-lashed almost like those of an albino, put him in mind of the goats that his mother used to keep as pets.

Gisborne merely smiled. The fellow was a deep one, thought Oakshott; though the hidden depths might well turn out to be hidden shallows if one took one's soundings with any skill. Certainly a fellow – forty-ish, pasty-faced, skinny, appalling bad teeth – who'd not run away with any prizes for being personable; but he had a brain inside that narrow skull, damn him for winning nine games of chess out of twelve; and he spoke of Prime Minister Pitt with the casual air of a man who lived in the pocket of the statesman who was regarded as his country's guardian in its day of need.

One wondered if Gisborne's mission had any connection with this unprecedented mustering of the French battle-ships. Or was one being fanciful?

'The Frogs are turning to port, sir!' From Rufus.

Oakshott aimed his telescope. They were turning in line, and not too badly – for Frenchies; till one recalled that the new stiffening of enemy seamanship generally – which had taken a bad tumble in the days immediately following the Revolution, when they had slaughtered the cream of their

14

officers – had been brought about by the mass conscription of Breton fishermen.

'They're for the Gironde,' said Oakshott. 'We'll follow in their wake and continue to close. They may be carrying deck cargo of some kind. Troops, perhaps. The more we know about them the better.'

The speedy sloop had by then closed the distance to within a couple of miles, so that the details of rigging, ships' boats and the tricolours that snapped from the mizzen gaffs could clearly be discerned. Also the ant-like figures that teemed on the upper decks and in the shrouds. The French squadron, upon turning, had presented its sides to a beam sea and wind – as evidenced by the quite considerable rolling that revealed the ships' copper bottoming. It was closing on eight bells, and the stormy-looking sun was as pale as a lemon against a duck-egg blue sky streaked with mares' tails.

Oakshott's servant brought two mugs of navy cocoa on deck for captain and passenger. Gisborne took his without a murmur of thanks and stood like a grey goat in the poor light, pale hands closed around the pewter mug, savouring its warmth.

'We're in their wake, sir,' prompted Rufus.

'Turn to port to follow,' said Oakshott.

'Port your helm!'

'You'd be prudent to hang on to something, Gisborne,' murmured Oakshott, as with a straining of canvas and a hissing of cordage through noisy blocks, the sails took on a new attitude to the beam wind, and the ship almost immediately heeled rakishly, rolled and heeled again – as the breaking sea crashed against her side and showered the upper deck with drenching spray.

'I – I think I'm going to be sick again!' muttered Gisborne, clinging like death to a shroud, his mug of cocoa dropped and forgotten.

'Do it over the lee side,' responded Oakshott unfeelingly, 'or you'll get your own back.'

The technique of close shadowing – one of the primary occupations of light naval craft in wartime – is to probe without undue annoyance, so as not to bring down the wrath of the bigger vessel; it was a convention which worked pretty well on a quid pro quo basis; a line-of-battle ship might compare the annoyance from such as the *Daisy* to that of a horse-fly threatening the rump of a well-horned bull; sufficient, in the bull's case, to dissuade the irritant with a lash of his tail; but to turn and present the full magnificence of the cornu at the fast-moving insect was an over-exuberance bordering on the absurd.

This mutually accepted ground rule being observed on this occasion, the *Daisy* closed with her quarry almost to within gun range, while the ship's three midshipmen – always on the alert for a chance to shine – were grouped up for'ard, telescopes aimed at the transom of the tail-end Frenchman, vying to be first to read off the name.

It was the senior among them – Charteris, who had been in *Daisy* throughout the commissioning – who won the game:

'*Le Mercure*, sir.'

'Thank you, Mr Charteris. Any deck cargo – troops?'

'Not a sign, sir. Nothing but a gaggle of Frog matelots gawping back at us as if they'd never seen real human beings before.' This contemptuous sally won him a snigger from his messmates.

'Number one's called *Le Guerrier*, sir!' piped the smallest and youngest of the mids, by name Thompson. 'Nothing extra on deck.'

'Very good,' said Oakshott. He turned to Rufus. 'We'll leave it at that, Number One. Stand by to wear ship.'

'Aye, aye, sir.'

A groan from the mizzen chains directed Oakshott's attention to his passenger: Gisborne was sprawled there like an elongated spider, long thin arms clutching at the cordage, head and shoulders bowed over the coaming, face down and staring into the boisterous waters of Biscay; an agonized spasm distorted his skinny form and he drummed his slippered feet in the agony of his retching; Oakshott, who was almost a complete stranger to seasickness, found it in his heart to feel compassion for the wretched victim.

'Bear with me in patience, Gisborne,' he said. 'The motion won't be so bad when we're close-hauled again.'

16

Rufus caught his eye. 'Ready, sir!'

'Wear ship, Number One!'

The helm was put over. The sails blossomed as, turning her elegant stern to the wind, *Daisy* ran before it for a few moments, went into the second part of the one-hundred-and-eighty-degree manoeuvre; the yards came across, well controlled by their sheets; the ship gave an almighty roll as she took the last of the oncoming waves on the windward bow – then stiffened, sails taut and thrumming like wet washing on a line.

'Nicely done,' said Oakshott.

He turned to throw an encouraging word at Gisborne.

Of the *Daisy*'s passenger there was no sign ...

'*Man overboard!*' came the cry from the masthead.

The convention attached to the difficult manoeuvre of picking up a man in the water under the very nose of the enemy had in it certain unwritten clauses. Since it called for either the lowering of a boat, or at best bringing the ship to a halt in the water, there was considerable risk involved. The first condition to be taken into account – and Oakshott did so – was whether the man was alive and swimming, for if not the ship would be put in hazard to no purpose.

It transpired that Gisborne could swim – or at least flounder. He was doing so, and waving frantically, two cables astern and falling back fast.

'Stand by to go about!' ordered Oakshott, thereby accepting the second, unwritten condition – scarcely spoken of – which was that a ship and her crew should never be put at risk for the sake of some fool of a common seaman who has been clumsy enough to fall overboard. For a commissioned officer – perhaps. For a midshipman – doubtful.

He met his First Lieutenant's inquiring eye.

'He's our only reason for being here, Mr Rufus,' he said. 'If we lose him, we might as well turn around and go back to Portsmouth.'

The *Daisy* went about again. And that was not all ...

'The *Mercure*'s turning, sir!' shouted Charteris from the bow.

'Oh, my God!' breathed Oakshott.

He sized up the situation in one glance. In that one glance, his keenly arithmetical mind accepted the equation and resolved the possible options open to him.

The man in the water – rising on wavecrests and falling from sight in the troughs, but continuing to wave, and no doubt yell his head off – was roughly equidistant from the oncoming *Daisy* and the tail-end Frenchman, who was in the act of wearing after the recent manner of the British sloop.

Lowering a boat, and the attendant delays, was out of the question. The slower battleship would be within range of everything down to pistol shot and the galley kettle before the boat was hooked back on again. The only chance – and it was so fraught with hazard as to cause the hairs on Oakshott's nape to stiffen – would be to put the *Daisy* in irons and still in the water alongside the swimmer – *at the first attempt!* – and accept whatever drubbing the *Mercure* might throw their way from bow-chasers. There was also the dreadful prospect of the enemy turning to fire a thirty-seven-gun broadside and reducing the *Daisy* to matchwood with one blow!

The white face in the water was directly in line with the sloop's bowsprit; the *Mercure* had completed its turn and was coming on on a reciprocal course.

'Steady as you go!' said Oakshott. The dice having been cast, he was all coolness. 'Have plenty of lines ready, and plenty of lively movers to get down there and grab at him. *And run out the guns!*'

By lively movers Oakshott referred to those members of the crew – known to him by name and repute – who could best be relied upon in a tight corner that called for supreme agility, physical strength and almost animal courage – or, alternatively, courage of the intellectual and analytical sort that the captain of the *Daisy* himself possessed.

In such a class belonged Bosun Cox, but his place was at the wheel – and, in any event, that veteran of a score of grim encounters with sea and enemy, in which his faculties had been strained to the limit – and a fair piece beyond, often – was a mite too long in the tooth for swarming down a rope's

18

end and assisting a half-drowned man back up again in a hurry.

Prime amongst the lively movers was Topman Tom Mudge, another *Daisy* veteran, pressganged at Oakshott's orders on his wedding morn in Dartmouth – but who nevertheless yielded to no man in his regard for his captain. This bull of a man was already over the side and clinging to his line, one foot braced against the bulwarks, the other trailing in the sea that surged past, before the order had scarcely passed Oakshott's lips.

The Frenchman came on. Sailing close-hauled on a good point, with white water creaming at the stem, the enemy must soon be within gun range with her bow-chasers – weapons that the *Daisy* did not carry: snub-nosed, light guns after the pattern of the British carronade, devastating at short range and capable of projecting a massive shot of sixty pounds and more, and extremely manoeuvrable. Oakshott could see the crews grouped around these pieces, right for'ard, one to each bow, port and starboard.

No time for contemplating what was to be, that was all in the hands of Providence; Oakshott dragged his gaze away from those two open maws that bore down upon him and must soon erupt – to the man who wallowed in the rising seas scarcely more than a ship's length ahead.

He called to Bosun Cox to put up his helm, but this worthy, nicely anticipating the order, was already bracing himself, and nodding to his two acolytes to do likewise. The order given, all three men bore down on the great double wheel. The *Daisy* spun like a top, so fickle and fine her responses to her rudder. Clawing her way relentlessly into the wind, she immediately lost her onward impetus; slowed, stopped with the sails backed.

The manoeuvre, considering the conditions, could scarcely have been more brilliantly executed: the sloop-of-war wallowed in the trough of a long wave, halted in the water, with her wretched passenger almost within reach of the hands that were extended to grab at him.

It was clear from his movements, from the ashen-faced fatigue, the staring eyes, the slack mouth, that Gisborne was at the end of his tether. It was likely that, had the *Daisy* been obliged to go about and about again, they would have found him gone below when they returned. As it was, Tom Mudge's massive arm reached out, his calloused hands grabbed hold of a hank of the wretched man's pigtailed hair, and dragged him to the safety of the rope.

At that same instant, the Frenchman's bow-chasers opened fire, one following the other in quick succession.

Impact came swiftly on the heels of discharge. Aft on the deck, Oakshott felt the wounds inflicted on his ship as nearly as if the iron had entered his own body. The *Daisy* tossed like a frightened horse as the two hurtling spheres crashed into her bows; the first demolishing the heads and unseating the bowsprit, coming to rest against the step of the foremast; the second sweeping along the fo'c'sle deck, carrying with it stanchions, guard rails and cordage, but miraculously passing over the side without doing any grave damage to ship or crewmen.

'Is he aboard?' shouted Oakshott.

Mudge's grinning, bovine countenance appeared over the coaming.

'All aboard and as right as a trivet, sir!' he cried – and produced a hand that held – supported – a now unconscious passenger by his hair.

A swift glance towards the Frenchman – now so near that he could see the expressions on the faces of the men ramming home the next charges of the bow-chasers – told Oakshott that the game was running to its close – one way or another.

One desperate stroke still remained to him ...

He called the order to pay off to starboard, hopeful that the *Daisy* would quickly respond and take up the wind again: she prettily obliged.

For a few brief seconds the sloop moved into a position when the entire length of her port side was presented to the oncoming Frenchman; anticipating this, Oakshott was at the quarterdeck rail and looking down into the gundeck, where groups of anxious faces were turned up to regard him, all grouped about their pieces; all crouching, naked torsos gleaming with sweat of effort, their slow-matches spluttering and spitting burning saltpetre – waiting in patient discipline for the order.

20

'We'll give the Frog a taste of a broadside, lads!' cried Oakshott. 'Fire when you bear!'

In succession – as the oncoming bows of the enemy ship passed before their gun-ports, the gun-captains called to their linstock men to apply match to priming powder, priming powder to charge, exploding charge to ball:

'*Give fire!*' Joyfully and exultantly.

'*Give fire!*' An echo of the same.

All along the port side of the turning – still turning – sloop, the 16-pounders cascaded into flame and acrid gunsmoke, as one by one the nine guns that could be brought to bear savaged the big seventy-four. Oakshott saw the *Mercure*'s starboard bow-chaser struck squarely and overturn midst a gallimaufry of rent rags and torn flesh; the enemy's foresail was miraculously peppered with a pattern of gaping holes; one ball cannoned off the mainmast at head-level, carrying away enough wood splinters to make a coffin lid.

And then they were gone away. Before the remaining bow-chaser could be brought into action, before the French captain could bring his ship broadside on to the speeding Englishman: the bull impotently presenting his horns to the stinging horse-fly.

When they were well clear, Topman Mudge knuckled his forelock to his captain.

'Passenger safely down below and fast asleep, sir,' he intoned.

'Well done, Mudge,' responded Oakshott. He grinned. 'You must surely be the only man in recorded history who ever carried a Knight Commander of The Most Honourable Order of the Bath around by his hair!'

Ding-ding. Ding-ding ...

Four bells of the first watch. Alone in his stern cabin, Oakshott pushed aside his half-eaten supper of the inevitable hard tack and ship's biscuit with its attendant weevils – and the little devils, in this particular batch, did not appear to quit their gritty abode when the biscuit was tapped upon the table edge. He had the wayward thought that, all his life, he had made an accommodation for small and obstreperous insects (not that weevils were noisy, only a nuisance): the death watch beetle, for instance, ran riot in the old family home, and one had practically been brought up with the tap-tap-tapping of the creature's head against the panelling. And, of all things, the death watch had followed him aboard the *Daisy*, nor all the efforts of Ship's Carpenter Henshawe had been able to eradicate him throughout the relatively long and happy commission.

Oakshott poured himself another measure of brandy, consoling himself that, after such a day as he had had, he was entitled to get a little tiddly and maudlin.

Back there in the quarter cabin, by grace of good seamanship and Topman Mudge's strong right arm, Sir Manvers Gisborne, KCB slept the sleep of the unworthy, having set ship and crew and his own mission to the Mediterranean (whatever *that* was!) in hazard by getting sick, incapable, and falling overboard.

A dark one, that Gisborne. No Member of Parliament, he – but clearly one who stalked close to the seats of power. He spoke of Pitt as one speaks of one's most intimate associates. There was a time, also – the *Daisy* was only a day out of Portsmouth – when Gisborne had left lying around on this very table that they sometimes shared, a letter with the superscription: *From His Majesty's Private Secretary, Windsor Castle.* Come to think of it, the fellow might well have purposely left it for him to see: that, along with the talk of Pitt, a ruse to impress – and by a fellow who was, by appearance and manner of address, not an impressive sort. Yet there must be something in that narrow head: the mastery in chess and the KCB might well go hand in hand.

And what of his mission to the Mediterranean?

Oakshott harked back to his own summons to the Flag Officer in Command, Portsmouth. He had been interviewed by the admiral's secretary; given verbal orders to receive aboard as passenger Sir Manvers Gisborne and proceed with all haste to Naples, there to remain till Gisborne had taken counsel with the British Ambassador to the Kingdom of the Two Sicilies, Sir William Hamilton. Next, upon instruction from either Gisborne or Hamilton (that was not made clear), he was to put to sea again.

And, upon losing sight of land, he was to open his sealed orders.

Oakshott reached out behind him and, lifting the lid of his old melon-topped sea chest, unlocked a drawer within and took out a sealed package wrapped in fine, transparent yellow oilskin.

The superscription, penned in a laboured clerkish hand, read:

Cdr Ld Chas Oakshott, RN
Officer Commanding HM Sloop-of-War 'Daisy'
To be opened upon leaving Naples, as per verbal orders.

He dropped the package back into the drawer and relocked it. Sufficient unto the day is the evil thereof.

From there, it was but a hand's breadth to his coat-tail pocket and the letter from what he supposed he still regarded as his home; though all of miasma-reeking Sennett Palace was irremediably depressing to him: the sagging roofs, rain-puddled stone floors; the Grey Ghost who was reputed to stalk when an Oakshott was about to die; his older brother, the incumbent marquess, temporarily reprieved by a marriage that he – Charles – had engineered with an excellently well-chosen daughter of an archdeacon, but now reduced to a brandy-sodden, pasteboard clown out of a toy theatre: fit only to sit in his high-backed chair and mutely gaze upon his estate collapsing about him, nodding and becking and chomping his toothless gums.

Wearily, Oakshott unfolded the letter for the umpteenth time. His sister-in-law's familiar, careful writing – the ink now smudged in places by spots of sea-water – stared up at him:

Dearest Charlie,
It is with a sad heart I have to tell you that our dearest little Charlie has taken sick and we fear for his life. Myself, I think it is on account of the unhealthy drains here at Sennett. Dr Constable opines likewise, and I would take him away to Bath for the waters, but where to find the monies for board and lodgings in Bath which is so ruinously dear?

I had raised 100£ by sale of willows in the stew pond, but was needed to thatch the cottages in South End, since the tenants gathered outside the gates & threatened violence if twas not done. I had thought me like Qu. Mary Antoinette at the openg. of the Fr. Revolution, and feared for all our safetys. Had I still that 100£, I could have betaken little Charlie to Bath. Still, all is not lost. I will endeavour to raise money on the estate by some means.

How can the ignorant envy the aristocracy in marble halls, not knowing the poverty as may go with the resounding title . . .?

Amen to that, thought Oakshott. He folded up the letter and replaced it. No mention, there, of his brother Jack, who was scarce likely to survive another twelvemonth. And after that – what? Young Charlie, the only defence against the damned marquisate and Sennett falling upon his – Charlie Senior's – shoulders, might already have succumbed to his malady.

So do the wiles and stratagems of cunning Man so often come to naught!

The bell clanged up on deck. Slipping his feet into his boots and clapping on his hat, Oakshott went up and joined the officer of the watch and quartermasters. The OOW – Lieutenant Shacklock – saluted his captain.

'Fine night, sir. And making good headway. Nothing in sight.'

Oakshott nodded. Shacklock had been a midshipman at the beginning of the *Daisy*'s commission, and a thoroughly unpromising specimen of that much-maligned breed to boot: scrawny, pimpled, sly and grubby. How had such an ugly duckling turned into a fine upstanding young cob like this? Nature was a wonderful thing. Might not little Charlie Oakshott similarly metamorphose from his sickly beginning (always supposing he had not been gathered in since his mother dispatched the letter) to a sturdy young seventh Marquess of Uffingham and Bow? The prospect of it was decidedly brightening.

Oakshott pissed over the leeward side, and went below.

'Call me according to my standing orders, Mr Shacklock,' he said.

24

'Aye, aye, sir. Good night.'

'Good night, Shacklock.'

Down below, kneeling by his cot, Oakshott said his customary prayers, then extemporized a short codicil:

'... and, if it be Thy Will, to preserve the life and health of little Lord Charlie Oakshott, for Thou knowest the special kinship in which we stand ...'

His last thought, lulled by the gentle motion of the ship, and before sleep overtook him, was that he must order work to begin on repairing the bowsprit and for'ard end on the morrow – sea and weather permitting.

Two

The *Daisy* shot the Pillars of Hercules in one broad reach, sighting the humped spine of the Rock in the dawn's light. Oakshott was on deck and making an al fresco breakfast of biscuit dipped in cocoa when Gisborne came up. The emissary – ambassador, commissioner? – had changed from his customary fustian into an extremely handsome coat of striped velvet, lemon-coloured waistcoat, nankeen breeches and striped stockings, over which he wore a silk-lined cloak with a fur collar. And a tall hat. Quite the Macaroni.

They greeted each other. 'When shall we arrive in Gibraltar, Oakshott?' asked the passenger.

'By noon, if the wind holds,' opined Oakshott.

'I'm straight for the Governor,' said Gisborne. 'Your orders, I believe, are to report to the Admiral Commanding.'

'That is so.' Oakshott dipped his biscuit into the steaming hot brew and let it rest there a while, to drown and broil the weevils.

Presently he became aware that the other's goat-like eyes were covertly upon him; nor did the other look away when Oakshott met the challenging gaze.

'Have you had much record of action in this ship since you commanded her?' asked Gisborne.

'Since Toulon, not a great deal,' replied Oakshott. 'An affair such as Toulon might occur only once in a commission. The rest – as far as the *Daisy*'s concerned – has been the workaday business of patrol and escort, patrol and escort, that makes up the daily round of a minor ship-of-war. I doubt me if we've had more than two weeks alongside a

26

wall in the last twelvemonth – but I'd have to consult the ship's log before I'd give my oath on it.'

'But you, yourself, have seen much action – much in the way of fighting?' persisted the other – and there was real persistence in his tone, as Oakshott readily perceived.

Oakshott shrugged. 'A little,' he conceded. 'It's unavoidable.'

The other's nose – long, pale and touching tapir-like – narrowed at the nostrils as he drew breath with a sudden annoyance, but he did not pursue that particular line of questioning; instead:

'Are you well acquainted with Nelson? I ask this because he appears to know you uncommonly well.'

'I'm surprised to hear it,' replied Oakshott, 'since we have met only once, when he was on the Selection Board at my promotion from lieutenant.

'Why do you ask, sir?' There was a keen edge to his question, and Gisborne discerned it. Then the latter gave a start of surprise, as the captain of the *Daisy* fixed him with a cold and unwavering glance, one eyebrow raised.

'Bless my soul!' exclaimed he. 'I always sensed there was something odd about your looks, Oakshott, and now I have it. You've got one blue eye and one brown!'

Oakshott, a trifle abashed, looked away. 'It runs in my family,' he muttered.

After a while, Gisborne said: 'Anyhow, touching upon my question about your acquaintance with Sir Horatio, I have to tell you that, when the issue arose of who was to convey me on my Mediterranean mission, it was his word that swung the balance.'

'I'm grateful to Sir Horatio,' said Oakshott. 'The admiral's more than generous.'

And there the conversation languished and died. And the morning sun, rising out from behind the Rock of Gibraltar, directed breathtaking fans of light across the wrinkled sea towards the speeding sloop, so that the merest wavelet was touched with its glory, and every man who saw it was elevated in spirit.

They warped against the southern mole shortly after noon.

27

Oakshott and his passenger took luncheon together from the proceeds of a swift dash ashore by the captain's enterprising servant – one Bantock – who secured in no time a dozen eggs, fresh vegetables and fruit, and a loaf of new-baked white bread. The resulting and most excellent repast consumed, the two men climbed aboard a summoned carriage and went to keep their respective appointments.

'Do you know Gibraltar, Gisborne?' asked Oakshott as they trundled out of the dockyard, high-walled and already reflecting the heat of the morning sun.

'I do not,' replied the other. 'Hot climes I find overly weakening to the spirit. I confess I have never been further south than Cornwall. There was no Grand Tour for me.'

Their driver, a Latin-looking individual, sizing up the two Englishmen and placing them in a discernibly high social status, interposed upon their discourse most helpfully:

'Gentlemens, we are now going along Main Street,' he said. 'And I tell you all things of interest. No extra charge.'

'How kind,' drawled Gisborne.

They passed under an archway into a narrow street. The height of its surrounding buildings, with their shuttered silence, meant that they were mostly moving through shadow.

'Shall you be able to tell me more about your mission,' asked Oakshott, 'when you have spoken with the Governor?'

'No,' replied the other, *tout court*.

'We are coming to cathedral,' intoned the driver and guide from the corner of his mouth. 'Cathedral of St Mary the Crowned, called Spanish Church. Used to be Moorish mosque till Spaniards capture Gibraltar, knock down mosque and build cathedral. When British capture Gibraltar, Spaniards bombard Rock, knock down cathedral. British build it again. I – Luis Villa – baptized there. God save King George!'

'Does it in any way concern – this mission of yours – the quite unprecedented movement of French battleships we encountered in the Bay?' asked Oakshott.

'Perhaps.' The other smiled enigmatically.

'I ask – merely because you seemed to imply that it might,'

persisted Oakshott. 'Or did I only fancy it?'

Gisborne smiled and looked ahead of him.

'Convent Place,' announced their driver. 'Residence of His Excellency the Governor. The building once house of the Franciscans. All things pass. It was ever so.'

'This is where you get out, Gisborne,' said Oakshott.

'Navy House and residence of admiral across street,' said the most helpful Luis Villa. 'Pity about admiral. Nice man.'

'Pity?' repeated Oakshott. 'Why – what happened to him?'

'Last week he die,' replied the driver. 'That will be eightpence for both gentlemens. Tips not included.'

Navy House was high-ceilinged, whitewashed inside and out. They kept Oakshott cooling his heels for ten minutes, he was then ushered by a marine corporal into a room with a wide window and verandah overlooking the Straits, with the humped forms of Africa in the violet distance under a staggering display of anvil-topped clouds.

Oakshott was received by a civilian functionary who introduced himself as Senior Admiralty Clerk Freakson – accenting the *Senior* most pointedly.

'I heard with great regret that the admiral ...' began Oakshott.

'Alas, Lord Charles, it was a great shock to us all,' interposed Freakson, who was a small, spindly man with a villainous squint behind pebble spectacles, wearing the seedy, shiny-elbowed black coat that seemed always to go with the position of Admiralty clerk. 'In the midst of life we are in death, or words to that effect. Sir Gervase rose from dinner table hale and hearty and was dead before midnight of what the doctor called a monstrous assault upon the brain.

'By the way, sir, you have a first lieutenant name of Rufus.'

'That is so.'

'I have received a signal appointing Lieutenant Rufus to the schooner *Muckle*, five guns, as Commanding Officer.'

'Well, Rufus will be pleased,' said Oakshott. And felt pleased for him. 'Where is *Muckle* lying now, Mr Freakson?'

The other brightened, tapped the side of his nose in a knowing manner and opened up a drawer of his desk, where innumerable small sheets of cards were packed in together, tagged with coloured flags and grouped under the letters of the alphabet from A to Z.

'Method, Lord Charles,' said the clerk. 'Method – method – method! You gentlemen who sweep the seas for England have your ways, we who are your bulwarks, upon whose shoulders you may build bridges, have our ways also. And they are informed by – *method!*'

'I'm greatly impressed,' murmured Oakshott, amused.

The functionary riffled through the cards and presently drew one forth with a small exclamation of triumph.

'Ha! HM Schooner *Muckle*, five guns,' declared he. 'Arrived Gibraltar on the seventeenth, and took up a berth alongside the south mole.'

'Well, that's handy,' said Oakshott. 'Rufus will be able to get his traps transferred straight away and sleep aboard his own command tonight. And now, as to his replacement – who's ... ?'

'Oh, dear me!' said Freakson, who had espied another item on the card. 'How very unfortunate.'

'What is unfortunate, Mr Freakson?' asked Oakshott.

'The *Muckle* sailed from Gibraltar the day before yesterday,' responded the other.

'And when will she be back?'

'Um – she will not, sir. She's for Portsmouth – to join the Home Fleet.'

Freakson's much-vaunted 'method', which had in truth elicited that poor Rufus had come all the way to Gibraltar only to have to chase his ship back from whence he came – was not equal to the question of how, and by whom, Oakshott was to replace his first lieutenant, save that the senior clerk was of the vague persuasion that such an officer might be available in Naples, where, thanks to the excellent terms with which Sir William and Lady Hamilton stood with the Royal Family, the Navy had till quite recently been received with favour in this neutral port. Yes, he opined, Lord Charles might very well find a replacement officer in Naples.

Lord Charles, who was of the opinion that Freakson was simply fobbing him off, abruptly changed the subject:

'I should like you, Mr Freakson,' he said, 'to dispatch a short memorandum for Admiralty which I have concocted. Let it go by the next ship to leave – and, since Lieutenant Rufus will presumably be travelling in pursuit of his ship, it had perhaps best be put into his charge.'

'Might I inquire of the substance of this memorandum, sir?'

'It concerns the activities of French line-of-battle ships in the Bay of Biscay,' replied Oakshott. 'The movement south of – by my own observation – five seventy-fours and one eighty. From Brest to St Nazaire, the Gironde. Southwards. Towards the Mediterranean. It seems to me like a fleet muster. Toulon or Marseilles. The Admiralty should be told. Perhaps, in conjunction with our spy system, which, as I understand, Mr Pitt has raised to a very high order, my observations may help to flesh out some dastardly plan that the Frogs have simmering – a landing at Naples, for instance. What do you think, Mr Freakson?'

Freakson was most willing to cooperate in the enterprise. Let Lord Charles place the memorandum in his hands, he said, and he would ensure that it was dispatched to England in the first fast ship to leave. And Lieutenant Rufus, in pursuit of his new command, would travel with it and be instructed to deliver same to Whitehall in person.

Oakshott handed over the memorandum and departed with a clear conscience of having performed his duty as he saw it; while Senior Clerk Freakson, pursuing his method, addressed himself to filing away the missive in such a manner that it must inevitably present itself as soon as the dispatch of the next fast ship to England passed through his hands, together with the cargo – human and inanimate – which would be on her bill of loading.

Oakshott who, eschewing a carriage, strolled through the quiet, shadowed streets back to the dockyard, bought himself a large bunch of luscious black grapes from a pretty Spanish girl on the way, and ate them in the Alemeda Gardens. He would have been less than happy if he had seen that the short-sighted and fundamentally inept senior clerk had filed his memorandum (mumbling all the time: 'Method – method, that's the ticket!') under the general heading:

31

England – but not, as he had intended, under *England, Sailings for* – but under *England, Quarterly inventory of Naval Stores to be requested from.*

It was Oakshott's custom, throughout the *Daisy*'s commissioning, to invite his officers to dinner at his expense on the last night in port when the ship was fair to bursting at the seams with fresh food and clean water (very speedily to be consumed by 130 officers and men of voracious appetite). These eve-of-sailing dinners were held in his stern cabin, the only sizeable compartment in the single-decked vessel that provided for his officers – most of them gently reared – scarcely better accommodation than the Jack Tars, that's to say about the level of prison or the workhouse – with, as Dr Johnson had pointed out, concomitant hazards thrown in. It had once been Oakshott's thought to turn over the stern cabin as a wardroom mess for all his officers' general use; but wiser counsel prevailed when it occurred to him that to set such a precedent would be to lay himself open to the obloquy of every small-ship captain in the fleet.

Dinner, the ingredients specially procured ashore by the captain's egregious servant Bantock, comprised on this occasion a fine hindquarter of Spanish fighting bull that had lately graced the ring in Algeciras, preceded by a beef soup largely fractionated from the same source and spiced with various Indian condiments from the captain's own chest. The main course was accompanied by an abundance of vegetables which, after the manner of men who lived most of the time on a diet of hard tack and biscuit, was greatly appreciated as a visual display, but largely eschewed by the diners, who went for the beef in large slices – all cut by themselves, round the table.

The meal progressing, and empty bellies largely having been filled, and the good raw wine of Spain having loosened tongues, the general conversation turned to speculations about their port of destination. Gisborne – guest of honour at the feast – proved to be a most bounteous fund of information on Naples, the Kingdom of the Two Sicilies of which it was the capital, the internal politics of the Italian peninsula, the progress of the war, and the personages involved therein. Though, as he freely admitted, he had himself set foot no further south than Southsea.

It quickly became plain, furthermore, that this loquacious Knight of the Bath had imbibed enough of the heady wine of southern Spain to make him – indiscreet ...

'To put it plain,' said he, 'Naples is ruled by King Ferdinand, whose brothers were mad and who was himself bereft of any education lest the strain of study would drive him insane also. Ferdinand in turn is ruled by his wife, sister of the late Marie Antoinette. This lady's method is to nag and berate her spouse till he performs her will. To a very large degree, Queen Marie Carolina is, in her turn, ruled by the wife of the British Ambassador.'

'And who is she, sir?' asked Oakshott.

'One Lady Hamilton, sir, wife of Sir William, who bought her from his nephew.'

'Bought her, sir – did you say "*bought* her"?'

'As good as. She was his nephew's mistress and had a bastard of him – or someone. Hamilton settled a fortune on the nephew and married the strumpet – albeit that she was twenty-six at the time, and he sixty-one.'

A silence that was significantly deeper than mere silence fell upon the table at the utterance of the epithet 'strumpet', for to raise the topic of the fair sex in the mess was solecism enough, but to impugn a woman's virtue, particularly that of a woman of title, at an officers' dinner in one of His Majesty's ships, was only to be compared with belching at the Communion rail.

To compound his fault, Gisborne appeared not to notice that he had given offence; or if he did, gave not a damn. Indeed, from the way his pale, goatish eyes slid sidelong up and down the table and his thin lips pursed in a puckish smile, one would have thought that he was thoroughly enjoying himself by deliberately teasing and taunting this circle of frowning, taut-lipped seafarers.

'When I say "strumpet", I speak advisedly,' he continued. 'In Whitehall, we have a dossier on her ladyship that pre-dates her present eminence. Kitchen skivvy at twelve. Graduating to posing in a transparent shift as the "Goddess of Health" for that charlatan Dr Graham's lectures at the

Adelphi. Then the besotting of Hamilton's nephew. Romney, also, fell for her charms and has painted her innumerable times. And then came Sir William.

'And others.'

He took a long draught of his wine and peered about him, amusedly, over the rim of the glass.

Oakshott cleared his throat and opined that it might well be a fine day on the morrow. This suggestion was taken up by Mr Quinch, the ship's sail master and arguably the only one present not of genteel birth; though, being older than any, and by religion of the Fundamentalist persuasion, more put down than most by the line of the guest of honour's discourse. Quinch also opined that the weather might well be fine in the morning, and that, should the wind hold, the ship might well make the entire passage on a landsman's reach. No one having a ready-made observation at hand to cap that, Gisborne was able to return to his scandalous diatribe.

'And when I say there were others,' he drawled, as if the topic of wind and weather had never been introduced, 'I could mention a specific name which might well cause a rustle of interest around this very table.' He paused and looked about him, soliciting interest.

'More wine, sir?' asked Oakshott mildly, passing the decanter.

The other took the vessel without thanks, replenished his glass and continued his peroration: 'As I have said, Naples – that's to say the Kingdom of the Two Sicilies – is ruled, in ascending order, by dunderhead Ferdinand, his harpie queen, and Lady H.

'The key, however, to the conundrum, as to why Lady H. has such pull with the Neapolitan Royals is – you cannot have guessed it, gentlemen – the Royal Navy!

'You are surprised? Consider. Naples and the Kingdom of the Two Sicilies are literally at the mercy of the predominant naval power in the Mediterranean. At the time of which I am speaking, which was during the Toulon affair – of which my friend Lord Charles Oakshott and the majority of you gentlemen have first-hand knowledge – the Royal Navy reigned supreme in these waters. That, gentlemen, was – and

34

still is to a degree – the basis, the bedrock, of the strumpet's power.' He sniggered and took a deep pull at his wine.

Whatever I do, thought Oakshott, I mustn't lose my temper with this unmannerly oaf, for not only is he the guest of honour at my table, but he's Pitt's confidant, the emissary for whatever mission we are upon, and almost certainly possessing enough pull to ruin me professionally. One must simply bite on the bullet and endure.

'To Naples, at the time of the Toulon affair,' said Gisborne, leering about him, 'there came the third-rater battleship HMS *Agamemnon*, sixty-four guns. Captain, Horatio Nelson. We are not privy to what transpired – even the confidential dossier in Whitehall is not privy – during the five days that the *Agamemnon* was anchored in the Naples roads, but the upshot of it was that Captain Nelson persuaded someone or other, and someone or other persuaded Queen Maria Carolina, who shrieked and vexed her poor husband into dispatching six thousand of his mostly unwilling soldiery to the defence of Toulon against the Revolutionaries.

'It has to be added that this – *interesting* – conjuncture of events, which almost certainly began in the boudoir of the egregious Lady H., resulted in this gallant six thousand being ignominiously bundled out of Toulon by the French.

'And there you have it. We are to Naples, gentlemen, where it is certain that the *Daisy*, due to the success and proximity of General Bonaparte, will not be welcomed with anything like the unctuousness that greeted the arrival of Captain Nelson in happier times. However the mission upon which I am engaged may well be assisted on its way by the Royal Navy – as on the previous occasion.' He leered across at Oakshott, whose face was very pinched, and whose eyes were dangerously narrowed, so that if Gisborne had been only slightly less intoxicated he must have seen the danger in which he stood.

The truly dreadful silence that followed was broken by Oakshott addressing the junior midshipman, seated facing him as vice-president of the *ad hoc* wardroom mess:

'Mr Vice – the King!' barked Oakshott.

'Gu-gentlemen – the King!' responded the boy: he was

thirteen, and was allowed only small beer.

The Loyal Toast was drunk, as custom and the proximity of the deckhead beams dictated, in the seated posture. After it, pipes and tobacco were produced. Oakshott had other ideas than a protraction of the dinner and what might follow.

He addressed himself to the master:

'Mr Quinch, do you not find it intolerably hot and oppressive below deck tonight?' he asked.

Quinch, who was quick on the uptake, after the manner of a man whose sensibility has been sharpened by a lifetime of experience in such matters as clawing a recalcitrant ship away from a lee shore, took his captain's point immediately.

He rose to his feet. 'You're right, sir,' he said. 'And by your leave, I'll take a turn round the upper deck before I retire. Your thanks, sir, for a most enjoyable meal.'

He left.

Nor was Lieutenant Shacklock, that former sly and unpromising midshipman of the first commissioning, slow to take the point. He also drained his glass and stood. 'We're for an early start, sir,' he said, 'and I'd be grateful for to lay my head down, since I have the morning watch ...'

Shacklock was followed in quick succession by the other lieutenants:

'Good night, sir. Splendid dinner. Many thanks.'

'Simply superb repast, sir. Thank you so much.'

''Night, sir. Thanks.'

'Splendid evening, sir. Most grateful. Good night. And good night to you, Sir Manvers.' This from Jobling, the senior lieutenant and one of the original commissioning. Now that Rufus had departed – in fact he had left for England that morning in a fast brig – Oakshott had decided to make up Jobling to Acting Number One, the more particularly since he had demonstrated his diplomacy by a courteous nod towards the unspeakable Gisborne.

One by one, they left as the contrivance dawned upon them. The midshipmen were last, for they had neither the worldly wisdom nor the assurance – and would never have come to it save for the precept of their seniors.

The last of them took his leave and departed. To Oakshott,

the emptying of the table was reminiscent of an excellent piece of music he had heard played at the Assembly Rooms in Bath before the war. Composed by Herr Mozart or another of those German fellows, it was so contrived that the ending came when, one by one, the musicians finished their particular piece, blew out their candle and departed, the last man snuffing the last candle and leaving the minstrel gallery in darkness.

'Well, Oakshott, that leaves just the two of us,' said Gisborne.

'Yes, Sir Manvers. Just we two,' responded Oakshott. 'Brandy?'

He pushed the brandy decanter towards his guest, and Gisborne poured himself a brimming measure – no doubt in emulation of the amount that his host had provided for himself.

'I pledge your health, Oakshott,' said he. 'And to our mutual success in the coming venture.'

'Amen to that,' murmured Oakshott. And he downed the entire contents of his glass and poured himself another.

Gisborne grinned his narrow-lipped grin and did likewise.

'You must not take me amiss, my friend,' said the emissary. 'The situation as I have described it in Naples is such that they might even refuse to extend the minimal courtesy of a neutral state towards a belligerent and tell the *Daisy* to go to hell. When one has an army of cut-throat French hovering on one's doorstep – particularly when it's commanded by Bonaparte – one's instincts for self-preservation are honed and sharpened to a quite astonishing degree.' He leered, hiccuped, and emptied his glass.

'What is your intention regarding Naples, sir?' asked Oakshott. 'You have a brief, I presume?'

'I have,' responded the other.

Silence – save for the faint gurgle of the decanter emptying another bumper into Gisborne's glass; which being done, Oakshott reached out and replenished his own.

'And no doubt you will apprise me of it,' said Oakshott. 'In good time.'

'In good time.' The other leered and raised his glass to his companion; in the act of doing which, his normally sallow-complexioned countenance turned a greyish yellow; it was as if a gossamer-thin curtain of the like colour had suddenly been drawn across his face. He dropped his glass on the table, overturning it. A long trickle of the spirit trailed across the table top towards Oakshott; he reached out and staunched it with his napkin.

By this time, Gisborne had collapsed, head downwards and pillowed in his arms. The captain of the *Daisy* crossed over and, taking the lightly built form of his guest, raised him up, threw him across his shoulder and brought him to the quarter cabin in the stern flat; where he laid him in his bunk, pulled off his boots, made sure that his head was to one side so that there was less chance of him choking on his own vomit – and went out on to the upper deck.

The night was fine. Only a faint wisp of drifting cloud – no more than a teased-out morsel of cotton wool – marred the dark blue of the moonlit night. The lights of an incoming vessel presented themselves, as the ship – a naval frigate – rounded the mole and made shape for the middle of the harbour. Oakshott watched with mild interest and professional appraisal as the frigate was brought aback, stood still in the water and dropped her bower anchor. A bosun's pipe sounded the secure. Then silence.

Fresh from England, he supposed. Maybe carrying mail.

Mindful of the letter that still burned a hole in his coat-tail pocket, Oakshott considered the possibility with mixed feelings.

The consuming of the best part of two bottles of raw wine and half of brandy not having had any marked effect upon the captain of the *Daisy*, he was on deck at sunrise to witness the raising of the ensign, having first apprised himself that his distinguished passenger was both alive and sleeping peacefully. The brief ceremony of 'colours' over, Oakshott watched the newly arrived frigate raise anchor and have herself towed by her own boats to a place alongside the wall a couple of ships' lengths astern of the *Daisy*. The manoeuvre was carried out well enough.

'Breakfast, sir. What'll you 'ave?' This was his servant

38

Bantock, a youth of most unprepossessing mien, with villainously crossed eyes. He was also an excellent contriver: would find roast beef and Yorkshire pudding in the middle of the desert and a glass of chilled wine for his master in hell.

'What's on offer?' countered Oakshott.

Bantock ticked off on his fingers. 'Sir, there's eggs any way you like 'em. There's the remains of last night's roast beef cold' – he gave his captain an anxious, hazed-eyed stare – 'and 'ow was it, by the way, sir?'

'Quite excellent,' said Oakshott.'But I'd not fancy it cold for breakfast.'

'Then I'll do you eggs the way you like 'em, sir. And oatcakes. Coffee. An' beer. That suit you, sir?'

'First rate.'

Bantock knuckled his forelock and departed at the double.

There then took place an occurrence which was not without note in the unfolding of *Daisy*'s mission to the Mediterranean, to *Daisy* herself and all who sailed in her, and also to the unfolding of Oakshott's life and career in many regards.

It was informed, in the first instance, by a procession . . .

The procession issued from the gangway of the newly-arrived frigate astern. Leading the file were two seamen carrying a brass-bound chest. Two more came after, similarly burdened. Next came a powder-monkey of a lad carrying a parrot in a cage. After him a nigger boy of about the same age – twelve or thirteen: he bore a large, furled umbrella under one arm and a crocodile-skin valise under the other. Bringing up the rear was the tallest, thinnest specimen of a British naval officer that Oakshott had ever beheld.

As to his dress . . .

The uniform of a lieutenant in the Georgian Navy possessed a certain austere elegance, being comprised of a swallow-tailed coat of navy blue or optional black, with white facings and silver-gilt buttons and a none too lavish display of gold lace. Add to that a white waistcoat, nankeen breeches, white silk stockings, optional shoes or Hessian boots, and a cocked hat with a plain black rosette. Not an attire, on the face of it, that permitted a great deal of idiosyncratic variation at the will of the wearer – one would have thought.

One would have made a faulty appreciation in this case ...

To start from top to bottom: the hat sported a plume of feathers garnered from the tails of gamebirds: pheasant, partridge, grouse, capercaillie and so forth. The coat, though nominally blue, was of a fugitive shade of blue that more nearly resembled the shimmering subtlety of a peacock's throat, because the material of which it was tailored was of a watered silk. There was also a considerable proliferation of gold lace. The boots were patent leather in mirror-like perfection of sheen and lavishly tasselled with gold knots. What one could discern of the stockings hinted that they were fashionably striped, violet and white. And he carried a silver-knobbed cane.

A Macaroni officer of the King's Fleet!

Oakshott watched, fascinated, as the apparition stalked towards *Daisy*'s gangway, waved aside his acolytes and proceeded aboard. Once on deck, he tucked the cane under one arm and raised his hat to the quarterdeck in an epitome of the correct manner. His eyes then lit upon Oakshott.

'Lieutenant Thomas A. Brewster, Royal Navy,' he announced. 'Designated First Lieutenant of HM Sloop-of-war *Daisy*. Do I have the honour – and, if I may say, the great pleasure – of addressing Commander Lord Charles Oakshott, Royal Navy?'

He spoke with an alien shade to his voice; with the curious metamorphosis of the English accent of Devon or Cornwall that had been adopted by – certain former Colonials ...

Lieutenant Brewster settled the issue there and then: 'From Boston, in the Commonwealth of Massachusetts, sir.' He grinned. The face, long and thin to suit the figure, split like a melon in the motion, displaying a heart-warming affability.

Oakshott managed to find his voice at last:

'Good morning to you, Mr Brewster,' he said. 'I trust you had a good passage to Gibraltar. Would you care to join me for breakfast?'

'We shall have a first-class navy of our own one day soon,

40

mark my words, sir,' declared Thomas A. Brewster. 'And I shall be one of its first admirals, never fear. In furtherance of this end, I am honoured to learn my profession in the Royal Navy, which is the best around - to date.' So saying, he stabbed another fried egg on oatcake from the dish before him and set to. He had an appetite and a half, and Bantock had been constrained to hold up the entire ship's company's breakfasts by monopolizing the tiny galley up for'ard with supplementary eggs on oatcakes for the stern cabin.

Oakshott diplomatically forbore to comment upon the other's declaration. 'What experience have you had so far, Mr Brewster?' he asked.

'Three years in coasters plying between Boston and Philadelphia, sir,' replied the American. 'My father and his father before him set up the Brewster Shipping Combination and by the time I was a younker of twelve, I'd put in plenty of sea time and knew where my dedication lay. My father put the ships of the BSC at the disposal of our country at the outbreak of our War of Independence ...'

'Your *revolution*,' interposed Oakshott mildly.

'As you say, sir.' Brewster shrugged, and speared himself another egg on oatcake. 'Right after the war ended, I went to sea and stayed there. Next after my experience in coasting, I worked my passage to Liverpool and 'listed in the King's Navy. Took my midshipman's rate at sixteen. Lieutenant at twenty-five. I've seen action in *Orion* at Groix, missed the Glorious First of June in *Gallant*, Teneriffe last year as gunnery officer in *Leander* - which is lying right behind us at the moment.'

Oakshott nodded approvingly. There was no shortage of the former colony's members in the Royal Navy, nor indeed aboard the *Daisy*, which in this instance might be said to be a microcosm of the Service in general, having among its complement of about 130 officers and crew (seldom up to strength on account of sickness and death, accident and death; but, let it be said, negligible desertion) no less than a dozen Americans, together with Swedes, Hollanders, Chinees, and all sorts of Blacks. They were all good, being volunteers, whilst the Britishers were for a great part pressed men; though - and it is an inexplicable conundrum - these same pressed sons of Albion were in no way inferior to the volunteers when the guns began to thunder; it was just that they grumbled and muttered more when all was quiet.

'So, sir, it's to Naples we're bound, so I understand,' said Brewster.

'That's right,' said Oakshott, and he narrowed his eyes against the keen morning sun which, glancing through the stern windows, hazed his view somewhat; his gaze was directed to the small and exceedingly skinny figure of the black boy who had accompanied the American aboard and whom (Oakshott, that most genial and incurious of hosts, could scarcely have omitted to notice) had stood behind Brewster's chair throughout their protracted breakfast.

'The – um – darkie . . . ?' murmured Oakshott, indicating.

'Name of Cuthbert,' said Brewster.

'Member of *Leander*'s crew?' suggested Oakshott.

'No, sir. He's mine.'

'Servant?'

'Slave, sir. Whither I go, he goeth. Like Gaul, though divided into two parts, we are indissoluble. Cuthbert is also a tip-top powder-monkey, and being stone deaf isn't greatly put about in the clatter of battle.'

Oakshott merely nodded and kept his peace; the advent of the Macaroni Yankee had curiously lightened his spirit.

The *Leander* had brought mail: a packet was delivered to Oakshott soon after breakfast. There were bills from his tailor, gunsmith and hatter, and a reminder from the secretary of his Pall Mall club that his annual subscription was greatly overdue, 'and would Lord Charles kindly give the matter, et cetera . . .'

There was also a short letter – much feared, he could have composed its anticipated phrases in his sleep – from his sister-in-law, informing him that his brother had departed this life, peacefully in his sleep, and that the young Lord Charles Henry Gervase Rupert Oakshott had succeeded as seventh Marquess of Uffingham and Bow. The bereaved widow added in parenthesis that 'little Charlie has greatly improved in health'.

Oakshott closed his eyes and tried to recapture a pleasing

image of his departed brother, but nothing would come –
save a half-forgotten remembrance of their childhood when
poor old Jack, stricken no doubt with a transitory pang of
remorse for mercilessly cheating his sibling at marbles, had
bent the rules to allow him to win a much-prized blood alley.

That done, Oakshott uttered a short and earnest prayer for
the young life which was all that stood between him and the
hated sucession to an empty title and a ruined estate which
would burden him for life and cost him his treasured naval
career.

Three

Watered, provisioned and topped up with powder and shot after her small encounter with the French, the *Daisy* took a handsome following wind the next dawn and was eastering with studding sails straining and the mountains of southern Spain fading into the dusk, all the Mediterranean open to her – and not a rope veered or hauled by so much as a smidgen in all that long day.

Sir Manvers Gisborne did not confide anything regarding his discussions with the Governor to Oakshott, nor did the latter presume to probe; but the emissary displayed a certain tight-lipped, self-regarding smile throughout that first day of the onward passage, which suggested to the captain of the *Daisy* that the discussions had not been unfruitful. Gisborne's tight-lipped smile faltered and faded after dinner that first night out, when, following a very excellent ragout of left-over Spanish fighting bull devised by the egregious Bantock, he became aware of a very slight dipping and swaying of the ship's motion and retired to his quarter cabin – after first renouncing his ragout over the side.

Lieutenant Thomas A. Brewster, citizen of the Commonwealth of Massachusetts, having eaten his way through three helpings of Bantock's excellent stew, having praised the latter to his face and dispatched his nigger slave to help with the washing up, excused himself of his captain and went to his hammock in the quarterdeck flat (the quarter cabin, customarily the habitation of the first lieutenant, being occupied by their distinguished passenger), because he was due to keep the middle watch.

'*Sails ho – three!*'

Oakshott heard the call quite clearly, coming from the mainmast lookout. Swallowing down the last of his post-prandial brandy, he snatched up his telescope and was up on deck before the beating to quarters had aroused all hands – though he was a mite outpaced by his new first lieutenant.

'What are they?' shouted Oakshott to the fellows up on the mainmast.

'Look like frigates, sir!' came the response.

As well as Oakshott had been able to glean from the dubious naval intelligence in Gibraltar, there were no British warships in passage in the western Mediterranean so far as was known – save for the blockade of Toulon that had been maintained by a squadron commanded by Nelson for so long that even his ships' parrots were contemplating desertion. It followed, then, that the sails were French: but, acting upon a little weevil of conviction that was burning in Oakshott's brain, he had to make sure.

'Call for the ship's carpenter!' he ordered.

The carpenter was called for, and came. By name Henshawe, he was a Northumberland man with all the Geordie's directness; he and Oakshott knew – and respected – each other well.

'Up with us both, Henshawe,' said Oakshott. 'I want you to take a glim at those ships before they sight us – as they soon must, for all that they've got the moon behind 'em.'

'Aye, aye, sir.' The ship's carpenter knuckled his forelock and gazed up at the soaring shrouds of the mainmast with the lack of enthusiasm that comes with late middle age and varicose veins.

Oakshott climbed up into the chains and set his foot on the first ratline, eager to settle his conviction.

'Maintain the present course, Number One,' he called back over his shoulder.

'Aye, aye, sir,' responded Brewster.

The captain of the *Daisy* was no great climber, for all that he had been mastheading since boyhood, and made no discernible lead over the older man who laboured up behind him. When they reached the devil's elbow, Oakshott took the quicker and more nimble course over the futtock shrouds;

Henshawe, mindful of his varicose veins, went through the lubbers' hole.

Upwards into the wind-whispering night, with the great sails straining all about them and the hundred and one musical notes of block and tackle, the bass note of wood groaning against wood; up the main topmast and on to the small platform – scarcely larger than a writing table and already occupied by two brawny tars, who pointed away into the night, towards three sets of sails moving across their bow about two miles distant. From that height, and with the moon behind the other ships, one could clearly discern the cut of their bows, the shape of their sails.

'They're Frogs, I'll lay a thousand,' said Oakshott, pulling his telescope from out of his belt and handing it to the ship's carpenter. 'Do you confirm it, Henshawe, for you know best.'

The old carpenter put the instrument to his eye and was not long in declaring that this was so. For had he not worked his apprenticeship in a French shipyard? And he was able to be even more impressively specific:

'The lead ship's *La Diane*, a forty-eight – as shouldn't I know, sir, for I had a hand in the building of her in Brest! I recognize the cut of that jib as well as I'd know my dear mother's face again, God rest her.'

That settled it: Oakshott leaned over and shouted an order down to the deck, contingent upon which the *Daisy* was brought on to a new course which led her further away from the French and into the safety of the night. It was no business of a little sloop-of-war of eighteen guns to try the game with three large frigates, all leaner and faster and greatly heavier armed than she.

On the way down the ratlines, Oakshott pondered on what he had seen, and in these terms:

Six French battleships in passage southwards towards the Mediterranean. Three frigates making course for – at a guess – Toulon, where Nelson's blockade could scarcely act as a net for three such speedy minnows as they, particularly if they approached upwind of the blockaders (who, in any event, were concerned with the more simple task of stopping ships from coming *out* of the port).

46

The French were up to something – but what?

Masters of northern Italy already, were they now massing for the seaborne invasion of Naples and Sicily and the toe of the boot?

And – more immediately – were the *Daisy*'s mission, and her eternally seasick and slightly unpleasant passenger, concerned in all this?

He went below and pencilled in the ship's log the following:

2 bells of the first watch: sighted 3 Fr. frigates 10 m. S. of Cap de Gata. The leader being La Diane, *48. Enemy steering N.E.*

That night, the weather worsened towards the middle watch. While Gisborne languished in his cot, no doubt, Oakshott, sleepless, went up on deck to keep company with his new first lieutenant.

Brewster was clad in a heavy boat cloak and a woollen cap, looking as unlike a Macaroni as an admiral on a donkey. His nigger boy was with him, curled up like a small black bear against the scuppers, covered with what looked like a deerskin, and fast asleep.

Brewster touched his strange headgear in salute to his captain and wished him a good night.

'And what construction do you place upon the Frenchies we sighted, sir?' he asked.

'Well, they were sailing on a broad reach northwards,' said Oakshott, 'which means that they might be steering for Toulon. On the other hand, it might mean nothing of the sort.'

In the dim light of the moon as it appeared through the scudding clouds, Oakshott perceived a broad grin splitting the other's countenance.

'I should be grateful if you would enlarge upon that observation and thereby enlighten me as to your thoughts, sir,' he said.

'Well, they haven't just come through the Straits ahead of us,' said Oakshott, 'for the *Daisy*, even at her best speed, couldn't possibly have overtaken them. It follows, then, that they're either in passage from somewhere on the coast of

Turkish Algiers – and why should they be doing that, I ask myself, since the Frogs have no interests in yonder arid, pestilential hell-hole? Or else ...'

'Or else?'

'Or else, they're on patrol.'

'Looking for *us* – seeking to intercept *us*?'

Oakshott glanced sharply at his companion. 'The thought had crossed my mind, Number One,' he said, 'but there's no reason why it should have crossed yours.'

The other's grin persisted. 'I don't want to pry, sir,' he responded, 'but I hadn't been aboard but half a watch and I'd gleaned (and us Yankees are almighty good at gleaning) from scuttlebutt that this ship's bound on a secret mission.'

'Did you now – did you?' responded Oakshott. 'Well, I have to be frank with you, Number One, and inform you that whatever this secret – if it exists – it is a secret from me, the captain of this ship. And I would be indebted to you, Mr Brewster, if you would pass the news to scuttlebutt to keep its gleanings to itself.

'Do you follow me?'

Brewster followed him all right, though by not so much as a wavering of his watermelon grin did the American show any dismay at what he might well have considered to be a snub from his captain; but merely saluted acquiescence.

On the fourth day, after variable winds, fair and foul, they came in sight of the hooked fingers of a great bay, with a sprawling white city rising above it, tier upon tier, dome upon dome, towers succeeding towers to the heights. And, beyond all that, to its eastern shore and behind all else, stood the lowering hump of a dark volcanic mountain crowned by a plume of smoke that ascended almost vertically into the windless sky of cerulean.

'Vesuvius!' declared Gisborne, quite unnecessarily. He was standing next to Oakshott on the quarterdeck, and standing exceedingly well – for him. The light airs that left untouched the rising of the volcano's plume were driving the *Daisy* through the pellucid waters of Naples Bay at a scarcely discernible rate and with no more motion than one would have experienced on a duck pond. Apparently in fine good

48

spirits after having survived another leg of his long sea journey, Gisborne had reverted to his Macaroni shore-going rig of striped velvet coat, striped stockings and lemon waistcoat – with the variant of a straw hat cocked fore and aft. He also reeked of patchouli.

'I think we should deliver a salute of guns, Oakshott,' he observed, with the air of someone delivering an original paradox.

'It is customary,' responded Oakshott, 'in the normal manner of things upon entering the harbour of a neutral power.'

'I doubt our former *gallant* allies are all *that* neutral,' sneered Gisborne, 'not with Bonaparte almost knocking on their gates. But one must observe the niceties. Twenty-one guns for a sovereign state, is it not, sir?'

'Twenty-one guns it is – sir,' replied Oakshott flatly. 'Fired in a rolling volley immediately upon coming to anchor. Some captains favour a quarter battery, or even a single gun. I, on the other hand, prefer to exercise the entire complement.' He turned on his heel and walked for'ard. God, he thought, that fellow stinks like a strumpet's boudoir.

The *Daisy* slid quietly to stillness in the glassy water a couple of cables from the shore, carefully upwind (such as there was) of a line of sardine boats. At closer acquaintance, the city of Naples was far from the wedding-cake pristine whiteness and sanitariness that had been suggested from afar. The whiteness of the handsome principal buildings off the splendid corniche – churches, palaces, public edifices and so forth – was found to be illusory: a trick of the intense sunlight allied to the overwhelming blueness of sky and sea; close up, they were streaked with verdigris and mould, rust, and heaven knows what; while their roofs sprouted small trees and foliage to abundance; nor was there scarcely an unbroken window to be seen. Inshore, moreover, even at two cables, the state of the water was of a nature that determined Oakshott to move out to sweeter pastures once the preliminary business of their arrival was dispatched.

'*Salute of twenty-one guns for a sovereign state – in a rolling volley, for'ard to aft, starboard to port – give fire!*'

The little sloop blazed forth, in orange flame and rolling clouds of white smoke, her accolade to the Majesty of the Kingdom of the Two Sicilies – representing as she did the end of a long arm of England's fighting Navy – whatever that counted for in that beleaguered and dubious part of the central Mediterranean to which she had been directed.

One round a piece, the odd rounds taken up by the three pieces to give fire first. And then silence.

'*Secure all guns!*'

'We have visitors,' said Oakshott, lowering his telescope, through which he had been quizzing the quayside during the firing of the blank rounds. He had remarked the masses of excited Neapolitans crowded there, on the quay and at every available window and rooftop; he had also observed the arrival of a small but ornate carriage, the alighting of a couple of personages in flamboyant uniforms, their descent by a flight of steps to a waiting boat – and the boat's departure from the shore, the strokes of its four oars directing it towards the *Daisy*'s gangway.

'Mr Brewster!'

'Sir?'

'Number One – accord the newcomers the honours to a ship's captain if you please.'

'Aye, aye, sir!'

The four-oared gig was brought alongside the gangway (not any too skilfully) by an extremely raffish-looking quartette of sailors, and from out of the vessel stepped two officers in blue and scarlet: blue coats and scarlet pantaloons well gold-laced, hats luxuriantly cockaded and plumed. Both men dark-avised, Latin, grave-countenanced.

Oakshott, who had been gazing with some fascination at the ensign that was being carried on the gig's stern – which was presumably the flag of the Kingdom of the Two Sicilies, and bore the quarterings, surely, of every royal and noble family in continental Europe – drew himself to attention as, to the shrilling of bosuns' pipes, the two dignitaries stepped aboard.

'Signor Captain...' The speaker – the older of the pair and the one bearing the most gold lace – cut himself short, as the bosun and his mates essayed yet another strident 'verse' of the

50

unintelligible cacophany delivered upon their silver whistles. The pause was beautifully done: a mixture of mild embarrassment and implied apology. The fellow was obviously a gentleman, thought Oakshott.

'Signor,' said the captain of the *Daisy*, to give his visitor a lead when the piping was finished. 'Welcome aboard. I am Commander Oakshott. This' – indicating his passenger – 'is Sir Manvers Gisborne.'

'And I am General di Castro, aide-de-camp to His Majesty,' responded the other. 'And this is my own aide, Captain Angioino. At your service.'

'Will you take wine, General?' suggested Oakshott.

Yes, they would take wine. And there was something about di Castro's manner that suggested a need to go into a huddle with the *Daisy*'s captain: the way he cast covert glances to left and right, his manner of sneaking swift looks back towards the crowded shore, and his obvious relief when their small party disappeared from sight of onlookers beneath the quarterdeck screen – all suggested to Oakshott that here was a frightened man. This impression was positively confirmed when, reaching the door of the stern cabin, the general delayed him for a moment with a hand on his arm and murmured into his ear:

'At an early opportunity, sir, you must raise anchor and take your ship beyond musket range of any sharpshooter on the shore!'

Safely in the stern cabin with the major part of a bumper glass of mixed brandy and port wine within him, the Neapolitan general was more explicit:

'Naples is in a turmoil!' he said. 'You will have heard that Bonaparte is turning the Italian peninsula, piecemeal, into a rag-bag of republics – all subservient to France. Genoa and the Cisalpine were the first to go. In February of this year, the French marched into the Holy City, declared the new Roman Republic and sent His Holiness packing.

'The would-be republicans in Naples – and they are many – are full of hope that we shall be the next.'

'It's your own damned fault!' This from Gisborne – the first comment he had made thus far, having been gazing

51

unwaveringly at the general over the rim of his glass with pale goat eyes.

'Signor!' Di Castro was visibly affronted by the imputation.

'After the fiasco of Toulon, you settled for making peace with France,' sneered Gisborne. 'Paying an indemnity – what *we'd* call Danegeld – of eight million francs a year into French coffers in return for being called neutrals. Now you whine because you think you're next for the knacker's yard!'

Tempers were running high ...

'The British fleet abandoned us to our fate!' cried di Castro. 'They left the Mediterranean!'

Oakshott, stung by his fellow-countryman's contemptuous reference to the 'fiasco of Toulon' – a hard-fought campaign in which he himself had played a not inconsiderable part – felt it was time to put an oar in:

'A British squadron is already back in the Mediterranean!' he declared. 'You must know that Nelson's blockading Toulon!'

The Neapolitan general nodded, not unkindly – indeed, with a certain degree of expressed pity, and it was not all self-pity.

'My friend,' he said, 'what you obviously do not also know – but what we learned only yesterday – is that Nelson's squadron – not a full fleet – was scattered in a storm, the admiral's flagship dismasted, and Toulon left with an open door!'

'My God!' grated Oakshott. He glanced to Gisborne, who made no comment, but looked down into his drink with inscrutable eyes.

'Worse is to follow,' said di Castro. 'The French slipped out of Toulon, their battleships in great number, more transports than could be counted. And headed south!'

'Is this true?' demanded Oakshott.

The other shrugged. 'My aide will read you the report given by one of our fast merchant ships in passage from Barcelona.'

The youngish captain produced from his pocket a paper from which he read in an execrable accent, quite unlike the near perfection of his chief's English.

'Ze translation iss: "Ay French armada wass sighted at dawn. Battleships to ze number off seven. Frigates. Transports spreaded beyond horizon. Heading – south."'

'Seven battleships!' exclaimed Oakshott. 'And there are at least six others at sea pointing to the Mediterranean! *Le Guerrier* and *Le Mercure* – both seventy-fours. Plus three more seventy-fours and a three-decker eighty. If they rendezvous with the Toulon fleet – and that's my guess, now – the French will have thirteen of the line in the Mediterranean!

'And for what purpose – with all those transports?'

Di Castro drained the last of his brandy and port wine, looked wistfully towards the decanters, but placed his hand over his glass when Oakshott made a motion to replenish it.

'The move will undoubtedly be made towards the Kingdom of the Two Sicilies,' he said. 'Either to Naples – which is the least likely, since we are easily open to assault by land – but more likely to Sicily, for the island would naturally call for a seaborne assault.' He looked towards Gisborne. 'What is your view, Sir Manvers?' he asked. 'You should be better informed than many – being Mr Pitt's special envoy to Sir William Hamilton, British Ambassador to our Court.'

Oakshott stared at the Neapolitan general, to whom no intimation had been given of the function of *Daisy*'s passenger. Then to Gisborne himself.

What he saw there in the latter's face gave him some cause for a wry amusement. Save when that unfortunate was struggling for his life in the Bay of Biscay, one had never seen that pale, goat's face so put out of countenance.

'How – how did *you* know of my mission here, signor?' demanded Gisborne in a tone of ice.

His addressee shrugged in the Latin manner, hunching his shoulders and spreading his hands.

'If you look out towards the shore, signor,' he replied, 'you will see the corniche packed with people, all agog to gaze upon the White Ensign of the Royal Navy. They are of all ages, all classes, young and old, poor and rich. Neapolitans all. News travels fast here. Of all that multitude – and that includes the many would-be revolutionaries who see the

53

British Navy as the only bar to the triumph of France in the Mediterranean – there can only be the little children, the *bambini* in arms, halfwits and idiots, the drunkards who do not care, and the dying who are past caring, who have not been fully aware for weeks that Mr Pitt's envoy was on his way here, and has now arrived!'

He smiled sadly across at Oakshott. 'You see, my friend, why I advised you to move your ship out of range of any sharpshooter,' he said.

That settles it, thought Oakshott. Those three frigates we met up with off Cap de Gata – they were looking for *us*!

The transparently well-intentioned di Castro and his aide having departed, Oakshott and Gisborne held an *ad hoc* council of war – at the former's insistence.

'Gisborne,' said the *Daisy*'s captain, 'the time has come for you to lay your cards on the table for me. We have come here on an ostensible secret mission which is now revealed to be the common knowledge of all Naples. On passage here, our time was not entirely wasted because we sighted what were undoubtedly reinforcements for the Toulon fleet. That force is now at large – is almost certainly at large – in the Mediterranean, and possibly heading for Sicily. Or it may be to Malta. Or anywhere. To oppose them – so far as we know – is a squadron under Nelson that to our best knowledge has been scattered by storm and the flagship dismasted.

'Do I make a correct summation of the present situation?'

'Exceedingly succinctly,' drawled Gisborne.

'Then I think the time has come for you to apprise me of the substance of our mission here – don't you?'

'No.'

'Not even if that mission is directly concerned with the perilous state of affairs that at present exists – as I have just summarized it?'

'No.' The envoy's smile was bland – sweet, even – as he regarded his companion.

Oakshott exhaled heavily through his nostrils; selected a four-digit number at random and calculated its square root – before he replied:

'Then when am I to be informed of the circumstances in

54

which I must hazard my ship and all in her? Perhaps you will tell me that!'

'When I have completed my business in Naples, and immediately upon our leaving here – as written upon the outside of the sealed orders which you were given,' responded Gisborne.

'And this business of yours – how long will it take?'

'Not long.'

'And when will it commence – this *business*?'

The envoy shifted in his chair, tapped the table with his well-manicured fingertips and glanced out of the stern windows.

'I imminently expect a summons,' he replied.

The summons arrived within the quarter hour. Oakshott, mindful of di Castro's warning, was about to give orders to shift further offshore when the duty quartermaster came aft with news that a boat was approaching. Upon reaching the upper deck, Oakshott perceived that the craft was a common bumboat sculled with some skill by a raggedly-dressed youth at the stern. Seated in the sheets was a man in servant's livery. He carried, under his arm, rather ostentatiously, a large sheet of paper, folded and secured with a seal of red wax the size of a galley spoon.

The servant – valet or whatever – came aboard and presented his missive. It was addressed to Gisborne.

Oakshott was with the envoy when the latter read it; which having done so he passed it over to *Daisy*'s captain with a sneer of amused contempt.

'You are marginally concerned in this, Oakshott,' he said. 'Read it – and see with what quality one is obliged to conduct the nation's business these days.'

Oakshott read:

The Palazzo Sessa, June 12th, 1798

Dear Sir Manvers,
I am askt by Sir Willm to greate yr arrival in Naples & to request the company of you & yr ships Captain this evening at eight. I much look foreward to seeing you and to assist yr enterprize, for you don't know the power I have hear in Naples, having the ear

55

of the Queen, a whoman ansome & reasonable and much engrossed in politicks as will further yr cause.

Be not late this eve. Intertainments is at 9 when I will perform my famous atitudes.

Sir, I remain yours,
Emma Hamilton*

He passed the letter back to Gisborne.

'So this is the lady,' he said, 'who, according to you, holds the key to power in Naples, having the ear of the Queen – as she herself puts it – and the Queen having sovereignty over her husband. Well, well! What manner of woman is her ladyship?'

Gisborne curled his lip. 'The information I have, my dear Oakshott, is that Lady Hamilton is – I quote – "In person, nothing short of monstrous in its enormity, and growing every day. Her manners perfectly unpolished, though not with the ease of good breeding, but of a barmaid."'†

He shrugged. 'We shall see for ourselves tonight, Oakshott. We shall see.'

Regarding di Castro's warning, Oakshott addressed himself to the problem of how best he and the envoy might reach the Hamiltons' residence without being assassinated by pro-revolution Neapolitans on the way.

There was the straightforward option of going ashore with an escort of armed tars under the command of a midshipman – a sort of pressgang; this he dismissed as being out of character for representatives of a belligerent country enjoying the hospitality of a neutral, and likely to cause more ill will than its effectiveness might secure. In the end – typically Oakshott – he opted for the old principle of softly-softly catchee monkey. As soon as the *Daisy* was safely anchored well out of musket range of the shore, and

---

*This scarcely believable document is in fact a pastiche of letters written by Emma to her husband, Nelson and others between 1786 and 1795 – spelling and all!

†Communicated (ungallantly) by Sir Gilbert Elliot, later Lord Minto, former Viceroy of Corsica during the British occupation, after he was thrown out and stayed with the Hamiltons in Naples (1796).

immediately surrounded once more by bumboats and suppliers of every comestible from pigs, chickens and calves (all live) to women, he ordered the bosun to perform a small diplomacy, to wit: pick out a trusty-looking bumboat man, offer him a gold half-guinea to take ashore a couple of officers in nearest proximity to the Palazzo Sessa where, by previous arrangement (by the bumboat man), must be waiting a discreet carriage to convey them the rest of the way. Half a guinea upon acceptance of the commission; another half-guinea on the safe return of the said officers. Very neat.

Bosun Cox's fractured Italian was equal to the task. His silver tongue, eased with bright gold and a tot of navy rum, won the compliance of the kind of moustachioed old Italian character with whom one would have trusted a nubile daughter. At seven-thirty precisely, with the three bells of the second dog watch clanging out over the glassy waters, the bumboat was being directed shoreward. In it sat Gisborne and Oakshott; the latter who, notwithstanding the apparent genuineness of the arrangement, was carrying in his coat-tail pocket a deadly little under-and-over pistol; the upper barrel loaded with ball for stopping, the lower with small-shot for relatively gentle persuasion.

They were brought to a secluded landing stage at the end of the corniche, where a carriage awaited. Bidding the bumboat man to remain, they mounted their new conveyance and went on their way.

It was a languorous, stifling evening, with the sun still unexpectedly high. As their carriage moved out of the quiet enclave containing the landing stage and emerged into a main street, they were embraced by the teeming charivari of the great city; where every man, woman and child, surely, was out parading in the shadows of the tall, eyeless buildings that made canyons of the narrow, rutted streets.

There were well-dressed personages, many of them affecting masks after the Venetian mode, most of them doubtless on their way to theatre or opera, balls and routs: lawyers and politicos at every street corner, declaiming and gesticulating; the hum and bustle of ordinary folk, dragging their wailing offspring behind them. Twice, the carriage was held up by the passage of priests and acolytes running, with the tinkling of bells proclaiming that the Host was being carried to the dying. And – everywhere – beggars: beggars who beggared description: eyeless, toothless, hairless, covered in sores, emaciated hands extended for alms, breathing heaven knows what foul emissions upon the objects of their solicitations. Above all, the stink – so that Oakshott and his companion – no strangers, both, to the miasmas of London, nor to the confines of a tiny sloop packed with 130 largely unwashed seamen – were constrained to cover mouths and nostrils with handkerchiefs.

'They say – the Neapolitans say – "See Naples and die",' essayed Gisborne. 'What do you think to that now, sir?'

'Sir,' responded the other. 'I would add that one should see it from a considerable distance – a couple of miles offshore and no nearer. And then die in peace!'

They came, at last, to the Palazzo Sessa.

The abode of His Majesty's Ambassador to the Court of the Kingdom of the Two Sicilies – and his lady – was palatial in the extreme; comprising a domed central block with pillared porticos at each face, atop of which groups of marble statuary gesticulated. Broad lawns set with shady cedars and noble cypresses surrounded the building, and the whole was entirely encompassed by a shallow moat, where swans glided in and out of sunlight and shade. There were stately peacocks on the lawns, and they were looking in some indignation at a group of laughing, tipsy roysterers who were playing blind-man's buff. As the men from the *Daisy* stepped from their carriage, Gisborne found himself seized by the blindfolded victim of the game, who whooped to have hold of a quarry – but was snarlingly shaken off by the envoy.

'Damned oaf!' growled Gisborne. 'Lathering me with his garlic-stinking breath.'

'It seems,' murmured Oakshott, amused, 'that Sir William is presenting quite a rout here tonight.'

The game in the garden was only a foretaste of the frolics at the Palazzo Sessa that eve. Upon entering the main portico at the head of a flight of marble steps (where, incidentally, they had to edge their way past silk- and satin-clad gallants and ladies seated on the steps in amorous dalliance), they found themselves in the spacious main salon under the dome. It was crowded. A five-piece string orchestra was sawing away at a minuet, and two lines of couples minced back and forth in opposition to each other. At gambling tables set around the dance floor, card players were engrossed in *rouge et noir* and faro, their silver and gold coins strewn in careless piles amongst spilled wine and broken meats. And all alone in that crowd, oblivious to the minuet and the gaming, a spindle-shanked old man in a coat of satin brocade was strutting up and down, flapping his arms and imitating the crowing of a rooster to every passing female.

'And still only eight o'clock!' mused Oakshott.

'Where to find our host and hostess?' said his companion.

And then – *she* came . . . gliding from out of the crowd like a first rater with all studding sails set. Junoesque would be the word to fit her, and that in an era where the slight appearance under a shift in the Grecian mode was more generally esteemed. Ungallantly to describe her as 'fat' would have been to show not only bad breeding but an undiscerning eye; she was larger than life – just as Classical statuary of goddesses is larger than life. Oakshott was attracted to her on the instant; and it was to him that she advanced, hands extended.

'Aaaah!' she cried. 'I seen the uniform of 'is Majesty's fleet from acrost the room! You must be our gallant Lord Charles Oakshott.' Her voice was powerful, musical, and heavily charged with overtones of Liverpool.

'Your servant, Lady Hamilton,' said Oakshott, perceiving whom she must be, and bowing over her proffered hand.

Gisborne, also, she knew by name and rank without any introduction, and her next declaration – delivered in a loud enough voice for anyone to hear who cared – made further mockery of the supposedly 'secret' nature of Gisborne's mission to Naples:

'Sir Willim 'as taken ill of the gout,' she declared, 'and is a-resting. You and me, Sir Manvers, will go to him right away. 'Tis as good a time as any to put us cards on the table, so we may present a united front when the King and Queen arrive.'

She beamed at Oakshott and ran her eyes over his uniform coat – like a small child with face pressed to the window of a pastrycooks' shop, as if she could have plucked off the silver-gilt buttons and gobbled them up. 'We'll leave the commander to amuse himself meantime,' she said. 'He'll not lack for comp'ny for long – not if I know sailors.' And she actually winked at him, turning as they walked away.

'Commander, may I present? . . .' It was General di Castro, and with him a young couple around their mid-twenties, of such identical features and colouring that they had to be brother and sister – as indeed proved to be the case: the Conte di Depretis and Signora Alicia Dante-Pergolisi.

'Charmed, ma'am,' murmured Oakshott – speaking the very truth. For Signora Alicia was stunningly like the woman back home, widow of a friend of his boyhood, with whom he had had a sporadic romantic attachment that was as likely as not to be a lifelong affair without benefit of clergy. The Neapolitaine had the same regarding eyes, finely-chiselled nose, firm mouth. But dark as a raven whilst Irene Chancellor was blonde.

'May one take it that you, and your ship, sir, are only the first of the many Royal Navy vessels we may expect in Naples?' asked her brother the conte.

'Sir, I'm not privy to Mr Pitt's intentions in this matter,' responded Oakshott.

The other smiled and exchanged a glance with his sister. 'But it is an open secret in Naples, sir, that Sir Manvers Gisborne is here to urge your ambassador' – again he met his sister's eye – 'and your ambassador's *lady*, to use their influence with the Royal Family so that, in defiance of the French and our declaration of neutrality, Naples will water and provision the British fleet, if and when it comes.'

'If that's the case, sir, then I'm unaware of it,' replied Oakshott in all honesty: di Depretis nodded and seemed to accept his statement on its face value.

The orchestra, who had been resting after the rigours of the stately minuet, now struck up a lively jig. Di Depretis addressed his sister, but with a sidelong look at Oakshott. 'My dear Alicia,' he said, 'I know you're dying to dance, but your brother and chaperon is no performer in the art of Terpsichore, as you are aware. However, perhaps the gallant commander might be persuaded to . . .'

'How very remiss of me, ma'am,' interposed Oakshott. 'Will you do me the honour, please?'

Her hand was soft in his, and dry as a snake's skin, for all that, the night beginning to close in, lackeys had lit the long line of chandeliers that spanned the chamber and the vault of the dome. Already the innumerable pinpoints of flame were adding to the general heat – and the smell of the burning tallow – to the combined reek of perfumes, over-rich food, and largely unwashed bodies.

They locked arms in the first figure of the dance: the forward skip.

'So your brother is also your chaperon, ma'am?' posed Oakshott.

'It is customary, sir,' she replied. 'For I am a widow.'

'Aaaah!' Another parallel with Irene Chancellor.

'Why do you exclaim?'

'I was expressing condolence, ma'am.'

'There is no need. My husband and I parted long before his untimely demise. What do you think of Naples?'

'I've not seen much of it, ma'am.'

'But what you've seen you have not greatly admired?' Her glance, sidelong and elfish, had a touch of coquetry.

'Not so by any means,' replied Oakshott. 'The scenic views are very fine.'

They moved into the second figure: the walk. When they reached the next turn, she slid her arm out of his. 'I find this rather tiring,' she said. 'Will you fetch me some wine?'

'Of course.'

The drinks and solid comestibles were piled high on a long table at the end of the room: bottles lined up in innumerable coolers, food enough to feed a fleet for a month, and all of the most extravagant and highly-coloured sort imaginable, including a whole cold roast pig on cut, its gleaming crackling dyed with saffron and a pomegranate in its open mouth. Oakshott took up a large, opened bottle, tucked two glasses into his coat pockets and elbowed his way out of the chattering crush to find Alicia Dante-Pergolisi again. He discovered her by the great double doors that issued out on to the marble steps and the lawns beyond in gathering shadow.

61

'It is so hot in there,' she complained. 'Bring the wine down to the water's edge and we'll sit on the bank.'

She turned and ran down the steps, light-footed as a gazelle because she had removed her pumps; nothing loth, Oakshott followed her at a more sedate pace.

The game of blind-man's buff was over; the lawns were deserted under the rising moon. Behind, the choruses of wild cries and shrieks of merriment indicated that the jig had degenerated into a gallop – a not unusual occurrence in Oakshott's experience, though a trifle earlier in the evening than would have been proper in London or Bath.

She was sitting by the moat, her bare feet trailing in the water, having removed cream-coloured silk stockings – now lying curled up with her dancing pumps. She reached out a hand.

'Wine,' she said. 'Give me some wine, and then sit down here and do what I am doing. It is so beautifully refreshing.'

Resigned to her lead, Oakshott did as he was bidden: poured out two bumper measures of chilled white wine and passed them to her, kicked off his shoes, peeled down his stockings, and joined her on the grass. The water was, indeed, deliciously cool.

'Your very good health, Signora,' said Oakshott.

'You may call me Alicia while we are alone,' she said.

'Alicia,' repeated Oakshott. They pledged each other, touching glasses.

She drained the wine in one long swallow and held out her glass for more: greedily, demandingly, like a spoilt child. After the second, she held up her perfect, heart-shaped face and closed her eyes.

'And now I think I should like you to kiss me, Commandatore,' she whispered.

Never one to turn up his nose at a good offer, the captain of the *Daisy* obeyed without question. The exercise he found most agreeable as to both quality and protraction of dalliance; indeed, he was constrained further to force the engagement by sliding his arm round her shoulders and afterwards enfolding her unbelievably slender waist, discovering during that short voyage – and not entirely to his surprise, for he had often remarked to himself upon the new

62

mode in female costume – that Alicia Dante-Pergolisi was wearing little of impediment under her Grecian shift, and certainly no stays.

Presently, he said: 'Would your chaperon entirely approve of this carry-on, Alicia?'

She tapped him on the nose playfully, with a fingertip.

'Silly man,' she murmured. 'You are in Naples now. We observe the outward proprieties – sometimes. But as for my dear brother being chaperon – ha ... !

'He picked you out for me!'

'Very prescient of him,' commented Oakshott, espying, and with no great dismay, that she was doing something complicated with the back fastenings of her shift. 'Can I assist you?'

'No, I've already ...'

Oakshott never did hear the end of her observation, nor were the implied delights ever made manifest; for from the splendid building behind them, and rising above the sweet strains of the violins, there came the unmistakable crack of a pistol shot.

This was followed by a woman's scream – and then by a voice calling out into the night: a voice that Oakshott had heard but once before – and quite unforgettably:

'Lawks a-mussy! Murderer! Stop that man – stop 'im!'

Four

'Good God!' exclaimed Oakshott. 'That was Lady Hamilton!'

Springing to his feet, he made a move to run to the house; but halted in his tracks when he espied a running figure come from behind the facing portico and light across the lawn; racing, head-down, at full stretch towards the driveway and the ornamental bridge that spanned the moat.

'You there!' bellowed the captain of the *Daisy* in a voice that had been honed and sharpened by shouting orders in many a gale of wind. 'Stop!'

The running man gave no heed. So Oakshott went after him, his keenly mathematical mind making an instant appreciation of the geometry required to make an interception of the fugitive at about five yards from the drive and fairly close by the bridge. A smart runner in his day, and unencumbered by shoes, he had not gone ten swift strides before it was apparent that his geometry was not at fault. The other runner must have perceived it at the same time, for changing his tack, he described a tight turn and made to pass *behind* his pursuer, disregarding the bridge and heading straight for the moat. He had leapt into the water, feet first, and was wading across it, thigh deep, when Oakshott jumped in after him.

The fugitive continued to wade. Oakshott went one better and, taking a forward plunge, struck out in a practised swimming stroke. The pair of them were scarcely half way across the moat when the *Daisy*'s captain wrapped his arms round the waist of his adversary and brought him to an unceremonious halt.

The other was to be no easy meat: Oakshott gleaned as much the instant he grappled with him and felt the leanness and hardness of the fellow's physique – as was presently put to good use in preventing his assailant from pinioning his arms to his sides from behind; in attempting which, Oakshott was constrained to bring his unguarded face in close proximity to the other's pigtail. In one deft move, the latter brought his head back with a stunning force, at the same time flinging his arms wide. Oakshott staggered back, his nose all but broken and spurting blood like a fire hose, while his opponent, turning, stabbed a knee – savagely – to the crutch. The heir presumptive to the Marquisate of Uffingham and Bow fell back in the water – which quickly filled his mouth, which was open in a howl of pain. Next instant, the other was at him again.

It was a life or death match; if Oakshott had had any doubt of it, the manner in which he was taken by the throat with two hands concentrated his mind upon the realities.

He saw only one trick to play – and it was a desperate manoeuvre.

Gulping in a massive lungful of air, he deliberately succumbed to his opponent's superior stance above him; threw himself back and submerged – at the same time seizing two handsful of the other's hair and ensuring that he went down with him. With luck – airless.

There followed a brief, bitter scrimmage under water, with the uppermost contestant fighting to free himself from Oakshott's deadly, cloying grip – and with the latter concentrating upon holding his breath – and holding on to those hanks of hair.

Before long, the frenzied struggles quietened; the grip on Oakshott's throat softened, relaxed and was gone. In for a penny, in for a pound, *Daisy*'s captain remained submerged – his limp opponent with him – till his own lungs were near to bursting point. Then he emerged into the air.

His late adversary – drowned or only half-drowned? – lay in his arms as he waded ashore. The lolling head, slack mouth, staring eyes, revealed the lineaments of the young Conte di Depretis, brother of the seductive Alicia.

And Alicia was waiting for them at the water's edge, her

lovely countenance suffused with mingled anguish and hatred.

'*Idiota senza cuore!*' she screamed in her native tongue. 'You have killed him!'

'Possibly,' responded Oakshott, wading.

There were figures approaching from the palace. Voices. Someone was carrying a lantern. They had been seen already.

Oakshott climbed up on to the bank and laid down his burden. He was about to kneel and tend to his victim, when, glancing, he saw the moonlight briefly make a flashing reflection on the blade of a sharp dagger that had appeared in Alicia Dante-Pergolisi's hand.

With a despairing cry, she lunged it at him. He had no difficulty in parrying the thrust; seized her wrist and twisted it. As the knife fell, he scooped it up and tossed it out into the moat.

'Don't be a sillier little fool than God made you,' he said. 'The game – whatever the game was – is up.

'Now to see if there's any life left in this brother of yours.'

They stood around him in a fascinated, chattering throng – all save Alicia Dante-Pergolisi, who knelt beside her brother's still form whilst Oakshott fought for his life. Hands clasped, eyes closed, head bowed in prayer and, between her slender fingers, a rosary (the same she had taken from her reticule that had also lately contained the dagger), she was a vision of piety and loveliness. There were many who remarked that her shift was unbuttoned at the back, she having forgotten to do it up again, and there were speculations as to how it may have come about. By a mild irony, it was certainly this oversight on her part which contributed to saving her pretty neck ...

The fascination of the onlookers, however, was more nearly directed to Oakshott's antics: in the attempt to rekindle life's feebly flickering flame in the drowned or near-drowned, he was resorting to the time-honoured sailors' expedient of standing barefoot upon the stricken man's back (the other lying face downwards) and gently bounding up and down upon his lower ribs, with the object of, firstly, expelling the water from the lungs and, secondly, to encourage those organs to reassume their role of viable appendages and draw in air of their own accord.

It was a long process. Alicia Dante-Pergolisi had passed from supplicant prayer to tears of despair long before Oakshott had done his work. A quarter of an hour or more must have passed before the stricken man gave a groan, opened his eyes, and vomited.

'Carlo!' cried his sister. 'Carlo - *caro mio!*'

'He'll live,' said Oakshott, stepping off his victim's back and addressing General di Castro, who had stood by him all the time, a cocked pistol in his hand.

'The bastard will live just long enough to talk and tell all he knows,' responded the other without heat - an observation that caused Oakshott to suffer the sensation of an icy finger trailing down his spine.

> *Heart of oak are our ships,*
> *Heart of oak are our men,*
> *We always are ready;*
> *Steady, boys, steady!*
> *We'll fight -*
> *And we'll conquer again and again.*

'Capital, my dearest, capital!' From the chaise-longue, where he lay with his bandaged foot propped up on a gossamer pillow, the British Ambassador to the Court of the Two Sicilies accorded his lady wife a heartfelt clapping of hands. A sharp-featured man of seventy with an aquiline nose and curiously pale eyes, Sir William Hamilton regarded his spouse with admiration that clearly bordered on the adoring.

Greatly embarrassed, Oakshott - for whom the offering of David Garrick's popular naval patriotic song had been rendered - clapped also. So did Gisborne, the only other witness to Lady Hamilton's *ad hoc* concert rendition, delivered in a powerful contralto voice of excellent timbre but uncertain pitch upon the captain of the *Daisy* entering the Ambassador's dressing room where he lay.

'Very fine, ma'am,' ventured Oakshott.

'Remarkable, ma'am,' essayed Gisborne. 'I don't recall having previously heard the ballad right through.'

'The last three verses I composed meself,' responded Lady Hamilton without a touch of side. 'Them as refers to Nelson.'

'Nelson was here, you know,' supplied Hamilton. 'He was here only five days during the Toulon affair, nor had we seen him before – or since – but he made a most remarkable impression upon my wife and myself. He was but a captain then, you know, and quite unknown and unacknowledged. But he said to me – and I have never forgotten his words – what was it he said to me at that time, my darling?'

'He said,' responded Lady Hamilton, '"I am now only a captain, but I will, if I live, be at the top of the tree!"' Her voice rang.

'And I believed him,' said Hamilton. 'Utterly! And still do!'

'Remarkable,' commented Gisborne dryly.

'Quite so,' said Oakshott.

'Well, now,' said Her Ladyship, 'we have had such alarums this eve as we won't soon forget. Did you hear the whole of it, Lord Charles – that part as preceded your gallant capture of the murderous scoundrel?'

'Madame, I did not,' replied Oakshott. 'We – that's to say I – heard the pistol shot and then your voice – I took it to be your voice, ma'am – calling out the alarm.'

'We were together in this room,' said Hamilton. 'We three – my wife, Gisborne and I . . .'

Lady Hamilton interposed: 'We was conferring as regards us tactics for the watering and supplying of the British fleet whensomever it might come. All of a sudden . . .' she pointed to the window.

'My wife cried out!'

'There was this face!' she boomed in her sonorous contralto.

'Staring in at us – through the open window!'

'I saw the levelled pistol!' And now Lady Hamilton was acting out the scene, striding to the centre of the room, where stood Gisborne. 'Levelled at Sir Manvers, 'ere! With one thrust, I pushed him sharply aside – *so!*' And she suited the action to the words, so that the lightly-built envoy was all but floored.

'You could have taken the ball upon yourself, my darling!' cried Hamilton.

'But I did not!' she responded, pointing. 'Instead, it struck and quite broke yonder very 'andsome bust of Hermes, the which I have greatly treasured!'

'So then he made his escape – di Depretis made his escape,' said Oakshott.

'Leapt from the balcony,' replied Lady Hamilton. 'But was not free for long – thanks to the Royal Navy!'

And her eyes feasted yet again upon his braided coat, now sodden wet through.

The Hamiltons' rout continued without further interruption throughout the night. It was the majority opinion that, far from being to the demerit of the affair, the attempted assassination of the British envoy and the brilliant action of Commander Lord Charles Oakshott had provided voluptuous entertainment for one's jaded emotional palate that was scarcely rivalled by Lady Hamilton's presentation of her famous 'attitudes'. The aforesaid spectacle began at the stroke of midnight in the withdrawing room of the palace, into which the guests were packed, with the most distinguished seated in the front two rows; centre of the front row being King Ferdinand; his consort Queen Maria Carolina – sister of the guillotined Queen Marie Antoinette; and the Prime Minister Sir John Acton, Bart, an Englishman born in France, a somewhat slippery adventurer of sixty years who had served in the navy of Tuscany and worked his way up by guile and stealth to his present eminence in Naples. Sir William Hamilton approved of Acton, saying: 'I can perceive him to be still an Englishman at heart'; Emma Hamilton was always less forthcoming in her opinion.

At the far end of the room was a raised dais, curtained. All the lights having been extinguished, save for candelabra which were borne on and offstage by lackeys to suit the requirement of each attitude, the spectacle began; the curtain was drawn, and the Junoesque person of Lady Hamilton stood posed as – announced by her husband through a speaking-trumpet offstage – the Goddess of Health. Much applause – as she stood tremulously for a minute or so in flowing draperies of near-transparency. After this came Diana the Huntress Chaste, The Birth of Venus, The Empress Messallina (which item caused something of a stir even among the Neapolitans), followed by a group of subjects inspired by paintings that George Romney had made of Her Ladyship. The whole was brought to a close by a rapturously received Rule Britannia, helmeted, with her trident and shield.

Oakshott, crammed at the far end of the room, stifling in his still clammily-wet uniform (though so intense was the heat that the garments were rapidly drying upon him), was greatly relieved to see the end of the spectacle, and was about to absent himself into the garden for a precious breath of fresh air when a lackey came up and informed him that he was to be presented to Their Majesties. Uneasily aware that thin plumes of steam were rising from his raiment, he went forward to where Gisborne was holding a halting conversation with the king through the interpretations of General di Castro.

Whilst waiting for his own introduction, Oakshot was buttonholed by the man sitting on the king's left.

'Acton,' he said. 'You may have heard of me, Lord Charles.'

'Indeed, Sir John, I have.'

The older man had a lofty brow; clever, shrewd eyes – though in conversation they were always fixed disconcertingly on a spot above one's shoulder.

'I've been told of your exploit, Oakshott,' he said. 'The incident was a surprise all round. Naples teems with revolutionaries – open, secret and potential. But young di Depretis was among the last of the secretives one would have suspected. His father was equerry at this very Court.'

'What will happen to him?' asked Oakshott.

The other looked surprised. 'He will hang, of course. That was a deliberate attempt to drive a wedge between our governments and hold up the secret negotiations for aiding the British fleet.'

Oakshott nodded, surprised to hear that a man in Acton's

position should still – considering that the issue was the talk of Naples – speak of secrecy. 'Will the negotiations be successful, sir?' he asked.

'I think so,' replied the other. 'If Nelson overcomes his present difficulties and is reinforced by St Vincent to the sum of – say – a dozen battleships, he will undoubtedly go in pursuit of the French armada – and will need to be watered and provisioned here or in Sicily. I have taken the opportunity of assuring Gisborne that this will be so – and damned to our neutrality.'

'You will accomplish it, sir?' asked Oakshott, intrigued.

'As like as not, Oakshott,' replied the Prime Minister. And almost for the first time he met his companion's gaze. 'But whether the matter is brought to a satisfactory conclusion by me or anyone, you may be sure of one thing ...'

'And what is that, sir?' asked Oakshott.

The other grinned wryly. 'Emma Hamilton will seize the credit for herself,' he said.

His presentation to the royals was informed by a stilted and largely incomprehensible tripartite conversation carried out in a mixture of halting French, English and Italian, only moderated by di Castro.

Ferdinand had the looks and superficial manners of a dockyard labourer; his wife carried with ease the beauty and bearing that suggested she might resemble her legendary, late, tragic sister – but made it perfectly plain that she had no more than a passing interest in an obscure naval commander; if an English queen, she might have closed the conversation, so far as she was concerned, with a definitive comment upon the weather; as the daughter of an Austrian empress, she merely raised her chin and looked away into the middle distance when she was done with him.

King Ferdinand had been told of Oakshott's exploit with the would-be assassin, and wanted to know the details. Oakshott answered as best he was able through di Castro; while wondering how a monarch so grotesque – with a mouthful of blackened fangs, belly almost bursting out of his waistcoat, hideous breath, and with lice teeming in his uncommonly ill-fitting wig – could ever remain in his present eminence for a minute longer than it took some bright fellow to depose him.

None too soon for the captain of the *Daisy*, the brief audience was over. He and di Castro moved away.

'What's happened to Signora Dante-Pergolisi?' asked Oakshott as casually as he was able.

'Oh, she made a great fuss about that scoundrel brother of hers, but as you must have perceived, there's no harm in her,' replied the general. 'I've recommended she be sent to her late husband's estate near Amalfi. A kind of exile. Keep her out of mischief – out of any contact with her brother's accomplices – if any.'

'He has accomplices, then?' asked Oakshott, thinking of the sharp dagger that Alicia Dante-Pergolisi had secreted in her reticule, along with her rosary. And wondered if, in any circumstances other than had turned out, that dagger might have been driven between his ribs.

'We shall have the answer to that before morning,' replied di Castro. 'The prisoner is at present being put to the question – that is the phrase we have, Commander – *put to the question* – in the most excellently equipped apartments set aside for that purpose, during less enlightened days than we now enjoy, in the cellars of the Castel dell'Ovo.' He took Oakshott's elbow and guided him to the door, smiling pleasantly the while. 'Come and take wine and a leg of guinea fowl with me, Lord Charles,' he said, 'and rejoice that you are alive and not being put to the question at this moment.'

Five o'clock in the morning.

The sun had not yet risen. Musicians dozed in their chairs where they had played, fiddles cradled on their laps. The buffet table looked like the detritus of a hard-fought battle, or a sacked city; huge piles of bones intermingled with empty bottles, broken glasses, squashed fruits and heels of bread. Every chair and sofa was occupied with recumbent forms, the carpets also. Yet, astonishingly, there were some who retained a liveliness and even an appearance of tidiness, with wigs not awry, linen still faultless, manners impeccable: for the most part these personages were quietly talking together

72

in groups, flirting decorously, or enjoying early breakfasts of grilled meats and oatcakes brought out from the kitchens by tired-eyed lackeys. Oakshott and di Castro were awake and spruce: they had been discussing the war and the turmoils of Neapolitan politics.

Presently: 'Here comes Sir Manvers,' observed di Castro. 'Fresh from his deliberations – if fresh is the word.'

The observation was well taken. Never a particularly fit-looking man, envoy Gisborne carried the appearance, that early dawn, of a person hard put-upon: goat eyes red and sunken from lack of sleep, shoulders hunched, footsteps dragging. He threw himself into an armchair that Oakshott had compassionately vacated for him and passed a trembling hand across his brow.

'Is it done, Sir Manvers?' inquired di Castro.

The other nodded. 'I think so,' he replied. 'I've been closeted with the Hamiltons and Acton since past midnight. Yes, I think the fleet will be accepted in Naples, or Sicily. My task here is done.' He looked up at the captain of the *Daisy*. 'Let's back to the ship, Oakshott,' he said. 'And we sail at your earliest convenience.'

'So soon, sir?' asked di Castro. 'Will you not tarry longer and sample more of the delights of Naples?' There was a touch of irony in his voice that amused Oakshott: anyone less likely than Gisborne – if his looks were any indication – to have been enjoying the delights of Naples would have been difficult to find.

'No, we must leave,' said Gisborne, seemingly unaware of the irony. 'For we still have far to go.

'One thing, Oakshott ...'

'Sir?'

'Lady Hamilton particularly commands that you say goodbye to her before we leave. She is in the withdrawing room. Make it not too protracted, there's a good fellow, for I'm dying on my feet.'

'Very good,' said Oakshott. 'Stiffen yourself with a glass of brandy. I'll soon be back.'

She was waiting for him in the withdrawing room, scene of her recent triumph.

The rigours of that spectacle, and the long night of deliberations that had followed, had laid not a featherweight of burden upon either her appearance or her spirits: the brilliant, wild rose and driven-snow complexion that marked out her essential beauty, the lustrous eyes, perfect teeth, Grecian nose, carelessly impeccable coiffure, were those of a woman fresh from her dressing-table. And her largeness – as Oakshott had remarked to himself upon first setting eyes upon her – was simply that she was larger than life and a goddess.

'Sir Willim is resting, poor darling,' she said, extending a plump and shapely hand, 'and did bid me say his farewells, Lord Charles, since he be quite wore out hisself.'

'I thank you, ma'am,' responded Oakshott, taking the proffered hand, which took a grip upon his and retained it for a mite longer than civility demanded.

Then she was all coquetry: tapped him lightly on the breast with her fan. 'La, you has been a right gallant this night, sir,' she declared. 'And not solely in the manner of pugnacity. I speak of your taking a lance to the lists of Hymen – to quote the poet whose name does evade me.'

'Ma'am ... ?'

'Come, sir, it was plain for all to see that you had inveigled that pretty young widow out into the garden for a little of the handie-dandie – as will doubtless place your visit to Naples high in your treasured memories. Come now – admit it.'

Oakshott, having the wry remembrance that it had been Alicia Dante-Pergolisi who had lured *him* out into the garden, and not the other way round, and for a reason that was hardening in his mind as a firm conviction, could only muster up a shy grin.

'Ma'am, you seek me out and find me,' he said.

Again, she tapped his chest. 'Sailors, I like,' said Lady Hamilton, 'for you are all of a piece. You sail straight to the sound of the guns and there ain't an ounce of the underhand in you.'

'Ma'am, you are too kind.'

'Touching upon the Navy,' said Lady Hamilton, and she walked away from him; paced up and down the room for a few moments. 'Touching upon your future movements, sir.

Where be you going next?'

'That I do not know, ma'am,' replied Oakshott. 'I am bound by the instructions of Sir Manvers, and also by sealed orders.'

'Shall you be joining Nelson, do you think?'

'That I can't say, either.'

She turned to face him. Oakshott had the distinct impression that what she was next about to say constituted her main – if not her only – reason for summoning him at such an hour to take farewell.

'I would 'ave you perform a small service for me, Lord Charles,' she said.

'I am your servant, ma'am.'

From somewhere about her person she produced a sealed letter – no more than a single, folded sheet – and held it out to him.

'If you do but join the fleet,' she said, 'I beg you to deliver this straight to Sir Horatio – personally.'

'Most certainly, ma'am.' He took it from her.

'Thank you, Commander.'

'My pleasure, Lady Hamilton.'

'Well, lawks-a-mussy!' exclaimed she.

'Ma'am, what ails you?'

She pointed. 'Your eyes!' she cried. 'I 'ad known from the fust that there were something about you, sir, as put my mind a-kilter whenever I did gaze upon you. And now I know what it is!'

'I have one blue and one brown eye,' said Oakshott wearily, reciting a litany that had been stuck with him since boyhood. 'It's a trait that runs in my family.'

On that inconclusive note, they parted.

Rejoining Gisborne and di Castro in the main salon, the *piano nobile,* he found the envoy still slumped in his chair, whilst the general was being addressed by his aide-de-camp Captain Angioino, the same who had accompanied him aboard the *Daisy.*

Gisborne roused himself. 'News of that murderous scoundrel who tried to assassinate me, Oakshott!' he croaked.

75

'Has he – talked?' demanded Oakshott, uncomfortably aware that a touch of anxiety had entered his voice upon the question.

'Unfortunately not,' responded di Castro. 'Angioino, here, informs me that di Depretis shrugged off this mortal coil an hour since, and without a word passing his lips, thereby saving the state the cost of a hangman's fee.'

'He must have been a very brave man,' said Oakshott.

The other looked at him in some surprise, but, upon consideration, nodded. 'I suppose so,' he conceded. 'Either brave, or stubborn, or – as is most likely – without confederates in the late enterprise.'

Not he! thought Oakshott to himself, as the riding lights of his ship drew closer across the glassy, moonlit waters of the bay. Di Depretis died under torture, saving his sister – at least. It's to be supposed that they had regarded me as Gisborne's bodyguard, or at least someone greatly to be reckoned with. And for that, the silly young chit offered herself as sacrifice to my lusts ... (It has to be said that, in many essentials, Oakshott was at heart a romantic and only dimly aware of the toxic effect that his unnerving parti-coloured eyes – to name but one of his physical attributes, not to mention his manner of bearing and address – had upon males and females alike) ... a sacrifice, to keep me occupied whilst the murder was being committed.

And, if it had been necessary, would she have used the dagger on me? On balance, I think she would.

So why am I shielding her? Why have I kept silence about the dagger – and all else?

He answered himself: because she is young, silly and vulnerable. Because the sweet curve of her eyebrow reminded me of Irene Chancellor.

'What boat?' The call from the gangway quartermaster.

'*Daisy!*' responded Oakshott, signifying that the bumboat carried the captain of the same.

Oakshott clambered aboard his command, and Gisborne after him. The envoy was half asleep on his feet, and Oakshott signalled to his own servant Bantock – who, beyond the call of duty, had waited through the night for his captain's return – to assist Gisborne to his bunk in the quarter cabin and settle him down.

'Any messages?' he then demanded of the Officer of the Day – Shacklock – who hurried up on deck, clapping on his hat as he came.

'No, sir. Save that the first lieutenant wished me to inform you that we complete watering and provisioning at noon, and will then in all respects be ready for sea.'

'Very well, Mr Shacklock,' said Oakshott. 'Pray make a note in the log that it is my intent to weigh anchor immediately after the stores are aboard. Have you break-fasted?'

'No, sir. But Bantock has made a pot of coffee in the galley.'

'Enough for two?'

'Ample, sir.'

'Excellent. I must remember to advance that lad to able-bodied seaman. Have him bring some to my great cabin, will you please.'

'Aye, aye, sir.'

In an odd kind of way, it seemed to Oakshott that the narrow confines of what he euphemistically referred to as his great cabin – which in truth was scarcely bigger in length and breadth than a condemned cell in Newgate, though more elegantly appointed, with finely carved panelling so light in construction that it could instantly be struck down when the ship went into action and the after cabin became part occupied by two 16-pounders and their sweating crews – was more to his taste than the stately palace of the Hamiltons, and infinitely more so than the miasma-reeking barrack of a place that was his family seat. The thought recalled him to the death of his brother: a man who, throughout his whole life, had never been known to perform a single generous act, or to exhibit the slightest manifestation of style and elegance that his rank and breeding should have impressed upon his mind. And yet, to give him his due, the poor old fellow's sins had all been of omission.

Bantock brought in the coffee and retired. Oakshott called after him for a shake at eight o'clock, and when he had

77

downed the steaming brew, laid himself upon the bunk and was fast asleep even before the vision of a woman's face had become fully imprinted behind his eyes: a frightened, lovely face, with something of Irene Chancellor's looks.

The arrival of stores called for all hands on deck. The casked meat and biscuit was hauled up from a lighter by sheerlegs and lowered into the hold, each piece checked over the side by the purser's mate.

'Did an almighty fine deal with the merchant ashore,' declared Brewster. 'Sir, I tell you that, when it comes to buying and selling, a Yankee can run rings round any old Eye-talian.'

'You're to be congratulated, Number One,' said Oakshott.

'That I am, sir, that I am,' declared the other with cheerful complacency. 'This feller was asking me three guineas a cask for beef and two for pork. Took him to a wine shop and drank with him till past midnight. In the end, he settled for two and one respectively.'

Oakshott nodded approval of the American's perspicacity.

It was well past noon before the supplies were aboard and battened down. Gisborne came up on deck. Mr Pitt's envoy was looking distinctly green about the gills, the more so because there was a quite tidy swell building up in the anchorage. He clung to the mizzen chains and cast his goat-like glance at Oakshott.

'Are we off, then?' he asked.

'I await your command, sir,' replied Oakshott. 'Do but tell me what course to lay, and I'll up anchor.'

The envoy pointed out of the bay. 'Head south,' he said. 'Once out of sight of this benighted place, turn to your true course.'

'Which is? . . .'

'East. It's to the east we go, Oakshott!'

They were off on a broad reach, with Vesuvius sinking into the horizon astern and the great arms of the bay flattening out. Bosun Cox was at the wheel with a quarter-master.

'Bosun, you have spent a good many years in the Med,' mused Oakshott. 'Where lies Amalfi?'

Cox pointed away to the port quarter, to the long tongue of land that encompassed the eastern end of the bay. 'That be a peninsula, sir,' he said, 'with the island on the end, which is Capri. Now, Amalfi, that's a little port on the eastern side.'

'Pleasant, this Amalfi?'

'I was there but once, sir,' replied Cox. 'Went ashore with a water party. In places, the cliffs do rise sheer up from the sea, with many fine villas, churches and such set atop 'em. I never did in me life see a place of such beauty. The Paradise that parsons do talk of must greatly resemble that coastline, I reckon.'

Oakshott nodded. So it was to there that Alicia Dante-Pergolisi was banished, there to eat out her grief and her folly. Well, he was glad to have kept his peace regarding her undoubted part in the assassination attempt. Alicia had learned her hard lesson, like as not: fair women should not dabble in politics – or murder.

The *Daisy* made good way. By six bells of the afternoon watch the last of Vesuvius had dipped below the horizon, and only its tell-tale plume of smoke remained to mark the dirty, dissolute yet incredibly colourful city of Naples.

'Lay her over on the port tack!'

'Aye, aye, sir!'

With a following wind and studding sails set, Oakshott went below, fired by an anticipation and a curiosity that he could barely contain. Seating himself at his desk, he opened up the melon-topped chest and took from out of the locked drawer the sealed package.

Now he would know the full nature of the *Daisy*'s cruise.

There were two sheets of paper within the package, one written upon in palimpsest, that is to say the Admiralty clerk who had limned the instructions had first written his page in the normal manner and then turned the paper sideways and penned another page over the top. Oakshott grinned to see such commendable frugality.

One sheet was addressed to him by name. It was brief and commanded his first attention:

79

Cdr Ld Chas Oakshott, RN.
HM Sloop-of-War *Daisy*.
By Hand of Officer.

Sir,
You are ordered by Their Lordships to proceed, upon reading
this communication and the appendix also contained, shaping
your best course to the Egyptian port of Alexandria, there to
make your best representations to the shore Authorities with a
view to remaining in that port till Sir Manvers Gisborne has to
his satisfaction concluded divers negotiations with the Mameluke governance there.

The said negotiations are of a highly confidential nature and
will not concern you in any way; yr sole regard will be to remain
in Alexandria, rest on good terms with the Mameluke
authorities there, and await yr further instructions from Sir
Manvers ...'

The usual closing, a dashing signature: that was the sum
of it. Oakshott, considering the anticipations he had
conjured up in many dark hours of the night ... visions of
heady action and the prospects of glory and promotion, not
to say prize-money – was somewhat put down to discover
that the second leg of the *Daisy*'s cruise was to be no more, in
essence, than its first: to act as transport to Mr Pitt's
eminently unlikeable envoy.

With a sigh, *Daisy*'s captain addressed himself to the
second document:

AN AIDE-MEMOIRE
Some Notes upon the Governance of Egypt by the Mamelukes,
by Gervase Scott-Waterfield, MA, Fellow & Tutor of Christ
Church, Oxford, dated March, 1797 AD
MAMELUKE – from the Arabic: *mamluk* – lit 'owned' – is the
name given to white male slaves of mainly Turkish & Circassian
origin, brought by the caliphs of Baghdad as unpaid
mercenaries (if one may be permitted the paradox) to stiffen the
shortcomings of Arab and Persian troops. Oddly, the Mamelukes suavely insinuated themselves into the government and
took over the direction of the state as an established military
caste.

The Fatimid sultans of Egypt (969-1171 AD) brought in
Mamelukes as soldiers, and the renowned Saladin and his

80

successors used them against the Crusaders. The pre-eminence of this military caste has reached what is probably an apogee in the present century in Egypt, now nominally under the Ottoman rule.

In short, at this present time, Egypt is virtually under the governance of the Mamelukes. This is exercised by the joint rule of two of their chieftains, to wit: Ibrahim Bey and Murad Bey.

In 1786, the Porte of Ottoman dispatched an expedition to Egypt to re-establish Ottoman authority. Ibrahim and Murad were desposed, and one Ismail Bey set up in their place. The latter's incompetence, culminating in his death from a plague that ravished Egypt in 1791, persuaded Constantinople that Ibrahim and Murad, for all their shortcomings, had the grit and ruthlessness to rule the ancient land of the pharaohs. And there the situation stands.

Ibrahim and Murad rule Egypt jointly. Not a ship enters Alexandria, nor a traveller sets foot upon those shores, save that these two chief Mamelukes set their seal of approval upon the venture.

To Egypt, then! The evocation had the power to thrill the spirit: uncounted centuries standing guard over a forbidden land. It speaks much for Oakshott's practical mind – rising above his essential romanticism – that he wondered how the *Daisy* would reprovision in a land that, for all one knew, had never yet determined the means to reduce the carcass of a bullock or a hog to the salted contents of a wooden cask as would last for God knows how long; nor master the art of baking ship's biscuit that, notwithstanding the attentions of the weevil, might last twice as long. The question of water, also, posed grave doubts.

He went up on deck; refreshed himself with the knowledge, nightly gained, that the great constellations were still in place: Cassiopeia, Andromeda and Perseus; Pegasus, Taurus and Aries; and the North Star – Polaris – beckoning him home when the time came.

He went back down, serene in the conviction that – notwithstanding the vagaries of common man – the essentials remain, and that the earth and the universe go about their ways, quite uncaring.

81

Part Two
TO THE NILE

Five

'*Sail-ho!*'

It had been 'Ship-ahoy' a score of times a day since leaving Naples, and the masthead cry was scarce enough to cause the watch on deck to desist from idling the hour by playing dice and jacks.

'She's a Froggie – carrying colours!'

'Beat to quarters!' This from the officer of the watch, who was Shacklock. 'Captain, sir!' he bellowed down the after companionway. 'Ship in sight bearing French colours.'

Oakshott was on deck, training his telescope along with all the rest, as the kettledrums, bosuns' pipes and the sketchy call of a bugle brought the *Daisy* to readiness for action.

He trained his glass on a sail that was now quite plain on the sloop's starboard bow, and making to cross the Englishman's track possibly a mile or so ahead on a roughly northerly course, bound for southern Italy maybe.

'She's a small merchantman,' declared Oakshott. 'A brig. No gun ports. But she's carrying the tricolour, and that's a damned cheek, for all that we may well be the only White Ensign in the central Mediterranean. Shape course to intercept her, Mr Shacklock. We'll make her heave to and explain why she dares to be so brash.'

He turned – to find himself looking into the goat's eyes of Mr Pitt's envoy. The other was in a thrusting, aggressive mood – that was clear from the start.

'There'll be no hanky-panky here, Oakshott!' he hissed. 'Let me make it plain. My mission demands that this ship remains on course for Alexandria with a full crew to maintain her. There'll be no skiving off a prize crew to take that vessel to Gibraltar so that you may benefit to the tune of a few guineas all round. Do I make myself plain?'

'Sir, you could not be more plain if you tried,' responded Oakshott. 'I am aware of the conduct of war, and also aware of the special conjunction that I have with you.

'However, sir,' he added, 'you will wish to enter a note in this ship's log book to the effect that you expressly forbade me to take the prize. You will agree to that, of course.'

'Of course, sir,' responded Gisborne.

The brig was closing the range, largely because the faster sloop had sharpened the angle of approach. She was now about five cables distant and fine on the starboard bow.

'Shot across her bows, sir?' asked Brewster, acting in quarters as gunnery officer – till his captain should be killed or incapacitated.

'I think so, Number One,' said Oakshott. 'That always clears the air of any lingering doubts as to one's intention, as well as providing a little target practice for one of the less able gun's crews. Make it so.'

'Aye, aye, sir,' grinned the American.

A gun crew – number three starboard side – was told off to load and make ready to fire, and the aim so judged as to strike water in direct line with the brig's course and half a ship's length in front. The wheel was brought over to allow a clear field of fire.

'*Give fire!*'

Thunderflash and billowing white smoke. 'Sippers' and 'gulpers' of rum ration having been wagered on the outcome of the shot, every man in the ship save the magazine party below followed the course of the 16-pound ball of black-leaded and beautifully polished iron as it soared to its apogee and descended – to strike water a clear fifty yards beyond the brig and well to the fore of intent. There was much ironical hooting and slow hand-clapping from the triumphant gamblers.

'Notwithstanding which,' commented Oakshott, 'I think the point has been made.'

So it was. The tricolour hastily lowered in response to the challenge, the brig's blunt bow was brought up to the wind and she was wallowing with sails aback when the British sloop glided sleekly alongside her at hailing distance.

'What ship – *quel vaisseau?*'

'*Marie Bord* – of Brest.' An English-speaker.

'I am putting a party aboard you. Your captain will come over here.'

A wave of acquiescence. The line of frowning 16-pounders commanded more than mere words would have accomplished.

'Number One, I want you to search her from keel upwards,' said Oakshott, addressing Brewster, who was girt about with a cutlass belt and pistols, as leader of the boarding party. 'Most particularly, I am after any information regarding the French armada – wherever that is, when it was last sighted, whither bound. Do you follow me?'

'Aye, aye, sir,' responded Brewster. 'And I take it, sir, that you will wish me to sail the prize to Gibraltar?'

'We'll speak of that later, Number One,' replied Oakshott with more evasiveness than was his wont. 'Get you gone. Make a thorough search of all aboard her.'

Oakshott rejoined the group on the quarterdeck as the *Daisy*'s jolly boat put out for the brig. From the Frenchman's waist, also, presently came a ship's boat bearing a standing figure in the stern sheets: clearly her captain.

'This is all a damned waste of time!' snarled Gisborne at Oakshott's elbow. 'Why do you not sink her and have done?'

'Apart from acting as your hackney cabbie, Gisborne,' responded Oakshott tartly, 'I am also the captain of a sloop-of-war. And one of the primary reasons for our being – what one might fancifully call our *raison d'être* – is to collect and pass on information regarding the movements of the enemy. That function I am now performing. If it offers you boredom, I suggest that you go below and take yourself a pre-prandial drink.

'Or – failing that – you may go to hell!'

With which, the captain of the *Daisy* turned on his heel and strode away. Gisborne's goat's eyes followed the tall figure; glowered as, with elaborate courtesy, Oakshott welcomed aboard the captain of the French merchantman: a reasonable-enough-looking fellow of middle years, fairly well dressed and in no way resembling the kind of louche gentry Oakshott had been acquainted with during the late Toulon campaign. Gisborne was still watching as the two men exchanged a brief conversation – though they were too far away for him to determine whether the discourse was in English or French.

He remarked that Oakshott was listening more than speaking; that the Frenchman was exceedingly voluble and coloured his discourse with the extravagant gestures – hand-waving, shoulder-hunching, eye-rolling – that the sons of Albion usually ascribe to their nearest neighbours. And, at the end of it, Oakshott nodded yet again, and, striding over to where the envoy stood, gravely addressed him:

'Firstly, Gisborne,' he said, 'I would apologize for my late incivility. Please forgive me. Secondly, you must know – and I wonder if it in any way affects the issue of your mission ...

'Bonaparte has taken Malta!'

The brig's captain was named Leclerc. He was pleased to take wine with Oakshott and Gisborne whilst Brewster was ransacking his ship that dipped and rolled close alongside. He also spoke perfect English.

'When did this happen, sir?' asked Oakshott.

'The armada came in sight of Malta only a week ago, on the ninth,' responded the other. 'General Bonaparte sent ashore a flag of truce and a request to enter harbour and water the fleet. This was refused – to be exact, the Grand Master of the Knights of St John replied that, in conformity with Malta's neutrality, only two ships at a time would be permitted entry – and that for a limited period.'

'And that, I presume, was all the excuse that your general needed,' said Oakshott.

Leclerc smiled, and accepted a refill of his glass. 'You have the general's character most perfectly expressed, sir,' he replied. 'And the taking of the island was no more than a bridegroom possessing his bride. The French Knights of St John vetoed a fight against their own countrymen. The native Maltese would as lief have France as the Knights to rule them. The fight – if you could call it a fight – was a farce.'

'And to think,' said Oakshott, 'that the Order of St John has held Malta through centuries against all comers – the Turks included.'

'And so will France, sir,' replied the other. 'You may mark my words: Malta will be French to the next millenium – and beyond.'

Oakshott made no comment. Gisborne, who had been listening to this exchange with perceptible irritation, broke in:

'And what are General Bonaparte's intentions now, hey?'

The Frenchman raised an eyebrow. 'The general does not take me into his confidence, sir,' he replied coolly.

'But you are detached from the armada,' persisted the envoy. 'You were on your way somewhere. Where – why?'

Oakshott cocked an eye to the Frenchman, wondering how he would handle the question.

'I was bearing dispatches, sir,' replied the other. 'Normally, this would have been done by a frigate or the like, but, since we were unaware of the presence of an English warship in the central Mediterranean ...' he shrugged expressively.

'And these dispatches ... ?' prompted Oakshott.

'I threw them overboard immediately upon your challenging me.'

'Of course,' said Oakshott. 'More wine, sir?'

'Please. It is excellent.'

Oakshott obliged him. 'I am going to sink your ship,' he said, 'and you'll not have the misfortune of being made prisoner of war. I take it that, being a merchantman, you have ample room in your boats for the entire crew?'

'Yes.'

'Be assured that I shall summons any suitable passing ship – and there are many – to take you aboard and on.'

'Thank you, sir. May I be given time to collect my personal belongings?'

'Of course.'

The foregoing civilities appeared to irritate Gisborne to utter distraction, for he listened to them whilst striding up and down the stern cabin, pouring himself more wine and tossing it down with all the desperation of a Devon tinner. Presently, unable to contain himself, he rounded upon the

Frenchman, goat's eyes palely blazing.

'And I suppose,' he cried, 'that as soon as you reach land, you'll report the presence of this ship to your masters, hey – you'll let them know that there's an English warship loose in the central Mediterranean? Excellent wine, or no excellent wine!'

Leclerc hunched his shoulders in the classic Gallic fashion.

'I must do what I must, sir,' he replied. 'But I do not suppose that this charming and hospitable little vessel will cause General Bonaparte any sleepless nights, nor her presence make the slightest difference to his plans.'

The *Daisy*'s crew was understandably chagrined to have lost the coveted prize money, but there lurks in every man an imp of destructiveness, and the prospect of sinking the French vessel was – almost – second best.

A barrel of tar and a slow match formed the classic way to kill a ship, but Oakshott, ever with an eye to improving the efficiency of his gunners, decided to sink the brig with roundshot – if only to afford the younger and less experienced members of the crew the sight of a ship going down, and – more precisely – to observe the *placing* of the shot that would rid her of buoyancy.

The order went out, then, to load with roundshot and to aim for the brig's waterline. One round each from every gun; so far from home and friends, the *Daisy* could afford no more than eighteen rounds for target practice.

'*Give fire!*'

The pieces fired from fore to aft, starboard first, then, when the sloop had gone about, from the port side. Dipping in the troughs a few cables distant, the three ship's boats of the Frenchman bore two score crewmen who gazed upon the death of their home with the sort of dull fatalism admixed with a certain sentimentality that is the sailor's reaction the world over to a like situation.

There were the usual wagers afoot – all in rum. Odds were offered for straight hits on the hull, shorter odds for the fatal strikes at the waterline; overs were outright losers. Shooting at a little over two hundred yards, however, the *Daisy*'s starboard battery scored no less than nine out of nine direct hits on the brig's hull, and four of them dead on the waterline. The vessel was filling up with water and sinking by the bow – quite palpably – before the sloop had gone about and brought her port battery to bear.

Oakshott stayed on deck long enough to see the Frenchman take the final plunge; but the sight did not afford him any pleasure.

The death of a ship – any ship – diminishes any sailor.

That night, Oakshott and Mr Pitt's envoy had their final break. It came about this way: First Lieutenant Brewster, having announced that it was his birthday and that he had a wish to make some small token of the same, short of entertaining the entire complement of officers, suggested that his captain and Sir Manvers might join him at dinner – with the captain's permission, sir – in the great cabin aft. The purser's mate having taken aboard, at Naples, various victuals extra to the general messing, all available to officers and men alike at the going rate, Brewster had apportioned for himself a fine leg of prime pork, which the purser's mate was glad to let go (since, being unsalted, it could scarcely keep for much longer) at a decent price. Oakshott was delighted to accede to the offer and so was Gisborne (the sea being glassy calm and the ship's motion barely perceptible). Accordingly, the very sizeable leg of pork was roasted in the galley that eve, and its rich scent – augmented by the addition of thyme, parsley, basil and onion – haunted all quarters of the ship throughout the last dog watch and drove officers and men alike to a bitter contemplation of their suppertime hard tack and biscuit.

The three of them sat down at eight bells. The joint was brought in with some ceremony by young Bantock, while Brewster's nigger boy Cuthbert served the wine – a light Chianti, purchased in Naples and provided by Oakshott.

'It cuts well,' commented Oakshott, carving.

'My father,' said Brewster, 'back home in our farm outside Boston, reared hogs for the table, the like of which were the talk of the county. Next to the traditional Thanksgiving Day turkey, Brewster's hogs were an integral part of the community's way of life. Not a village junketing was

91

complete without a whole, roast Brewster hog on cut, nor a wedding, nor a funeral. Sir, those hogs will be long remembered after I am forgot. This is good,' he added, helping himself to a first mouthful – as provider of the feast.

'Not too much for me, Oakshott,' said Gisborne, offering his plate. 'I find myself short of appetite.'

'As regards our present voyage,' said Oakshott, when they were all provided, 'I read the aide memoire from the Admiralty with some interest. I take it, Gisborne, that you will be making some sort of negotiation with these Mameluke chiefs, Ibrahim Bey and Murad Bey. Do I have it right?'

'Quite correct.'

'Is there any way – apart from simply lying alongside the wall in Alexandria – in which I can further your enterprise? I ask this in all sincerity, for it seems to me that we have come a long way together, and I would not wish you to think that I am not entirely at your service in all regards.'

The other's pasty face – for Gisborne had never ventured out into the sub-tropical sun without his wide-brimmed straw hat – was turned upon him, the goat's eyes narrowed and suspicious; suspicion and venom were writ in every line of his uncomely countenance.

'Mark this, Oakshott,' snarled the envoy, 'and mark it well. This enterprise will be the making of me. The entire Mediterranean strategy, as conceived by William Pitt, depends upon my present endeavour. My success – my sure success – will see me into the House of Lords.' He grimaced, threw aside his knife and fork and pushed aside his plate. 'And I shall not require the interfering hand of a damned sprig of the peerage and captain of a minor ship of war to steal my laurels. And the same goes for Nelson and the rest of the damned Navy!'

In the awful silence that followed this most intemperate outburst, Brewster remarked that the pork crackling was excellent, and helped himself to another piece of the same. Oakshott made no response to the envoy's vituperative declaration; but observed that Gisborne's brow was beaded with sweat, and that his choler was quite clearly inspired as much by physical malaise as by simple spite.

'Gisborne, are you not well?' he asked.

92

'I am – damned sick!' declared the other. And, suiting the action to the remark, rose to his feet, staggered to the stern windows and, throwing one open, vomited bitterly out into the night.

'Bantock – fetch the carpenter!' ordered Oakshott of his servant, who, with little black Cuthbert, had been the silent observer of the preceding scene. Henshawe was the nearest thing to a surgeon they possessed, being a good hand with the drawing of teeth, lancing of boils, setting of broken limbs and suchlike. He was brought from his supper of hard tack and biscuit (his nostrils quivering towards the largely uneaten leg of pork upon the captain's table) to attend to the envoy, who was by this time slumped by the open stern window and clutching himself slightly above the level of the navel.

'Tell me what ails you, sir,' asked the makeshift ship's surgeon in a mellifluous voice that he had learned to assume, when the need arose, in his part-time trade.

'Damn you, I'm sick!' snarled the other. 'Can't you see I'm sick, you fool?'

'Be you in pain, sir?' asked the patient amateur surgeon.

'Pain? Yes – that also.'

'Where be the pain, sir?'

Grimacing, Gisborne indicated the area immediately below his rib cage.

'And when did the pain begin, sir?'

'Just before we sat down. I – I found myself in not very good appetite ...'

'Did you, sir – did you now?' The carpenter stole a wistful glance towards the prime leg of pork – part consumed and emitting its succulent odour and rich juices. 'No appetite, hey? And what next, sir?'

'Next began this grumbling pain – and then sickness.'

'Aah.'

'Well, give me some physick, man!' snapped Gisborne. 'And have done with your idiot questions!'

Henshawe glanced towards his captain with a certain appeal. 'I could give the gennleman a draught of emetic to hasten the sickness, sir,' he said. 'But I would not advise.'

'Be ruled by Henshawe, Gisborne,' responded Oakshott.

'He's a wise way with him in these matters and with much experience – though not formally trained.'

Gisborne muttered something under his breath and withdrew himself into his pain and discomfort, crouching, eyes closed, in a corner of the window seat and clutching the hurt.

'Permission for a word with you, sir?' murmured Henshawe to his captain, behind his hand and with a meaningful cock of an eyebrow towards his patient.

Oakshott nodded, and himself led the way out into the lobby.

'Well?' he asked. 'What do you think ails him, Henshawe?'

''Tis too early to say, sir,' responded the other. 'Come morning, and the gennleman will be sitting up and demanding his breakfuss – or mayhap he won't. And then we'll have cause to worry.'

'You think it's something serious?'

'I've seen similar many times, sir,' replied the other. 'But there's no cause for concern till the morning watch. Till then, a sup o' spirits wouldn't do much harm and might help him to sleep.'

'And if he's worse in the morning – then what?'

''Twill depend upon how the pain does move, sir,' replied Henshawe. 'If the pain haven't gone – yet have moved – then we may expect a stormy passage for the gennleman. I've seen it many times.'

'What is this – malady – that you suspect?'

''Tis an evil humour of the gut that he may have, sir.'

'And how long does it persist, this evil humour?'

'Till the man be departed this life, sir. And the sooner that do happen, the more merciful.'

Observing that his captain had absorbed his grim prognosis, and that his presence was no longer required, Henshawe knuckled his forelock in salute and took his leave.

When Oakshott re-entered the stern cabin, Brewster was assisting the wretched Gisborne to his – Oakshott's – cot and settling him down there.

'He's been sick again, sir,' said the American. 'Reckon he's in for a bad night.'

'You can stay there, Gisborne,' said Oakshott, 'and I'll sleep in the quarter cabin.'

The former did not reply, or even open his eyes – but merely groaned.

'He said – Henshawe said – that a drop of spirits might be of help,' said Oakshott. 'Pour him a tot of brandy from my tantalus over there, will you, Brewster.'

They fed him the brandy as one might feed a motherless calf with milk from a titty-bottle, and the patient first made as if to throw it up, but in the end managed to consume half the tot before he brushed it aside with a petulant gesture and slumped back against the pillow.

'Best we leave him, don't you think, sir?' opined the American.

Oakshott nodded, and they left.

'Pity about the magnificent leg of pork, Number One,' said the captain of the *Daisy* when they had closed the door, 'but I have to tell you that my appetite, also, is quite gone.'

Brewster grimaced. 'And mine also, sir.'

'Join me up on the quarterdeck,' said Oakshott, 'and I'll pass the word for my servant Bantock to bring us some cocoa laced with rum.'

The night sky was in total stardom, with no more than a few teased-out driftlets of cloud. A full moon. And the sea like dark glass speckled with a rich froth of luminescence trailing from the sloop's bows and fading out astern.

'Sir Manvers, before he was taken sick,' said Brewster, 'sure did deliver a fine broadside against the Navy. Not to mention your good self, sir. And Admiral Nelson.'

Oakshott took a sip of the laced cocoa and savoured the rich warmth on his palate. 'The Navy has broad shoulders,' he commented. 'I don't give a damn about Gisborne's opinion of me. But if he hadn't taken ill, I might have had a few words to put forward in Nelson's defence, since he once did me a considerable service. Indeed, I can think of only one other person in my life to whom I owe a like debt of gratitude.'

'You know the admiral personally, sir?'

'I encountered him personally only once,' said Oakshott.

'It was at my *viva voce* for promotion to commander. I had been out drinking with an old shipmate – now, unhappily, no longer with us – and my drunken tongue had all but ruined my chances before the Board, when Nelson came in, having been delayed. He swung the Board in my favour.'

The American eyed his captain over the rim of his mug. 'That he wouldn't have done simply because he took to the cut of your jib, sir,' he opined. 'You must have earned the commendation, I guess.'

Oakshott shrugged. 'I'd been travelling passenger in a Dutch brig out of the Hook,' he said. 'It chanced that we were set upon by two Frog frigates and I had the luck to lure one of them on to a sand bar. Nelson saw it happen from *Agamemnon*. That was all.' He fell silent.

'Fine sailer, the *Agamemnon*,' observed Brewster presently. 'I did a stint aboard her.'

'Finest sailer in the fleet, Number One.'

'Undoubtedly, sir. But you were saying that there was another to whom you owe gratitude ...'

Oakshott grinned into his cocoa. 'That's so,' he said. 'And the recounting of the story doesn't redound much credit on me. I was a junior midshipman at the time. Aboard the *Mayfly*, frigate, thirty-six. Our captain was one Abraham Spear. A good seaman, but a brute, a bully and a bad captain. He took against me from the start, for I gave him some lip, being in those days somewhat uppity. Spear mastheaded me on average thrice a week, nor did that break my foolish boy's spirit, and I think if it had gone on, he might have killed me with exposure to the elements up there, or I could have fallen from the icy rigging one mad, stormy night.

'Our first lieutenant was Henry Darby (and the last I heard he was captain of the *Bellerophon*), a fine officer, though on the taciturn side. He reasoned with me, often, to quell my high spirits when the captain was around, but he did not have the powers of persuasion to convince me. I persisted in proving to my messmates of the gunroom that young Charlie Oakshott could not be broken by the likes of Spear.

'It happened one eve off Finisterre. I had the last dog watch that I kept with Darby. Spear came up on deck, all fuming with rage. He had with him my midshipman's log, with the day's journal, in which I'd made an observation that he took to be directed against him – and it was.

'To paint the scene: it was blowing a half-gale and promising worse. A February night and cold enough to freeze Old Nick himself. Spear ordered me to the main topgallant – the main topgallant, mind you – and I was to stay there till dawn. Barefoot and all.'

'Barefoot!' echoed Brewster.

'The very same,' said Oakshott. 'Darby made some considerable protest, but Spear silenced him. Up went Charlie Oakshott.'

'It's a wonder you survived it, sir,' opined the American.

'I wouldn't have,' replied Oakshott soberly, 'but for friends. Some time in the first watch, all hands were called to shorten sail when the full force of the gale fell upon us. One of the topmen, finding me crouched up there and frozen stiff, put a rope around my middle and lashed me to the mast. On that account, I didn't fall, as fall I must have.'

'But you could still have perished of the cold,' said Brewster, 'barefoot and all.'

'Like as not,' conceded Oakshott. 'But I would have known nothing of it, for I presently fainted clean away. Next I knew, I was waking in my warm hammock and my messmates were chafing me and feeding me with cocoa.

'It was Lieutenant Darby who brought me down. In the middle watch, and contrary to orders. He saved my life – the life of an uppity young sprig – and I shall be beholden to him till the end of my days.'

'And what was Captain Spear's reaction, sir, to this flagrant disobedience of his orders?' asked Brewster.

'He threatened Darby with a court martial, but thought better of it upon mature reflection,' replied Oakshott. 'And he was afterwards killed in quite commendable circumstances at the Glorious First of June, so it could be said he's set the record straight as far as I am concerned. But, as I say, I am still in Darby's debt.'

Six bells of the first watch rang out. Oakshott drained his mug, and his companion did likewise.

'I'll turn in, Number One,' he said. 'Tomorrow morning, it's to be hoped that our egregious passenger is quite his

97

repulsive self again. Good night to you.'

'And you, sir,' responded the American, touching the brim of his outrageously befeathered hat. His lean face was directed towards his captain's back, and the clever eyes regarded Oakshott as the latter swung down the companion-way.

It's like peeling an onion, thought Brewster. The longer one knows that fellow, the more one listens to his converse, the greater becomes the complexity of his character, as fresh levels of his being emerge.

Aloud to himself, he added: 'Ho-ho, we are in a philosophical mood this night, Thomas.' And added: 'By God, the clean air has quite restored my appetite. Pity we left that fine leg of pork. Still – it will serve well cold with apple sauce. If we have any apples.'

Morning brought another blistering sun, and the officer-of-the watch had thoughtfully ordered awnings to be rigged over quarterdeck and fo'c'sle, where they afforded blessed shade and were scarcely disturbed by the light airs that barely filled the sloop's sails.

Oakshott rose early and went to see Gisborne, to find him in a wretched state: the envoy lay half in and half out of the cot, bathed in sweat and moaning piteously.

'Are you no better, Gisborne?' asked *Daisy*'s captain – somewhat superfluously.

'I – I am dying, Oakshott!' came the hoarse response.

Henshawe was sent for. The carpenter became grave-faced at one glance, and addressed his patient gently: 'Be the pain shifted, sir?'

'Yes,' breathed the sufferer. 'Now it's – here!' And he gingerly touched the right lower side of his abdomen.

'Aah!' said Henshawe, and looked wise. 'Do you please open your mouth, sir,' he requested.

Gisborne, whose natural choler seemed quite to have abated, and who was taking to obeying his 'physician' with a childlike meekness, did as he was told; Henshawe peered closely into the other's open mouth – and again nodded sagely. 'Let us lift up your shirt and have a closer look at the place of pain, sir,' he then said.

As Oakshott looked on, the amateur ship's surgeon gently touched the area on the right lower abdomen. 'It feels very hard and tight, the skin here,' he said. 'Sir, does it greatly hurt when I do - this?' He did no more than tap the tightly stretched skin - and Gisborne gave a shrill yelp of pain. Then let his head loll back against the pillow, closing his eyes.

Henshawe glanced at his captain and inclined his head towards the door; discerning his message, Oakshott went out, and the carpenter followed.

'Well, Henshawe?' said Oakshott. 'I take it the malady has developed as you feared?'

'Yes, sir,' responded the other. 'The pain has moved to that part of the gut where the evil humour does rest till merciful death ends the victim's agony.'

'Are you sure - *quite* sure?'

'If there were any doubt in my mind, sir, 'twas the smell of the gennleman's breath as laid such doubt to rest. I smelt it plain - the reek of rank hay or grass. In every such who'm I've met with this evil humour of the gut, I've smelt rank hay or grass on the breath, so I have, sir.'

'And what now, Henshawe?' asked Oakshott. 'Must he die?'

'As sure as night do follow day, sir,' came the reply. 'I never saw one as did recover.'

'In great pain?'

'In most agony, sir.'

'But there must be some way to relieve him. Tincture of opium, perhaps?'

'Yes, sir, I do have some laudanum in my ditty box.'

'Use it, Henshawe. Keep him out of pain to the end.' Oakshott turned to go up on deck, but paused after a couple of paces. 'You are free of all duties, to attend Sir Manvers,' he said. 'Feed him laudanum at your discretion.' He walked on a little further - then turned again. 'You are *sure* there is no hope, Henshawe?'

'As sure as I believe anything, sir.'

Oakshott nodded, and went on up.

'Man that is born of a woman hath but a short time to live,

and is full of misery. He cometh up, and is cut down, like a flower; he flee-eth as it were a shadow, and never continueth in one stay ...'

It was cool, that dawn, under the quarterdeck awning, with the sun barely up, and a light breeze gusting fitfully over the bare heads of the men gathered there around the corpse wrapped in the bolt of sailcloth and covered by a Union flag.

Oakshott, long familiar with the Order for the Committal of the Dead, both in hearing and latterly in the reading thereof, could have repeated the words in his sleep.

'Forasmuch as it hath pleased Almighty God of His great mercy to take unto Himself the soul of our dear brother here departed ...'

The word 'brother' tripped none too lightly off the tongue, for Oakshott had to admit to himself that, with the greatest of Christian forbearance, he had found it – and still found it – quite impossible to contemplate Gisborne with other than distaste; though the poor wretch's last days (he had shrugged off this mortal coil not forty-eight hours after the first onset of the 'evil humour of the gut'* – and, notwithstanding the laudanum, in dire agony) had softened his memory to a very large degree. Oakshott had taken turn and turn about with Henshawe to watch over the dying man and tend to his needs. There had been times, in his delirium, when the envoy had called out such declarations as: 'I shall win my glory ... the House of Lords for me ... a waterway carved through the desert ... highway to India!' And the theme of his elevation to the peerage constantly reiterated.

'... we therefore commit his body to the deep, to be turned into corruption, looking for the resurrection of the body, when the sea shall give up her dead ...'

The brief obsequies finished, four sailors lifted the wrapped corpse upon a plank and tipped it over into the ship's wake, where it sank out of sight in a trice, weighted as it was with two spheres of roundshot.

---

*Which the reader will have discerned to have been peritonitis – at that time undiagnosed and unnamed.

Whatever the mission of Mr Pitt's envoy, it had been cut short most precipitately.

Straight after the committal, Oakshott had his servant bring all of the dead man's gear to his stern cabin, where, seated at his desk, shirtsleeved against the heat, with the windows wide open and a quite pleasant draught moving through the compartment, *Daisy*'s captain addressed himself to his duty, which as he saw it, was to determine the exact nature of Gisborne's brief from Prime Minister Pitt (if such a thing existed on paper), and himself do whatever lay in his power to advance it.

There were three main pieces of luggage: two chests and a leather valise. The latter he found to contain linen, some tins of snuff, a pot of gentleman's rouge, and half a dozen calf-bound books of an erotic nature. Laying aside this mute evidence of the deceased envoy's secret proclivities, Oakshott next opened up the larger of the two chests – after which, since it revealed nothing but outer clothing and footwear, he was reduced to his last option.

The smaller chest was crammed with a jumble of items of a personal nature: writing materials, a diary (to be examined later), comb and hairbrushes, hair ribbons, an account book, gloves, soap, a night-cap, scissors, some soiled handkerchiefs, and a large packet of letters – which Oakshott doggedly read, only to find that all were of a private and frequently embarrassing nature.

And there was a rather ill-concealed false bottom in the chest. In it reposed a sheaf of papers dated six weeks previously and addressed from Number 10 Downing Street, Westminster.

The main body of the matter was a memorandum penned by Pitt's private secretary. It was addressed to Gisborne and marked *Highly Confidential* – thrice underlined.

Sir,
The **PM** has instructed me to summarize the burden of yr discussions with him on the 10th instant, and to repeat the instructions that were given you verbally on that occasion.

1. Our information is that by a secret decree of 12th April last, the French Directory has instructed Bonaparte to assemble an expedition to sail to Egypt, wrest that country from Turkish suzerainty by overthrowing Mameluke rule, and make the way clear for French advancement to India, Ceylon and the Orient generally.
2. It is accepted that our source for the above information may be unreliable, even tainted – and indeed that the same may be a deliberate stratagem to deceive us as to the enemy's true intent.
3. Notwithstanding which, Ld St Vincent has been ordered to augment the squadron under the command of Admr. Sir H. Nelson and detach this fleet to the pursuit of the French, with the intent of destroying same before (a) it reaches Egypt, or (b) when the expedition has been landed, thus isolating Bonaparte's land forces.
4. Further notwithstanding, the PM is doubtful that Nelson's fleet will be able to catch the enemy in the wide range of the Mediterranean either before or after the possible Fr. landing in Egypt, and that the same Fr. fleet may remain in being to support their land forces.
5. In anticipation of this, you are to proceed to Egypt with all dispatch (first calling at Naples to arrange the supplying of Nelson's fleet – See Appendix 1, attached), and make representations to the Mameluke Beys; offering them the total support of Britain against the threat of French invasion, warning them of the Directory's secret decree of 12th April last, and negotiating a draft treaty between our two countries in accordance with the schedules contained in Appendices 2 and 3 (attached) . . .

And that, thought Oakshott, accounts for the aspired seat in the House of Lords. Baron Gisborne of Wherever, Proconsul of Egypt!

He read through the Appendices, and Numbers 2 and 3 were composed of mightily heady stuff, sufficient to fire the spirits of considerably less ambitious men than he judged Gisborne to have been. Reading and re-reading with growing wonderment, he digested Pitt's plan to virtually colonize Egypt as a British vassal – pre-empting Bonaparte and the French.

102

There was provision, in the proposed draft treaty, to reorganize the Egyptian land forces and fleet under British officers. It was proposed immediately to commence upon the project – long dreamed of since pharaonic days – of carving a canal to join the Mediterranean to the Red Sea, all directed by British engineers with native labour. There were further plans – more woolly, even more fanciful – for exploring the dark hinterland of the great African continent to the glory and profit of Britain by navigating the River Nile to its source. All these grandiose projects, and teeming others, were to be fired and fuelled by ... gold!

A large section of the third schedule was devoted to the funding of the proposed treaty: an astronomical sum of gold guineas would mark the ratification of the same. There were other inducements: the two beys were each to receive similar amounts upon signature, and there were provisions for lesser 'gifts' for lesser functionaries, gifts which, as the writer pointed out in the schedule, were a classic ingredient of political and business transactions east of the Pillars of Hercules.

That, then, was Pitt's plan: a two-pronged reaction to the supposed French move; if Nelson failed at sea, diplomacy must win on land, with Egypt organized to defend the gate to India in the interests of Albion.

A slight increase in the breeze that refreshingly cooled the stern cabin, an almost imperceptible motion underscored by the faint creaking of block and tackle, signalled that the wind had shifted. Laying aside the papers, Oakshott went up on deck. The awnings were already being taken in, and Quinch the sail master was conferring with officer-of-the-watch Shacklock as to a re-setting of the sails. They both saluted their captain. Oakshott left them to their deliberations and walked forward to the bows where, supporting himself on the rail, he looked out ahead to the south-east and his next landfall.

There had never been an instant's doubt in Oakshott's mind where his duty lay in the matter. A captain of the Georgian Navy was the end of a long arm of Albion's might. As such, he possessed the power of life and death over his command. The advancement of his sovereign's will was his sole criterion, and in following this duty the captain's will was also sovereign.

Envoy Gisborne, rudely cut off, had been given his orders, and he – Oakshott – would take on the mantle of envoy, since there was none other present to perform the orders given in the king's name by the king's chief minister.

The equation, to Oakshott's intensely mathematical mind, was perfect and indisputable.

In this ethic of a captain's sovereignty, of course, there was one small snag: it permitted of no allowance for failure.

There were no second prizes for trying!

Six

The *Daisy* closed with the North African littoral and coasted it for two days, taking continuous soundings and finding the depth good and also constant. At noon on the third day, the lookouts reported a lighthouse and a city. Oakshott ordered Bosun Cox on deck: he who, of all the crew, was most thoroughly versed in the landfalls of the eastern Mediterranean.

'Aye, 'tis Alexandria, sir,' confirmed Cox, sighting through his captain's telescope. 'Yonder's the Pharos light, as was put there by the Emperor Pompey, so they do say.'

'What of the approach?' demanded Oakshott.

'A straight run-in would be advised, sir,' replied the bosun. 'Keeping well to port, as I recall. There be plenty o' room in the roads, with anchorages in abundance, and quays galore. Mark you, sir, it have been twenty years since I were here last. There ain't likely to have been many improvements – indeed, the port is likely to have been greatly run down, considering the idle ways of folks in these parts.'

Mindful of Egypt's neutrality, and aware of the Ottoman Empire's notorious xenophobia – particularly towards Christian nations – Oakshott was dubious about sticking his neck into a hornets' nest without a careful plan; he had already given it some thought.

'We will beat to quarters before entering harbour, Number One,' he said presently.

'Aye, aye, sir.'

'Not too ostentatiously, mind. Load with alternate ball and langridge. But don't run out the guns. And have a few fellows lolling and smoking up in the heads. It might be an idea to have some washing hanging up. A couple of fenders over the side. A rope trailing in the water – you know the kind of thing.'

'A little – *dégagé*, as the Frogs say, sir,' responded Brewster, grinning at the thought of so tight a ship as the *Daisy* entering harbour in the state that his captain had sketched.

'Precisely,' said Oakshott, grinning also. And to Cox: 'From your recollection, Bosun, what hour of the day are things most quiet in these parts? Do they partake of the siesta, like the Spaniols?

'Indeed they do, sir,' replied Cox. 'Most religiously they do. Betwixt four bells of the afternoon watch and the end of the first dog you could fire a broadside of langridge down the main street all unbeknownst.'

'And what happens at six in the evening?'

'The first dog being over, sir,' replied the bosun, 'the whole town do take to the streets for a promenade.'

Oakshott rubbed his chin. 'Do they now,' he mused. 'Well, that will suit us very well. As good an introduction to Alexandria as one could wish for.

'Bosun, have your quartermaster pass the word for the purser's mate to muster here on the quarterdeck.'

'Aye, aye, sir.'

As a minor ship-of-war, the *Daisy* did not rate a qualified purser, but the purser's mate, one Butterworth, was as honest a man as the purser's department went, and a mathematician after Oakshott's heart. He was quick to attend his captain's summons; a man in his late forties, earnest-faced, bespectacled, plump and heavily-perspiring.

'Butterworth,' said Oakshott, 'when were the hands last paid?'

'Sir, they were paid in Gib, sir,' replied the other.

'And are they spent up?'

'Sir, a little money may be passing around in cards and dice,' replied the purser's mate, 'but I would say that ninety-nine per cent of what was paid out in Gib was frittered away in buying trumpery gee-jaws from the Gib bumboats. Likewise in Naples.'

106

'So, substantially, they are on their uppers?'

'Yes, sir.'

'Very well, Butterworth. Lower deck will be cleared at noon today, and you will pay all hands - officers included - three months in advance.'

The honest Butterworth's slack mouth went agape; he eyed his captain - whom, as a fellow mathematician, he looked upon with considerable esteem - as one might regard a beloved dog who has gone berserk.

'Thu-three months', sir?'

'That is so, Butterworth.'

The purser's mate's eyes swivelled from side to side, probing the glances of those who stood around - the first lieutenant and the bosun and others - as if seeking confirmation of his belief that the captain had gone mad. Three months' pay in advance - why, it flew in the face of all reason and naval discipline! What devilment might not a common sailor get up to with three months' pay in his pocket?

'Attend upon the first lieutenant at six bells, Butterworth,' said Oakshott, 'who will open the ship's safe. Every man must have three months' pay in hand before we enter Alexandria harbour.'

'Aye, aye, sir,' breathed Butterworth feebly, and took himself off to prepare his nominal list for payment - by now thoroughly convinced that his beloved captain's brain had been addled by the sub-tropical sun.

Oakshott, aware that all eyes on the quarterdeck were upon him, took a few paces to and fro, smiling quietly to himself the while.

Presently, he paused, 'Bosun ...'

'Sir?'

'How is the dancing aboard us?'

'The - *dancing*, sir?' Now it was Cox's turn to glance round and seek confirmation from those present that the old man had gone quite loopy.

'The Hornpipe and the Morris dancing, Bosun.'

'Ah, I follow you now, sir,' said Cox, much relieved.

'The reason I ask is because I have not seen or heard any dancing in recent weeks.'

107

'Ah, sir. That would be on account of the heat, you see. The hands prefer to lie under the awnings when they're off watch, rather than get in a lather of sweat with the Hornpipe and such.'

'Well, there will be dancing in the last dog. See to it. Muster, also, every fiddle, penny whistle and drum. And the bosuns' pipes shall augment the merry noise.'

'Aye, aye, sir.'

Oakshott nodded agreeably and swung himself down the companionway.

'Very good. Number One, maintain the present course and have me called when Alexandria harbour entrance is nearly abeam.'

'Aye, aye, sir.'

Brewster exchanged glances with Bosun Cox, but neither man gave any sign to the other of what might have been in his mind.

'By the mark – seven!'

It was five o'clock in the afternoon – two bells – and swelteringly hot; the *Daisy* wallowed slowly towards the harbour entrance in light airs, with the leadsmen taking prudent soundings all the way, there being no charts of the Egyptian littoral.

'A deep six!'

'Beat to quarters – quietly,' ordered Oakshott.

This was done; the guns loaded but not run out. Already, a delighted pair of midshipmen were rigging up some particularly unaesthetic small-clothes on washing lines for'ard, and fenders and a trailing rope had been put out, as ordered.

'By the mark – four!'

'Does this look about right to you, Bosun?' asked Oakshott, passing his telescope to Cox, who trained it on the scene ahead.

'Not a body in sight, sir,' replied the other. 'I mark that the Pharos and the mole are unchanged, likewise the citadel, which, when I was last here, fair bristled with cannon. And like still to be.'

'By the mark – three!'

108

'Number One, if we are challenged, we dip the ensign in acknowledgement and continue to proceed.'

'Aye, aye, sir.' Brewster had put on, for the occasion, a dress uniform coat of some ephemeral material that might have been the finest and filmiest of Irish linen, and a high stock that reached to his earlobes, with an extravagantly frilled shirt. And, surely, thought Oakshott, the fellow was adding an extra plume to his hat for every new week of his life.

'If we are fired upon directly, we will return fire, turn about and make ourselves scarce – back the way we came.'

'By the mark – three.'

With eighteen feet of water below her waterline, the *Daisy* slid past the end of the mole unchallenged; stole under the shadow of Pompey's lighthouse, and came broadside on to the frowning walls of the citadel, in whose machicolated ramparts could be seen the frowning muzzles of cannon.

'Make ready to come to anchor! I'll have her close by yonder quay,' said Oakshott, pointing. 'A cable's length from the shore, no more. There's a large brig alongside the wall, so we should have plenty of water under our keel.'

Barefoot pattering on the decks, silent haste to carry out his order, most skilful handling of the great wheel to bring the sloop precisely to the spot that he had indicated. The *Daisy* turned on a half-guinea, spilled the wind from her sails; the best bower anchor splashed into the scummy waters of Alexandria harbour and held fast.

'Dress ship overall!'

Already, every signal flag in the locker, and the courtesy flags of all nations, had been brought out and strung together; the hands swarmed up the shrouds, and in no time the *Daisy* bore a brave crest of colour stretching from the end of her elegant bowsprit and sprung from masthead to masthead, to the taffrail.

'Very pretty,' was Oakshott's comment. 'Gives us a singularly unwarlike appearance. And I observe that our arrival has already begun to arouse the populace from its siesta.'

From out of the dark alleyways that led off from the corniche there appeared nightgowned and turbaned figures;

at first they came in driblets of twos and threes, but presently they were issuing in tides of excited humanity from every hole and doorway; crowding to the edge of the quay; chattering and gesticulating towards the tall ship just out of throwing distance, all in its beflagged splendour.

'Muster the dancers!' ordered Oakshott. 'And keep a sharp eye on the citadel.'

'They've manned the guns up there, sir!' cried a midshipman.

'By God, they have,' said Oakshott, training his telescope, to observe that the pieces up in the ramparts had been run out and that a row of dark faces was regarding them. 'Let us hope that our peaceful intentions are manifestly apparent.'

'Dancers mustered, sir!' Cox touched his forelock.

'A lively air to begin with,' said Oakshott.

'With respect, might I propose "Bean-Setting", sir?'

'Make it so.'

And so, in that far-flung corner of the Mediterranean, in the late afternoon sunlight, before the rapt eyes and ears of the silent and awestruck multitude, the fiddles and whistles struck up the jaunty air more familiar by far in the village greens of rural England; and out of the fo'c'sle screen there issued a dozen Morris men in pairs – Devonians, all – in ribboned hats and jangling bells, and carrying thick cudgels.

The drums and tambours joined in, quickening the tempo!

Jingle-jingle went the bells with every stamp of foot!

Clack-clack! Clack-clack! as the cudgels were struck together with high disregard for barked knuckles!

'Captain, sir – the gunners up there have lit slow match!' cried the midshipman lookout.

Oakshott pointed his telescope to the ramparts. Sure enough, the thin plumes of smoke from lighted matches – six of them – rose in the still air. The fortress guns were loaded and trained, awaiting the order to give fire.

'Run out the guns, sir?' suggested Brewster.

'Not yet, Number One.'

The 'Bean-Setting' ended with a flourish, a jangle-jangle, a clash and a clatter.

'Now we give them the Hornpipe!' cried Oakshott. 'Clear

lower deck! The whole crew – officers and all!'

Slowly, teasingly at first, then building up in tempo, the traditional double-double beat of the catchy Hornpipe brought the men of the *Daisy* advancing and retreating, arms folded, barefoot and prancing, officers and men alike, crowded across the narrow, scrubbed and holystoned decks from fore to aft. Oakshott, alone, eschewed the dance, though he was a fair performer; his whole attention was upon the silent multitude that watched them from the quay, gauging its mood, speculating upon the effect which the rumbustious gaiety of the Hornpipe might or might not be having upon the dark suspicions which the arrival of the *Daisy* must almost certainly have aroused. But the impassive, dusky faces told him nothing; the people – men, women and children, all – stood like statues, immobile and expressionless.

'Quicken the beat, lads!' cried Bosun Cox.

Fiddlers and pipers responded mightily; the dancers picked up the step – and now it was a wild, demanding step, a high and capering step.

'Faster – faster!' called Cox, and close on 130 perspiring men obeyed him; the whole ship rocked to the pounding of their bare feet.

And then – it happened . . .

Oakshott saw the beginning of it: the immobility of the watching multitude on the shore was broken, almost imperceptibly at first, as one or two started jigging to the beat of the Hornpipe. And then a whole row of them were at it, and more joined in.

And then all Alexandria seemed to be dancing with the crew of the *Daisy*; men, women and little ones, old and young, whole and lame, the straight and the crooked; all doing the Hornpipe as if they had been at it all their lives.

'We have them!' said Oakshott, elated.

It was then, as if upon a signal, that the bumboats put out from the shore, from every quay and inlet; they swarmed like lice upon the anchored sloop-of-war, gunwales scarcely above water with the abundance of their wares: great green watermelons the size of prize pumpkins, live fowl screeching in rickety small cages of papyrus stem, tiny lambs trussed fore and aft and bleating most piteously, bloody haunches of cow-beef that patient children fanned against the teeming flies, mountains of sweet corn, cabbages, peas, beans, lentils, yams and potatoes; and the purveyors of gaudy finery, the trumpery of the bazaars, cheap shoddy and spurious velvets from Baghdad, Basra, Damascus and Constantinople; imitation Damascene work from Cairo, jewellery wrought in Smyrna, camel whips plaited by patient women in the villages of the lower Nile, embroidered slippers, curious skullcaps such as the Bedouin wear when smoking the hookah at their ease, fancy waistcoats sewn with beads of coloured glass; rings, bracelets, necklaces, earrings, nose jewellery, toe jewellery; and then the gully-gully men who produce tiny chicks from their ears for a tossed coin, the vendors of small snakes and baby crocodiles, coneys, desert rats, mongeese, jerboas; Delta falconers offering trained vultures, kites, hawks, eagles and owls. And there were veiled girls on offer also.

Oakshott watched with satisfaction as, the dancing finished, his crew crowded to the rails to do business with the bumboatmen, tossing down their hard-earned coin (paid three months in advance), and counted that there must have been at least fifty small craft surrounding the *Daisy*, with another hundred jockeying for position to move in.

'I think we've been accepted here, Number One,' he opined. 'They'll not fire on us from the citadel – not with all the bumboats in Alexandria lying around us and giving us their protection. And *they'll* remain here for so long as the crew's money lasts.'

'They've run in the guns up there, sir,' replied Brewster, 'and put out their matches.'

And so it was.

The crowds remained on the quay all through the long evening and twilight; the bumboats continued to carry on their trade. *Daisy*'s sailors, after the manner of sailors since time immemorial, vied with each other to spend and spend again on items that were either edible or drinkable – or were of a trumpery enough nature, or sufficiently bizarre, to catch their fancy. So it was that much unripe fruit was ingested that eve, and a lot of dubious fruit drink imbibed. Embroidered caps and slippers adorned many of the hands off watch; others strolled the decks in the cool of the evening with small coloured snakes looped around their necks, or carrying baby crocodiles adorned with ribbons. Yet another parrot had appeared aboard and the messmen who had clubbed together to buy the bird were already teaching the innocent creature to repeat lower-deck expletives. There had been sundry attempts to bring aboard veiled ladies at vastly inflated charges – but they had all been turned back at the gangway by the officer of the day.

Oakshott sat at supper alone, feasting off a thinly-cut steak of cow-meat that, by smothering it with fried onions to mask the decided aroma of dissolution and by hammering it with a marlin-spike, the most expert Bantock had contrived to translate into the illusion – as regards both flavour and texture – of a cut from a prime Hereford bull.

Brewster knocked and entered.

'Visitors coming aboard, sir,' he said. 'Looks like the great panjandrum himself. Do we pipe him aboard?'

'By all means,' replied Oakshott. 'Plenty of ceremony, then bring him down here to me. Important-looking personage, you would say, eh?'

The American grinned. 'Sir, if he ain't the biggest man in town, I'd be surprised. There's a diamond in his headgear that you could weigh against a plover's egg!'

Shoving the remains of his supper out of sight, Oakshott shrugged into his full-dress coat, clapped his hat on his head, buckled on his sword belt – and awaited the arrival of the newcomer in an attitude suggestive of a busy, important man hard at work upon papers of great pith and moment.

He only looked up when, Brewster having tapped discreetly upon the door and having opened the same in response to a gruff order to enter, the visitor was ushered in. The captain of the *Daisy* then put down his pen, stood up to his full height, and extended a hand.

'In the name of King George, I greet you, sir,' he said with as much portentousness as he could muster.

The great panjandrum – an apt term – was immensely obese, bearded, with narrow-set eyes; dressed in gold-embroidered coat over a shift of fine linen, with a vast turban of patterned silk adorned at the brow with the huge diamond to which Brewster had alluded.

Oakshott's greeting was not understood by the dignitary, who inclined his head to a personage standing at his elbow. The latter, a dark-eyed mercurial-looking manikin clad all in black, gave his master what was apparently a translation in Arabic, to which the other replied, looking and gesturing towards the *Daisy*'s captain.

'His Excellency Mohammed el-Korain, may his shadow never grow less, Governor of this city, likewise greets you in the name of The Most Serene Sultan Selim the Third,' said the little man in black, his clever eyes twinkling good-humouredly at Oakshott. 'He wishes you a long life, and asks if you are perhaps from the British squadron that appeared off Alexandria last week and then departed.'

Oakshott's heart beat faster: so Nelson had been already, and finding no sign of the French had gone on to continue his search!

'No, I am not,' he replied; then, striving to keep the excitement out of his voice: 'How many British ships?'

'Fourteen battleships,' was the reply. 'And now, His Excellency wishes to know how long you are hoping to remain in Alexandria. I would add,' he continued in his perfect, almost imperceptibly-accented English, 'that it will cost you mightily to remain more than the statutory two days allowed by a neutral power.' At the end of this delivery, he *winked* at Oakshott with the eye furthest away from his master.

'Tell His Excellency that I wish to remain here only for so long as it takes me to present certain proposals from my government to your ruling beys,' replied Oakshott.

This declaration, duly translated, wrought a remarkable change in the Governor; in place of a former attitude of lightly-veiled boredom, he became extremely animated and had a lengthy and voluble exchange with the translator.

'What did he say?' asked Oakshott, when it was over.

'Their Excellencies Murad Bey and Ibrahim Bey reside in Cairo, sir,' was the reply. 'To reach there would take you two

114

or three days on horseback. You would, of course, require horses. And a guide.'

'How much?' demanded Oakshott.

The manikin winked again – covertly.

'Start him at a hundred English guineas and let him beat you up to a hundred and fifty,' he replied. 'But not too quickly.'

The transaction – haggling – was considerably protracted, during which time Oakshott ordered tea for his guests. It was four bells before Governor Mohammed el-Korain nodded with ponderous gravity and condescended to accept 150 guineas for the loan of four horses and a guide.

And the guide . . .

'I shall be your guide and interpreter, sir,' said the little man in black. 'Pepe Lopez, at your service.

'And if I may say so without giving offence, sir' – he added with a wink and a metaphorical nudge – 'you handled His Excellency extremely well. One might have thought you had Turkish blood in your veins. *Such* intrepid bargaining.'

'Thank you,' said Oakshott, amused.

They set off at dawn the following day: four of them. For companions, Oakshott had chosen Lieutenant Shacklock, that former midshipman of no great promise who had grown in stature both physically and as a steady and reliable young officer, and Ship's Carpenter Henshawe, not only for his steadiness but also because of his wide knowledge – and, though Oakshott did not admit it to himself, the Geordie chippy was, amongst the officers and crew of the *Daisy*, perhaps the man with whom he had the most rapport.

Along with them went the surprising Pepe Lopez.

The *Daisy* remained where she was: close by the wall of the corniche, still surrounded by bumboats who would act as leeches upon the sloop until they had sucked every penny of the sailors' three months' advance of pay – and incidentally provide a protective shield against any possible treachery on the part of the Governor.

Upon leaving Brewster in temporary command, Oakshott had given him specific orders: 'Trust no one ashore, Number

One. They'll take our bribes, but it's been proved time and time again that the Turkish Empire doesn't like us. As for that fellow Mohammed el-Korain, who took our hundred and fifty guineas and looks the sort who'd grow cabbages on his mother's grave, trust him least of all.

'You'll be safe from the guns up in the citadel for so long as the bumboats remain, so encourage the crew to make their pay spin out.

'If Nelson returns, inform the admiral that I am in Cairo carrying out the mission entrusted to the late Sir Manvers Gisborne. Lastly, if the French are sighted off Alexandria, don't get caught with your breeches down. Get out of here. Cut your cable if needs be. Stand off downwind at your best point of sail – and run like hell from their frigates!'

'And how shall you locate us if we're at sea, sir?' asked Brewster.

'By a simple stratagem,' replied Oakshott. 'Listen carefully ...'

They rode at walking pace through the dawn, with the new eastern light touching the prim fields of the delta, turning them from grey to green and from mere green to shimmering emerald; where patient toilers were already stooped at their work, gathering, tending, irrigating; whole families from ancients to infants, and many of the women carried babies on their backs.

'Nothing here has changed since the days of the pharaohs,' said Pepe Lopez. 'Conquerors may come and go, empires may wax and wane, but the Egyptian fellahin will still remain to work the Nile's annual miracle.'

'You are something of a philosopher perhaps, Pepe,' opined Oakshott.

The other flashed him a sidelong glance, a grin, a twinkle of berry-black, clever eyes. 'I am well schooled in the philosophy of life, sir,' he rejoined. 'By birth, I am a Spanish Moor, born in Cadiz. I was educated by the imams of the Saracenic university and also by the Jesuits. My calling was the sea, and I served in a British Indiaman plying between Bristol and Bombay, rising to the post of captain's secretary. When I had made enough money, I retired from the

116

merchant service and set up as a ship's chandl'er in Las Palmas.'

'And what brought you to Egypt, Pepe?' asked Oakshott.

'The Corsairs raided Las Palmas,' replied the other. And now the smile had faded and the dark eyes were broodingly shadowed. 'My two fine sons died in trying to protect their mother. I never saw my wife again. They took me to Algiers, where I was sold in the slave market to a buyer from Alexandria, who sold me to Mohammed el-Korain, whose chattel I remain.

'That is the hard school where I have learned my philosophy, sir.'

Before Oakshott could frame a suitable comment upon the remarkable account, Pepe Lopez dug his heels into his mount's flanks ands urged the animal forward in a gallop towards a small hillock just off the rutted road. Reaching the summit, he drew rein and gestured to Oakshott to join him up there.

This low mound afforded a surprising extension of vision across the flat fields of the delta with their criss-crossed irrigation canals. Tiny clusters of hovels succeeded each other to the far horizon, where – astonishingly – a ribbon of bright silver was etched against the skyline.

'The River Nile,' said Pepe Lopez, pointing. 'Where civilization was born.'

Their guide reckoned that the distance from Alexandria to Cairo was about one hundred and twenty miles, and proposed that they attempt no more than thirty miles a day – this in the coolness of dawn till mid-morning and from late afternoon to dusk. He had made the journey many times, he said, in the company of his master and his entourage. At various large villages and small townships along the way, they could seek the hospitality of the local sheriffs and headmen – for the writ of Alexandria's Governor stretched the length of the Nile valley from Rosetta at the main mouth of the great river as far as Cairo.

Pepe Lopez was a seasoned horseman. Oakshott was not bad. Shacklock had used to ride to hounds in Devon since early boyhood, and Henshawe, a country-bred man also, had

117

learned to ride ponies in his native fells. Their mounts were arabs, though neither young nor in prime condition: Mohammed el-Korain had exacted a stiff price for the hire of second-rate horseflesh.

On the evening of the first day, they rode into a middling-sized town and were immediately the sensation of the decade in that backwater of the delta, for the sight of two British naval officers and a Jack Tar was as rare as may be imagined in so remote a part of so isolated a country: isolated by distance, by religion and culture, by the dead hand of the Sublime Porte and the Sultan in far-off Constantinople and the dictatorship of the Mamelukes.

They supped that night from a communal dish of goat stew in the house of the sheriff, dipping their hands in the pot as their guide and mentor instructed them; afterwards they slept on suavely soft rugs in a cool verandah that was part open to the blue-black sky and all the heaven of stars. They were off again in the dawn. And on the second evening, they reached the road that ran alongside the left bank of the Nile as far as Cairo.

When the sun had risen high on the third day, and they had shortened their journey by short-cutting a snaking loop of the river, a smudge of whiteness in the blue-grey haze to the south revealed to them their goal. By the time they had picked up the river again, the vision had hardened itself into a pattern of domes and minarets.

Cairo ...

'That is the mosque of the Sultan Hassan,' said Pepe, pointing. 'On the hill – see? And below it the citadel, built by Saladin, now the abode of the Mameluke beys.'

'And the pyramids?' asked Oakshott.

'Away to the right – at Gizeh, over there.'

'Tell me more about the Mamelukes – and about the beys, Pepe.'

'They are bad people, sir,' replied the other. 'In all the world there have never been such men. Trained in mind and body from infancy to war and brutality, they are without mercy, without culture, wisdom, or honour. They are simply – killing machines. Brilliant horsemen, skilled in all arms,

118

fighters to the last. They never surrender.'

'One would tend to feel quite sorry for their adversaries,' said Oakshott, thinking of Bonaparte and the French. 'And what is their manner of fighting?'

'Always mounted,' said Pepe. 'Dressed, as they always are for the fray, in numerous long robes and a surcoat of chain mail, they are forced to remain in the saddle till victory – or death.'

'Weapons?'

'A cavalry carbine, pair of pistols, a long lance, a mace, and a heavy scimitar – every man.'

'A veritable armoury! And how does this cavalry – this extraordinarily heavy cavalry – dispose itself in battle?'

'Always the attack, sir. Massed charges against the enemy with the lance. Then in again, firing from the saddle. And then, the enemy ranks broken, they ride in amongst them with mace and scimitar, sparing none.'

Oakshott, who had survived several hand-to-hand encounters in boarding parties, could well imagine the shambles and the butchery involved in the kind of fighting that his companion described. He pictured the possible outcome of his present mission: this barbarian cavalry riding stirrup to stirrup with the British heavies – the Blues or the Greys perhaps – against massed French infantry. There was a certain – incongruity. Was that really what Mr Pitt had in mind?

'As to the beys,' said his informant, 'Murad is the stronger character and more intelligent by far than Ibrahim. He also speaks passable English, having been taught by an English seaman who was captured, like myself, by the Corsair pirates.' The clever eyes flashed towards Oakshott speculatively. 'Murad is also corruptible to an unbelievable degree. To serve his own ends, he would gladly see Ibrahim skinned alive. Does that direct your mind to the method of dealing with him, sir?'

'It might,' responded Oakshott. 'Would Ibrahim have a similar disregard for his associate's skin in like circumstances?'

'By all means,' replied Pepe. 'Only, it is my belief that Murad would find some way to turn the skinning knife

119

against his executioner.'

The curious spectacle of masts and sails moving slowly to and fro behind the sandbanks ahead revealed the presence of the river again. By the banks of that wide and murky waterway, Oakshott called a halt for rest and refreshment.

In the afternoon, they came to the city.

The outskirts of Cairo were informed by mud huts of the kind they had passed during their passage through the delta – together with hordes of barefoot and near-naked children who followed the quartette with hands extended to beg, beseeching eyes aswarm with totally disregarded flies, and yelping pie-dogs gambolling at their heels.

An ancient archway pierced through the city wall brought them into a teeming street of lowering façades and roofs that nearly touched overhead; a place of shadow, relative coolness, and most unbelievable varieties of perfume and stench. Every open doorway and window displayed the wares of a shop or eating house, where there was constant shouting and haggling, consuming of indescribable comestibles and beverages, the smoking of hookah pipes, playing of elaborate board games, much tinny music and nasal singing. The men from the *Daisy* and their black-garbed guide progressed through an ever shifting throng that gave way to them with some reluctance, much curiosity, and more extending of palms.

'*Baksheesh – baksheesh, effendi!*'

'More beggars in this bit of street than you'd see in all of Portsmouth,' observed Shacklock.

'Begging is the largest single national occupation, sir,' said Pepe Lopez. 'A wearisome occupation that is encouraged by Egypt's rulers. Like the pharaohs and sundry conquerors since, the Mamelukes know that revolutions are started by the poor and hungry – but not by the jaded and apathetic.'

'You are ever the philosopher, Pepe,' said Oakshott.

Their guide gave his gently cynical smile.

Saladin's citadel stood upon the heights, its ochre towers and ramparts lowering over the low-roofed city. Entrance to its stark walls was by a portcullised archway beyond a bridge that spanned a dry moat. It was here that the Englishmen had their first sight of Mameluke soldiery: two dismounted guards stood sentry at the arch, both wearing the long, loose robes and chain-mail surcoat, the headgear and trappings that Pepe Lopez had described. One of them stepped forward: he was a giant of a man, pale-skinned, bearded, scowling. He snatched from the guide the passport that Mohammed el-Korain had provided and scrutinized it with glowering suspicion for longer than could possibly have been necessary, before thrusting it back at him and brusquely beckoning them on.

'Wouldn't like to knock over his ale pot in a tavern,' muttered Henshawe.

'Nor I,' said Shacklock. The young officer gazed about him, at the high-walled courtyard through which they were passing. Oakshott saw him pale, saw his lips part, his eyes widen with horror – before he, himself, divined the cause of the other's reaction.

'Good God, sir!' breathed Shacklock. 'See over there!'

One slab of the high wall bristled with great iron hooks – reminiscent of cup hooks on a kitchen dresser, though they served no such homely purpose; a dozen or so of them, displayed in no formal order, but set at random, some high up on the wall, some near to the ground, supported what at first glance appeared to be anything from bundles of limp rags to undressed marionettes – but which on more careful inspection proved to be corpses in varying degrees of dissolution. The ochre walls were streaked from hooks to ground with ominous stains, some dark and dried, some brightly fresh. And one of the impaled figures was still kicking out its feeble life.

'The condemned are thrown from the ramparts daily at noon,' explained Pepe Lopez. 'Those not caught on the higher hooks die more quickly.'

'And their crimes?' demanded Oakshott.

'Any action deemed to be against the rule of the Mamelukes,' replied the guide. 'Even the unguarded word. Or a thought accompanied by a certain glance.'

'S'welp me, they run a tight ship here!' declared Henshawe.

At the end of that courtyard of hideous death was a flight of steps leading to an arched, open doorway guarded by another pair of Mameluke soldiery. The procedure of inspection and appraisal was repeated in the like, hostile manner before they were permitted to enter the building, to find themselves in a vast, echoing stone-built hall with a domed roof. There were no windows in that forbidding chamber; a line of guttering torches burnt sullenly in iron sconces along one wall.

Summoned by some means unknown, a stout figure in orange robes approached from out of the shadows and crossed the flagged floor towards them. Bald, porcine, waddling, of indeterminate age, the apparition fixed them with button-bright eyes encircled in rolls of loose skin, and he appeared to care little for what he saw; his dislike seemed mostly directed towards Pepe Lopez, whom he addressed in high-pitched, sibilant Arabic, to which the guide responded.

'What was that?' asked Oakshott. 'And who might this be?'

'This is the eunuch Habiba,' supplied Pepe. 'Like so many of his sort in the East, he wields more power than you would think possible. He knows me and my master the Governor, and mistrusts us both. I think there may be grave impediments to your obtaining an audience with the beys.' He re-addressed the porcine individual, but won from him only another diatribe well laced with venom, followed by a narrow-eyed stare at Oakshott.

'Surely,' said Oakshott, 'as a representative of my king and Government, supported by a passport from the Governor of Alexandria, I am not to be turned away from the door by this Jack-in-office?'

'He could keep you waiting for days, maybe weeks,' said Pepe. 'However' – he directed his eyes towards the gloomy underside of the dome high above them and contrived to look detached – 'there are ways and means, in the East, of circumventing the obstructions and delays of officialdom.'

'How much?' demanded Oakshott.

'I would say four gold guineas,' replied Pepe Lopez. 'Or perhaps five. No more.'

Uncomplainingly, *Daisy*'s captain counted out five coins from the purse which he had had the foresight to fill from the ship's safe in anticipation of such a contingency. Pepe Lopez took the money and passed it to the eunuch with a comment. The other received it with no sign of appreciation, examined each coin and bit at it, gave one back to the guide and hid the remaining four in some part of his costume. He then fluted a brief pronouncement, turned on his heel and waddled away into the shadows from whence he came.

'Habiba says he will apprise their Excellencies of your presence, sir,' said the guide.

'Good,' commented Oakshott. 'And, by the way, why did he give you back one guinea?'

With an expression of sublime incorruptibility, the other replied: 'That is my commission on the transaction, sir.' And when Oakshott frowned: 'It is the custom, sir. You are astounded. I commend to you the words of St Ambrose, Bishop of Milan: "When in Rome, live as the Romans do."'

'As you know, sir, I learned in hard schools – and the Jesuits taught me as much as any.'

The pure gold content of Albion's coinage notwithstanding, for over an hour Oakshott and his companions were left cooling their heels in the great gloomy hall, before the eunuch reappeared and summoned them to follow him into the presence of the lords of life and death over Egypt's teeming millions, whose unquestioned power extended to the meting out of hideous death for so much as an unguarded thought accompanied by the concomitant glance.

Seven

Their progress through the dark corridors and tortuous staircases of the citadel was greatly protracted. At every door, at the foot of each staircase, armed Mamelukes stood guard, and their credences were checked, notwithstanding the presence of the eunuch; at length they came before a massive, double door of dull bronze banded with brass, upon which the epicine Habiba knocked and was given admission by a guard.

The eunuch hissed an instruction to Pepe Lopez ...

'Sir, I am reminded that we must approach Their Excellencies with eyes averted,' whispered Pepe to Oakshott. 'Likewise, when we reach Their Excellencies' thrones, we must prostrate ourselves on hands and knees and touch the floor three times with the forehead.'

'Damned if I'll do any such thing,' growled Oakshott, 'or my men either.'

Their guide's dark eyes were tragic with apprehension. 'Sir, you do not know what you are saying,' he breathed. 'Remember – *the hooks!*'

'Sheer rubbish!' cried Oakshott. 'We declared war in Spain in thirty-nine because they boarded a British merchantman and cut off her captain's ear. Let the Mamelukes but lay a finger on me or my men, and our people will dispatch a fleet of gunboats up the Nile and pound this pestilential city to rubble!'

'Oh, sir – sir!' bleated Pepe Lopez. 'You make things very difficult for me!'

'Gird your heart high, man!' said *Daisy*'s captain. 'We'll

carry the day, never fear. Forward!' So saying, he doffed his hat, tucked it under his arm and strode with a steadily measured pace along a wide sweep of tiled floor towards the far end, where two robed and turbaned figures sat regarding the newcomers from the eminence of richly carved thrones set upon a stepped dais. The others followed him.

The first impression Oakshott received of the two beys was scarcely calculated to raise the spirits: it seemed to him that they were both of a piece with the brutish-looking guards whom they had encountered; if anything, Murad and Ibrahim were cast in even more barbaric moulds and carried an additional patina of overweening arrogance. They were both Caucasians, and the eyes that glared down from out of the craggy, sallow-complexioned faces were of a pale tawny hue, almost yellow – the eyes of predatory big cats.

Oakshott halted at the foot of the steps and inclined his head in a civil greeting that excluded any suggestion of sycophancy. From the corner of his eye, he observed that both Pepe Lopez and the eunuch had prostrated themselves and were making deep obeisance. He assumed – rightly – that Shacklock and Henshawe were standing to attention behind him.

'My name is Oakshott, commanding officer of His Majesty's sloop-of-war *Daisy*,' he declared. 'I bring greetings from my Sovereign King George the Third.'

There was no response to his formal announcement. In the silence that followed, Pepe Lopez, still on his knees, gestured towards Oakshott and nervously stammered a translation of Oakshott's words – and elicited a quite surprising rejoinder:

'Is it that English captain come to seek protection of Mamelukes?'

The question, delivered in heavily-accented English, came from the bey seated on Oakshott's left: this would be Murad.

No stranger to sudden squalls and unexpected landfalls, Oakshott took this unexpected query in his stride:

'Sir, I do not come to seek protection,' he declared, 'and I am surprised that you should think I have. The fact is I have been sent, in the first place, to apprise you of an item of secret, privileged information which should be of vital interest to the well-being of the Egyptian state.'

He paused, glanced towards Pepe Lopez, and allowed him to translate his response into Arabic for the benefit of the non-English-speaking Ibrahim Bey.

This done, it was Murad Bey who again made reply – and as before, his words were indirectly inflected, and addressed to the interpreter:

'We will hear this information from English captain.'

Oakshott nodded. Armed with the late Gisborne's brief – which he had committed to memory, chapter and verse, appendices and all, it was perfectly plain sailing: he simply repeated Mr Pitt's private secretary's memorandum – colouring it up slightly, as an actor might round out a jejune monologue:

'The British Prime Minister's agents in Paris have information that on the twelfth of April last, the French Directory instructed General Bonaparte to assemble an expedition of troop transports escorted by a fleet of battleships with a view to sailing to Egypt ...'

He paused at the end of each paragraph to allow Pepe Lopez to interpret for Ibrahim Bey.

' ... the object of this expedition being to conquer your country and thereby secure a gateway to the far Orient ...'

He had not gone very much further in his peroration – indeed, only as far as the phrase: ' ... it is acknowledged that this information may be false and no more than a stratagem to deceive us as to their true intent ...' when Murad Bey interposed:

'*Malta.*'

Taken somewhat aback, but by no means put out of countenance, Oakshott riposted smartly: 'Granted, sir! Bonaparte has taken Malta, but this is not to say he will not ...'

'Bonaparte take Malta – therefore English captain seeks protection of Mamelukes. English captain fears to return home through Mediterranean.'

Smouldering with high indignation, *Daisy*'s captain was obliged to swallow this direct slur upon his courage while Pepe Lopez was translating the foregoing dialogue; having heard which, Ibrahim Bey joined his colleague and fellow

126

ruler in nodding and grinning agreement with the proposition that Pitt had been gulled, Bonaparte's object of capturing Malta had been achieved, and that the miserable English sea captain standing before them was scared to brave the Malta narrows and run home with his tail between his legs.

Oakshott let a little time go by, then he returned to the attack:

'Sirs, I do not know what might be the extent of your intelligence regarding the capture of Malta,' he said, 'but I had it at first hand from the captain of a French ship present at the time. The island surrendered virtually without a fight – as might have been expected, considering the collapsed state of the Order of St John.

'Sirs, I ask you – is it likely that the French would assemble such an armada to take so easy a prize?

'I tell you that, in my opinion, Bonaparte has not finished his adventure in the eastern Mediterranean! That armada is still at large – *and the richest prize within its grasp is Egypt!*'

Whilst Pepe Lopez was rendering a translation of his outburst, Oakshott was gratified to observe that his words had struck home at Murad Bey – leastways, the other was looking directly at him for the first time since the commencement of the audience. And when, after Ibrahim Bey had digested the translation (and he was visibly quenched by the same), his English-speaking co-ruler addressed *Daisy*'s captain to his face:

'Sair, will you take tea?'

'Most certainly, sir,' responded Oakshott. 'And with pleasure.'

'We take tea together,' declared Murad Bey. 'And we speak more of this.'

He clapped his hands, and obsequious slaves came running.

'And what does Mistair Pitt propose?'

They were seated in a circle in a small, comfortable apartment adjacent to the 'throne room'; luxuriating upon suave rugs, with an open balcony that looked out across a pleasant arbour of palm trees and tinkling fountains. It was

Murad Bey who posed the question.

Oakshott lowered his tea bowl. 'The Prime Minister, sir, offers you Britain's total support against the French,' he replied.

'Britain is far away,' came the shrewd reply.

'There is a British fleet in being in the Mediterranean. And they are seeking out the French armada.'

During the pause while all this was being translated, Oakshott continued to meet Murad's gaze, conscious that he was achieving a contact with the Mameluke leader – though acutely aware that it was rather like supping with a tiger.

'And if British fleet does not catch armada?'

'It will.'

'And meanwhile?'

'Meanwhile, we will have a treaty.'

'Treaty?'

'Between our two countries, sir. This will provide for Britain to send troops to Egypt to support the Mameluke armies. With them will come veteran officers who will train your soldiers in the modern methods of warfare, without which you could never hope to withstand the discipline and fire power of the French infantry and artillery, which has set Austria on its ear and conquered most of northern Italy, Rome included ...'

There had to be a pause while Ibrahim Bey was acquainted with the development of Oakshott's argument, during which time the latter's eyes never left Murad, but continued to weigh his adversary's reactions.

The interruption over, Oakshott tried another tack:

'There is more to it, even, than that, sir,' he said – and now his memory was seeking out the detailed extravagances of Appendices Numbers 2 and 3 – 'Mr Pitt had a proposal completely to reorganize your sea and land forces under British officers. To drive a canal through the desert and join the Mediterranean with the Red Sea, to the manifest advantage of both our countries ...'

Murad laughed shortly: it was more of a snarl.

'Hey! You mean that Mamelukes deliver themselves for destruction at the hands of the British instead of the French – and British conquer Egypt without fight!'

This appraisal, once the burden of Oakshott's outline had been communicated to the other bey, drew forth a similar outburst. Oakshott, who with the detachment of a natural-born logician more than half agreed with the Mamelukes' conclusion, felt his arguments slipping away from him. The image of the death wall of the hooks danced before his imagination as he racked his brain for a way out.

In sheer desperation, he said: 'By the way, gentlemen, Mr Pitt pledges a transfer of gold to the Egyptian treasury upon the ratification of the proposed treaty. Er – and similar sums will be paid to each of you gentlemen upon signature of the same.'

He paused to allow Pepe Lopez to translate; he need not have troubled; Murad Bey pointed to the latter, eyes blazing.

'Still your tongue, infidel!' he hissed. 'One word and it will be the hooks for you tomorrow's noon!'

Pepe Lopez' mouth hung open – and silent.

'How much, English captain?' demanded Murad Bey.

Oakshott named the astronomical sum mentioned in the appendix.

'For – *each?*'

'For each, sir,' confirmed the captain of the *Daisy*.

Murad Bey exhaled a deep breath and looked towards his fellow-ruler, who looked back at him questioningly.

Murad Bey nodded, and rose to his feet.

'Audience has finished for today,' he declared. 'Will be resumed tomorrow.'

He snapped an order to awestruck Habiba, contingent upon which the eunuch leapt up from his knees and bustled Oakshott and his small entourage out of the audience chamber.

'Sir, I never would have believed it – never! 'Tis like living in the wardroom, or sharing a table with you, sir, in the stern cabin, with silver plate, bright cutlery, wines, fine victuals and all.'

Edgar Athling Henshawe, ship's carpenter and amateur surgeon, made this declaration that eve as he and his captain, Lieutenant Shacklock, and guide and interpreter Pepe Lopez took supper together in the sumptuous apartment that had been apportioned to them. Oakshott had been offered accommodation on his own, but had insisted that his party remain together, notwithstanding their relative ranks and stations. The apartment included a large parlour which was faced on walls, ceiling and floor with blue faïence tiles in the Moorish manner, and had in it a sunken bath filled with cool water in which floated freshly-cut lotus flowers. They were eating the inevitable goat stew, but it was of a vastly different quality from that which they had endured during their journey down the Nile delta and valley; being young and tender as to flesh, it was flavoured with saffron, garlic, coriander and other spices.

'Glad of your company, Henshawe,' responded Oakshott, dipping his fingers into the communal pot and placing a fine sliver of lean meat upon the patty of unleavened bread that lay upon his lap. 'And you, also, Pepe.' He glanced towards the latter. 'Tell me, what is your summation of my audience with the beys – do I guess right about Murad's intention regarding his partner?'

'Sir, undoubtedly Murad will cheat Ibrahim out of his share of the promised gold,' responded Pepe Lopez. 'Indeed, for a fraction of that sum, he would condemn his whole family: mother, father, brothers, sisters and cousins to the hooks.'

'And for that he would deliver Egypt – for this is the truth of it – into Britain's hands as a vassel state,' said Oakshott.

'Sir, the Mamelukes do not regard Egypt as their native country,' replied Pepe, 'but only a plot of land to be milked for every copper coin, every ear of corn. The beys' power is tremendous, but the revenues of Egypt, despite the rapacious tax-gatherers, would not yield the sum you mentioned in five good years. Furthermore, both Murad and Ibrahim, in the phrase of your great poet Andrew Marvell, are uncomfortably aware of "time's wingéd chariot hurrying near", and seek to garner nest-eggs against their old age.'

'Then it seems as if Mr Pitt's alternative strategy may bear fruit,' mused Oakshott. 'I only hope that this business can be speedily concluded so that we can return to the *Daisy* in time to be in at the kill with Nelson when he arrives.'

Pepe Lopez smiled his world-weary, cynically-sweet smile.

'Sir, with respect, you must know very little about the manner in which such business is transacted in the Orient if you think that this matter will be done with any speed,' he said. 'Even the anticipation of the gold will not hasten Murad. Indeed, so serious a consideration will only serve further to excite his caution.'

Pepe Lopez never spoke a truer word. Two days of idleness and luxury passed before Oakshott was again summoned – this time to attend Murad Bey alone. The Mameluke leader made no secret of the fact – whilst not overtly alluding to it – that he intended to take advantage of his colleague's ignorance of English in order to cheat him of most, if not all, of the gold. That consideration set aside, Murad took Oakshott through each and every point in Pitt's memorandum, appendixes included, as the former was able to recite them. And quibbled over every item.

How many British officers, military and naval, were to be detached to Egypt? And how many troops? Cavalry was not required, but the Egyptian forces stood in dire need of modern artillery. A few regiments of the famous British infantry would not come amiss. And when would the work commence upon the proposed Red Sea canal?

More importantly, he implied, by what means would the gold guineas be transported to Egypt ...?

Oakshott returned to his quarters with a brief to sketch out a draft treaty for Murad's approval. This he began in collaboration with Pepe Lopez, the former ship's captain's secretary and man of liberal education.

Pepe proved to be an excellent draftsman of treaties. His spare and unequivocal handling of the English language far exceeded Oakshott's competence at the same. They progressed, item by item, clause by clause – and Oakshott insisted on Murad's approval of each before they progressed on to the next. And this was all time-consuming.

The two men – the aristocratic naval commander and the stateless slave – worked every morning from sun-up till noon, at which time the screams of the victims brought to the hooks echoed and re-echoed throughout the citadel. And again in the evening.

In the fullness of time, the draft treaty was completed, each section provisionally endorsed by Murad Bey. It only remained for the Mameluke leader to initial the whole document and – so far as Oakshott could reckon – his self-imposed mission of duty in Egypt was finished and he could return to his ship, and by some means arrange for the draft treaty to be transported to England.

Not displeased with his brief essay into amateur diplomacy, *Daisy's* captain tucked the document under his arm, clapped on his hat, and went to call upon Murad Bey.

Of the eunuch Habiba, who arranged these meetings, there was no sign; indeed, the entire citadel seemed deserted, and there was a curious air of tension about the place. Come to think of it, the screams of the condemned had not made the noon hideous that day.

Oakshott wandered through the deserted courts, the empty corridors, till at length he came upon a wild-eyed functionary, whom he buttonholed. The man, who clearly did not wish to be detained, spoke a few words of English; he blurted out the news to Oakshott before wrenching himself free and rushing on his way.

Bonaparte had landed and taken Alexandria, and his army was even now marching on Cairo!

It was days before further reports fleshed out the bare bones of the first intelligence which had reached Cairo by relays of fast riders ...

The French armada must have appeared off Alexandria only days – perhaps hours – after the departure of Oakshott and his companions.

Avoiding the risks that Oakshott had braved, Bonaparte eschewed the harbour and anchored off Marabout, a small fishing port about a league and a half to the west, in the shadow of Pompey's column. There he disembarked 5,000 men and marched upon Alexandria. Governor Mohammed el-Korain ordered resistance, but the walls were in a ruinous state and the French quickly forced several breaches, through which they poured almost unopposed into the city and commenced an indiscriminate massacre. According to one of their own officers, a certain Adjutant-General Boyer, in an intercepted letter, men, women, old and young and children at the breast were all put to the sword. The entire city was abandoned to sack and pillage for four hours.

Within a week, the whole force of the French army was disembarked, mustered in column of route, and set off on the long march up the bank of the Nile – the same path that Oakshott and his party had taken, though not close enough to the river as to allow the soldiers to break ranks and quench their burning thirst, encumbered as they were with heavy clothing and equipment. A small flotilla of gunboats ascended the river to protect the army's flank. News of the French advance, continuously relayed to Cairo, told of brilliant spoiling attacks by hard-riding Mameluke cavalry patrols, who cut off stragglers and carried them away for questioning – doubtless with the cruelty for which the masters of Egypt were notorious. From these prisoners it was learned that a discontent, despair and melancholy had descended upon the French who, having expected a land flowing with milk and honey, much loot and fair women, were appalled at the desolation of the desert and the grinding poverty of the delta villages. It was all Bonaparte could do, said the reports, to keep his troops in subordination.

All this news, relayed by the eunuch Habiba to Pepe Lopez, was brought to Oakshott's ear. *Daisy*'s captain, ruefully aware that the march of events, coupled with Murad Bey's procrastination, had turned his amateur diplomacy to a dead issue, had only one thought – which was to regain his ship with all speed, supposing that First Lieutenant Brewster had obeyed his last order smartly and extricated himself from Alexandria before the French took the port. Accordingly, he made representations to the beys, through Habiba, for permission to leave Cairo. No such permission was granted; for the present, came back the reply, the English must remain within the confines of the citadel for their own safety, till the French had been brought to battle and – in a word – annihilated. To reinforce this edict, two armed Mameluke guards were posted to watch over Oakshott and his party, day and night. They were confined to their quarters; but from the balcony of their parlour, which looked out across the great courtyard and the wall of hooks, they had – in Oakshott's phrase – a seat in the front row of the balcony to view the Mamelukes' preparations for war.

First, there was a rash of executions: the wretched victims being, no doubt, those whose fealty to the Mamelukes stood in the slightest doubt. The killings were protracted well beyond noon, and soon every hook was occupied, and the ochre wall washed anew with bright blood.

The hours from dawn till dusk, notwithstanding the executions, were taken up in military parades of the Mameluke forces, inspected by either Murad Bey, Ibrahim Bey, or both. For hour after hour, the pride of the finest heavy cavalry known rode past their leaders in close formation, line after line, column after column; plumes waving, lance points glittering, bright steel and snow-white linens dazzling in the searing sunlight; their arab steeds high-stepping to the beat of war-drums and the brassy notes of great trumpets.

'They look well,' opined Oakshott. 'If I were a Frog infantryman of the line, the sight of those fellows coming at me in a massed charge would give me food for thought.'

'And me, sir!' said Henshawe fervently.

'But how would they stand up to a broadside of grape or langridge?' mused Shacklock.

'A good question,' said Oakshott. 'And it's to be remembered, in this context, that Bonaparte was an artilleryman before they made him a boy-general.'

Touching upon artillery, the watchers had an introduction to the Mameluke disposition of this arm on the third day of the parade, when some forty pieces of cannon were marched past in the courtyard below. Following the splendour of the cavalry, this display was something of a shambles. To begin, the pieces were not mounted upon wheeled carriages, but upon clumsy wooden frames, each manhandled by a team of sweating peasantry. Nor did the guns' crews commend themselves to the critical eyes of the professionals from the *Daisy*: not Mamelukes, but raw peasants like the gun-porters, they shambled along in rear of their pieces, clad in filthy rags; linstocks, ramrods and searchers sloped over their shoulders like so many rakes and pitchforks.

'With any of *that* lot to crew my gun,' said young Shacklock, 'I'd as lief be before the muzzle as behind it!'

And still the daily parades continued. The sight of the Egyptian infantry – all irregulars – inspired confidence only by reason of the vast numbers of their companies. More admirable were the battalions of negros from the Sudan: wild-looking barbarians with frizzed hair and saffron-coloured skirts, all bearing broad-bladed spears as would splice a man in half with one thrust. And the desert Bedouin, on horseback and on camels: they rode in proud silence, eschewing trumpets and drums.

The great parade ended. The courtyard was empty. The Mameluke army had gone to meet the French.

'Pepe – we have got to get out of this place!'

It was Oakshott who spoke. News had been received on the grapevine that several squadrons of the beys' best cavalry had been engaged in what was variously described as a skirmish or a small battle somewhere on the French line of march. The Mamelukes and Bedouin had charged on a broad front, as was their custom, but Bonaparte had fought back in formation of squares – British fashion – and had beaten them off. The lesson may have been lost on the Mamelukes, but not on Oakshott.

'If the French play that tactic in open battle,' he argued, 'and make good use of their artillery, we can expect them in Cairo within a week. And we had better not be here when their advance patrols ride in!'

They were holding a council of war, the four of them. At the far end of the parlour, their two guards scowlingly barred the door.

'First, we have to give those merchants the slip,' said Oakshott, 'then we need rope – plenty of rope, enough to scale down the outer walls. And four fast horses waiting out there.

'Pepe, can Habiba be trusted to supply us?'

'At a price, sir.'

'Half on agreement, half on delivery – and successful escape.'

'That will be the most satisfactory arrangement, sir.'

'How much?'

'Um – say, twenty guineas, sir.'

'Does that include your commission?'

Pepe Lopez contrived to look incorruptible; no easy feat.

'Considering the circumstances, I shall be happy to waive my commission in this case, sir,' he said piously.

Night. The whirring of cicadas in the sage brush that overflowed the citadel's unkempt gardens. A waning moon.

Oakshott came in from the verandah, a tiny porcelain bowl of honey-sweet and scalding hot Turkish coffee between his fingers. His three companions were still seated round the remains of their supper, and Lopez was preparing the coffee over a tiny charcoal burner.

'The place is as quiet as the grave,' said Oakshott in a loud voice, casually inflected. 'It wants five minutes to the hour. I think we begin, gentlemen.

'Make it so, Pepe.'

'Aye, aye, sir.' Pepe Lopez had begun to adopt the naval response.

'Are you ready, Mr Shacklock?'

'Yes, sir.'

'Stand by to give fire,' said Oakshott with a fierce smile.

The sequence of events, which depended for its success upon split-second timing, had – for obvious reasons – been impossible to rehearse, save by constant vocal repetition.

Upon Oakshott's executive order, Pepe Lopez, squatting over his stove, looked across to the two guards and invited them – in Arabic, naturally – to partake of some coffee. The two Mameluke soldiers, who had been subjected to the delicious temptation of the aromatic brew for the past quarter hour, needed no second bidding. One of them, leaving his comrade alone at the door, came over, spear still in hand, his surly face sketching an approximation of a grin.

Next – Pepe poured out two bowls of coffee, while the Mameluke stood over him, mouth watering.

136

Two bowls. Two hands. But one hand carrying a spear.

'Allow me,' said Shacklock, in the honeyed tone of civility that is acceptable the world over and goes beyond the bounds of mere language. He took the second cup and brought it over to the guard by the door, smiling ingratiatingly as he went.

Oakshott watched in two directions at once – more or less.

He waited till the first guard was reaching out to take the proffered bowl, and the man by the door doing likewise from Shacklock.

'Give fire!'

Pepe Lopez and young Shacklock simultaneously tossed the scalding coffee into the eager faces of the guards, temporarily blinding them.

Oakshott was on his feet. One arm wrapped around his opponent's throat from behind, he quickly brought him to limp unconsciousness.

A blow to the point of the jaw, delivered by the rugged young Devonian, downed the second guard like a felled ox.

'Bind and gag them both,' said Oakshott, consulting his watch. 'We are a minute behind schedule.'

The eunuch was waiting for them outside in the shadowed corridor. Habiba was terrified: sweat stood out on his bald scalp like dew upon a watermelon. He hissed something venomous at Pepe, who shrugged it off and gave the other a slight shove which sent him waddling off down the corridor. The others followed after him.

They came to a low arch leading on to a spiral stair. Habiba went up, moving in terrified haste, his wheezing breath laboured. One flight. Two flights. Three. They were now on the uppermost floor of the citadel and level with the ramparts. A touch from the eunuch's plump hand and an iron-bound door creaked open. They stepped out into the starlit night.

'Still!' breathed Oakshott. They froze to silence and edged themselves back into the shadows, as a pair of spearmen came loping along the ramparts towards them, muttering between themselves. They passed so closely by the five hidden figures that Oakshott distinctly caught their acrid

tang of dried sweat and crudely tanned leather trappings.

The danger past, the five moved on.

They quartered the courtyard, passing the wall of hooks and the balustrade from which the victims were daily thrown, till they came to the section of the wall which fronted that part of the citadel facing a spread of open ground covered with the dark clumps of prickly pear. Below them, the dry moat; beyond that, good cover and freedom.

From about his porcine person, Habiba then produced a rope. It was of no great thickness, but twisted from fine hemp and enough to bear a man. Making one end fast around one of the granite machiolations, young Shacklock swung himself over and made the first descent, silently and expertly swarming down, for all the world as if he were descending the mainmast of the *Daisy* on the back-stay.

His low whistle from the darkness of the dry moat signalled success.

'You next, Henshawe,' said Oakshott.

Exercising his inestimable privilege as captain, Oakshott was to be the last to leave. He turned as the eunuch scrabbled at his sleeve and fluted a bird-like phrase of entreaty. *Daisy*'s captain took from his pocket the second half-share of guineas as bargained.

'You've played your part, Habiba,' he said, 'and I don't think you'll betray us at this late hour, for that would be to condemn yourself to the hooks for your part in it.

'Good luck to you, poor deprived fellow that you are.'

So saying, he swung himself over, hands and feet gripping the slender rope, binding himself to it like a spider, and swinging on down.

They were beyond the edge of the city and moving out across hard-packed sand – and nothing but sand.

Climbing out of the dry moat had been the work of moments; the progress through the small forest of prickly pears cost them no more than a few tears and scratches – more than offset by the advantage of cover afforded from anyone looking down from the ramparts. The way through the outer suburbs of the city had been enlivened by pie-dogs that snarled at them from every dark doorway, and by occasional challenges from suspicious householders fearful for their pathetic crops of yams and sweet corn pricked out in narrow back gardens.

And now they were free of Cairo, heading northwards at Pepe Lopez' direction, making back to the coast across the desert – the Garden of Allah.

Away to the north-east, on their right, there came from time to time the muffled rumble of gunfire and occasional flashes in the night sky betokening that Napoleon's cannonry was engaged against marauding skirmishers raiding the French line of encampments. For the rest, there was only silence, as their mounts plodded at walking pace through the sand.

'As to our destination, Pepe,' said Oakshott, 'the prevailing wind being at present in the north, my ship – if she indeed made good her escape from Alexandria – will have shifted to the east, in accordance with my orders, since her best point of sail is on the port tack. Do you please bring us to the east of Alexandria.'

'Aye, aye, sir – I will do my best,' responded their guide.

'We will ride through the night till dawn,' said Oakshott, 'and then rest up through the daylight hours – somewhere in good concealment, in an oasis or some such. Do you follow me?'

'Perfectly, sir.'

'You are a good fellow, Pepe. Tell me, what shall you do with yourself when we have gone?'

The other hunched his shoulders and pulled a long lip. 'Sir, I have not given it any thought,' he replied.

'Well, one thing's for sure, you will not be able to go back to Mohammed el-Korain – assuming he survived the taking of Alexandria. Nor – supposing that the Mamelukes drive out the French – can you show your face again in Cairo, or it will be the hooks for you.'

'Both thoughts had occurred to me, sir.'

'Well, do you give your mind to the problem, Pepe. And if there is anything I can do in the way of counselling you, don't hesitate to ask.'

'Thank you, sir.'

They rode in pairs, Shacklock and Henshawe following:

139

maintaining a steady walking pace and not pausing for rests – Oakshott's intent being to put as much distance between them and Cairo as possible before dawn. He constantly scanned the darkness ahead, mindful of the need to take cover before daylight. Several times he questioned their guide as to the feasibility of their line of advance, and Pepe Lopez constantly assured him that most excellent cover lay not far distant.

At the hour before dawn, when spirits are at their lowest ebb and the soul most readily quits its tabernacle, Oakshott repeated his question – and with some asperity.

'Keep your eyes on the horizon, sir,' enjoined the other. 'You will presently see the finest hiding place in all Egypt!'

Oakshott did as he was bidden. The concentration demanded by staring into the darkness was such that his mind fled away to other, less demanding, matters: the memory of Irene Chancellor's cool green eyes that so well complemented his own two-coloured gaze, the soft curve of her brow; all about her ...

What was that ahead ...?

He stood up in the stirrups, struck with a sudden disbelief, as from out of the dark horizon there seemed to appear a trio of geometrical shapes which, by their size, must only be a few hundred yards ahead, a cable at the most; and yet, by their very insubstantial greyness, they must be hull down below the horizon – as the nautical saying went. But, surely, his reason told him, that must mean they were huge beyond all belief ...

They could only be ...

'Good God!' he breathed.

'Do you see them, sir?' asked Pepe Lopez, amused.

'*The pyramids!*'

'Where, sir – *where?*' From both Shacklock and Henshawe.

Oakshott pointed ahead.

They rode on, silent with awe. And all the while, the vision hardened and took shape, size, bulk. As they drew closer, the three vast forms – one discernibly larger than its companions – loomed ever higher above them. Presently, the eastern faces of those massive monoliths took on a pinkish hue with the first light of dawn.

When daylight thinly broke, they were standing in the shadows of the oldest, largest man-made monuments on Earth.

There was cover in plenty in the environs of the pyramids: a small army could have concealed itself amongst the tumbled masses of broken granite blocks as high as a house and vast shards of limestone facing – mute testimonies to the innumerable generations of vandals who had robbed the pyramids of some of their outer fabric, without making any real impression upon the whole indestructible mass.

Between the Great Pyramid of Cheops and the famous Sphinx, whose head and shoulders rose from out of the soft sand a few cables distant, were lines of tombs: stone mausoleums that had once housed the embalmed mummies of the pharaohs' priests and courtiers – long since sacked and violated by tomb robbers. Each was as large as a decent-sized stable, and it was in these that they hid the horses, having watered them from a well nearby.

The mounts having been cared for, the four lay themselves down behind cover and slept the whole day through in the serene knowledge that they were safe from disturbance; that French and Mameluke alike could never touch them within that silent enclave which had kept its secrets for forty centuries.

Oakshott awoke in the early evening from profound dreams of safe landfalls and complaisant women, but with the nagging impression that he had been disturbed by something which had caused him some unease. He rolled over and sat up – to see that Shacklock was similarly aroused.

'Sir, unless I'm mistaken, that was a bugle call!' said the latter.

'I think it was!' replied Oakshott.

'From the nor'ard, sir. The damned Frogs!'

'And damned close! Follow me, Mr Shacklock!'

Daisy's captain was already running towards the bulk of the Great Pyramid, by whose southern base they were sheltering. The huge blocks of granite of which the monolith was constructed were too large to be used as

141

stepping stones, but some were broken, some worn down by the attrition of time and vandalism, many had deep interstices between them where a man might find a foothold. In short, the pyramid could with difficulty be climbed.

Oakshott set his foot in a deep cleft and hauled himself up, hand over hand. Young Shacklock followed.

Oakshott, climbing slowly but steadily, so shaped his course that he was not only going upwards, but sideways, with his goal of aspiration about one third of the way up the pyramid at the edge where the southern and eastern faces met. From that vantage point, he reckoned, there would be an excellent view of the desert and the Nile valley to the north and north-eastward.

And so it proved to be ...

Half an hour's hard scrambling brought Oakshott to the point he had fixed for himself. Shacklock, younger and more nimble, was by then very close behind him. Both reached the edge of the two vast rock faces more or less simultaneously, one below the other; and both peered round.

'Look, sir!' cried Shacklock.

There was no need for him to have drawn Oakshott's attention, or to have pointed. Ahead and to their right, in the lengthening shadows that the low sun was casting across the desert, they saw in the distance an enormous dust cloud stretching from the silvery ribbon that was the River Nile to a point almost directly in front of them. Allowing for the drift of the wind, which was coming from the north-east, the dust cloud must have been stretching for nigh on fifty miles. As they clung there in awestruck silence, they heard again the far-off blare of a bugle. It was answered from another segment of the horizon. And again.

'The French – and they'll be here by dawn!' declared Oakshott. 'No use our moving on tonight, for we'd ride straight into the hands of their skirmishers.

'Best we stay where we are.'

It was then, turning to look behind them, the way they had journeyed, that the two Englishmen saw yet another sweep of dust cloud, scarcely less impressive than the other, on the horizon to the south. Furthermore the source of this disturbance was closer than the other: the low-cast sun glinted from a thousand pin-points of bright metal. And straining their ears they could just discern the double-double beat of war-drums.

'And here come the Mamelukes to meet the Frogs!' said Oakshott. 'By heaven, Shacklock, tomorrow you will see such a clatter as you will remember all your life; a sight with which you'll regale your sons and your sons' sons to their intolerable boredom.

'Tomorrow, Shacklock, there'll be a battle to remember – and we shall see it all from the front row of the gods!'

Eight

The long night of waiting began.

Henshawe and Pepe Lopez joined their companions on the Great Pyramid. Oakshott, who rightly supposed that they would be invisible to any onlooker amidst the scarred stone mass of the monolith, led the way to the summit, which was composed of a flattened area the size of a tennis court, strewn with broken facing-stone; this was to be what he had wryly referred to as 'the front row of the gods'.

The night wind, after the baking heat of the desert below, blew with delicious coolness about their lofty eyrie. They lay at their ease, chewing at the cold remains of their supper which they had brought with them and passing round a water-skin. Then, sleepless with mounting excitement, they lay and watched and listened. And the dying moon rose to its apogee.

At one in the morning by Oakshott's watch, there came the sound of the massed French drums beating the call to arms, indicating that Bonaparte, having been apprised by his skirmishers that the Mameluke army was directly in front of them, was making his dispositions for the coming battle.

'If only there was more moonlight,' complained young Shacklock. 'I can't see anything.'

'There'll be sights a-plenty on the morrow, sir,' Henshawe assured him.

'Who will likely be commanding the Mamelukes, Pepe?' asked Oakshott.

'Murad Bey, undoubtedly, sir,' replied the other. 'And

Ibrahim Bey will remain with the reserves in defence of the city.'

'There'll be no defending Cairo if the French win here tomorrow morning,' said Oakshott. 'Bonaparte will carry all before him.'

Other sounds reached them, coming up from the dark plains below and beyond: more bugle calls, the snicker of a restless horse, a shouted command far off, rumble of gun-carriage wheels; once, they automatically crouched closer to their cover and kept their heads low, as, with a thunder of pounding hooves and the jingle of harness and equipment, a group of cavalry passed close by below – all unseen by them in the Stygian gloom.

Dawn brought a revelation of the coming battlefield, with the participants set out like toy soldiers in a war-game.

To the east, the bright ribbon of the Nile. To the south and south-east, the domes, minarets, palaces and hovels of Cairo, whitely clear under the rising sun. Between the pyramids and the river, a vast plain of sand and scrub, with a few mean villages set amongst the cultivated land towards the river bank.

Murad's forces were drawn up in lines parallel to the river, facing the plain of the pyramids; cavalry in the centre, regular and irregular infantry on the flanks, with artillery interspersed. It was nakedly obvious that the Mameluke field commander was intending to risk his all on his cavalry arm.

From their high vantage point, Oakshott and his companions saw the French marching to their final positions; swinging into line to face the enemy, marching like guardsmen all, to the tap-tap of their kettle-drums. And their right flank was no more than a musket shot from the base of the Great Pyramid of Cheops.

'How many a side would you say?' mused Oakshott. 'They look about equal as to numbers. As to quality – well, we shall see . . .'

'Twenty to thirty thousand each, at least sir,' opined Henshawe.

'Do you see the centre of the French line?' said Oakshott. 'A group of staff officers, mounted, and the fellow in the middle of them? See – he's pointing . . .'

'By heaven, he's pointing up here!' cried Shacklock. 'Do you suppose he's seen us?'

'Out of the question,' said Oakshott. 'But I tell you, gentlemen – that is Bonaparte himself, I'll stake a purse of guineas on it. Mark how the others are deferring to him. See – he's given an order, and that officer in hussar's rig is galloping off to take a message to the flank. That is Bonaparte, right enough. Conqueror of northern Italy, scourge of the Austrians. The fellow who threw us out of Toulon.

'Toulon . . .' his expression grew wistful. 'You know – did I ever tell you two?' – looking at the men of the *Daisy* – 'I had an encounter with a French artillery captain whom we briefly captured in Toulon. Fellow with an outlandish name that I immediately forgot. I've half a mind, when I look back on it, that it may have been Bonaparte.'

'Pity you didn't put a bullet through his head there and then, sir,' declared Shacklock. 'It would have saved a lot of people a very great deal of trouble.'

'Sir!' interposed Pepe Lopez. 'The Mameluke cavalry – see – they are on the move!'

'By God, so they are!'

'And the French infantry's forming squares!' cried Shacklock.

'Best tactic for them,' said Oakshott. 'It would be folly for them to throw their own cavalry against the Mamelukes. Best by far to hold them in hand till the rout. And I have a notion that there will be . . .' he did not complete his remark.

The Mameluke cavalry, with their irregulars and Bedouin horse and camels bringing up the rear, moved forward across the wide plain at the walk-march, while the French infantry unhurriedly formed squares with artillery disposed at each corner of the squares and the cavalry tucked neatly behind.

''Tis now that the Frogs should be loosing off a few long-range cannon shots!' cried Shacklock. 'A broadside of ball would carve swathes through that massed cavalry, even at that distance.'

'Maybe Bonaparte doesn't want to put 'em off,' murmured Oakshott laconically. 'He'll have all morning to do that –

and at point-blank range!'

The oncoming horsemen were by now almost entirely masked by the kicked-up sand of their passage; but what they lost in visibility they gained in sound: the war-drums were beating out their strident, nerve-tingling rhythm, and this was augmented by an eerie ululation rising in barbaric chorus from uncounted throats.

'Heaven help the Frogs if them demons do ever get amongst 'em!' breathed Henshawe in awe.

'Amen to that,' responded Oakshott.

The cream of the Mameluke cavalry, mounted as they were on the finest Arabian horses in the world – trained to obey the lightest touch of rein or heel, to advance, wheel, or fly with wonderful rapidity – kept most marvellous formation throughout their long approach, though it was plain to the onlookers in 'the front row of the gods' that the irregulars at the rear, and even the desert Bedouin, had no such mastery; their ranks were bunched together and constantly colliding, straggling, sprawling across the landscape.

'If the crack troops in the forefront ever want to make a quick retirement to re-group,' said Oakshott, 'they are going to find their friends in the rear more of a burden than an asset.'

It was seven o'clock in the morning when someone in the leading line of the Mameluke cavalry – it may have been Murad Bey himself – raised aloft his lance, pointed it to the tight-packed French squares and gave the order to charge.

The splendid arab horses picked up the canter, then the trot – and within two hundred yards of the blue-clad infantry, stretched into a solid, irresistible gallop.

And then the French musketry opened up. And the cannon.

They came thundering on like a whirlwind, and even when the lead flew into them, they still came on. The first of the French squares to be struck was immediately thrown into confusion, pierced, with the enemy amongst them and making terrible execution with pistol and scimitar: but the French officers rallied their men, ordered the gap to be plugged with flesh and bayonet. The Mamelukes who had

147

smashed their way inside the square were dragged from their horses and bayoneted by former farm-lads from Perigord, shop assistants from the rue Royale, wine-growers from the Midi.

It was Murad Bey's first, flawed success; his last and only.

Murad, who had boasted that he would cut up the French like 'gourds, succeeded in getting no closer than bayonet length to the remaining squares. Their horses mowed down by musketry and artillery, those Mamelukes obliged to fight on foot, grossly encumbered by their armour and weaponry (not to mention all of their personal valuables,) fought till they fell, and when they had fallen, crept forward on hands and knees to slash at the Frenchmen's legs with their unblooded blades. But to no avail.

All this the onlookers observed from the summit of the pyramid.

They saw the Mameluke cavalrymen flinging their discharged pistols into their foes' faces in despair; watched them backing up their horses in the vain hope of breaking them by kicking and, finding all unavailing, fleeing.

As Oakshott had discerned, the support cavalry irregulars and the Bedouin, having no ghost of a hope where the finest heavy cavalry had failed, served only to impede the latter's retirement – more nearly a headlong retreat.

'It's over,' said Oakshott. 'The real fighting's over. The rest is only mopping up.'

And so it was.

There were twenty thousand infantry in a hastily-entrenched position on the Mameluke right; but these were no more than a rabble of pressed fellahin, taken from the fields, armed with old muskets and set to support the forty cannon that Oakshott and his companions had seen being carried around the parade ground in the Cairo citadel. They played no part in the battle. The guns loosed off a few rounds apiece, but the ill-timed shots rolled wildly away across the empty desert like bowls thrown against their bias. When Bonaparte sent a wing of his light cavalry against them, they fled like sheep before the curved, swinging blades of the hussars and chasseurs – and, like sheep, they were slaughtered.

As for the French heavy cavalry ...

These – the pick of the *sabreurs* who had slashed a swathe of terror from the Rhine to the Tiber – Bonaparte unleashed upon the Mameluke cavalry when they turned and fled; they fell upon the enemy in the utter confusion of the latter's entanglement with their irregulars and the Bedouin. Dragoons and cuirassiers carved through the mêlée of jostling, cursing riders and their wild-eyed, by now unbiddable mounts. Those who survived the first part of that death-ride made for the river, which they then attempted to swim. They did not get far. Mameluke heavy cavalrymen, weighed down by their mail coats and weaponry, were either drowned or picked off by the dragoons' carbine fire from the bank. All this was observed by the civilian population of the city, who watched with horror from the far side of the Nile.

The men on the crest of Pharaoh Cheops' pyramid saw it also.

They witnessed the wholesale surrender of the wretched fellahin who had never traded a blow, the rout of the proud Bedouin, galloping for their lives into the deep desert from whence they came; as the day wore on, they saw the French troops gleaning a second harvest of death from the corpse-strewn field, rifling the pockets and the baggage of the slain Mamelukes for such assorted coin and valuables as would provide many a soldier with the means to buy a farm or a café upon his retirement.

'All gone – finished!' said Oakshott. 'And the sun not yet over the yardarm.'

By nightfall, the French had gone on into Cairo, which they entered without the need to fire a shot. On the plain of the pyramids there remained two thousand despoiled corpses. The battle – if such a rout can be graced with the term – had cost Bonaparte thirty killed.

At sunset Oakshott led his companions down the pyramid. The horses were safe and sound. A short ride through the night brought them to a small oasis where the mounts were able to water and graze upon the sun-parched herbage; their riders quenched their thirst, filled water-skins, and tightened their belts against the promise of going hungry for quite a while. They set off again within the half-hour.

Under the dying moon and a whole heaven of stars, the trackless desert unfolded before them like an unending carpet, featureless, unchanging, inhospitable. Guided by the North Star, they rode without ceasing till dawn, when Oakshott gave the order for a short rest. Then, reckoning that as the French had moved down to Cairo and there was only a slender chance of falling foul of a wandering cavalry patrol, he opted to carry on through the day in the hope of finding water and shelter. Blessedly, with the blistering noonday sun right overhead and their mounts flagging, they came upon a brackish water-hole and a clump of stunted palm trees and prickly pear where they rested till the late afternoon. It was there that Pepe Lopez' horse was bitten by a horned viper. Not possessing the means to put the poor beast out of its misery, they were obliged to leave it to die. From then on, it was four men to three horses, watch-and-watch about, navy fashion.

The second day of their long trek through the wilderness to the coast brought them to the end of their water. It was then that Oakshott, knowing that the time had arrived when their true worth as men would be put to the real test, took stock of his companions and liked what he saw ...

Henshawe, despite the minor infirmities resulting from his advanced years coupled with the hard life, bad food and appalling living conditions of the naval service, was stolidly uncomplaining; the phlegmatic Geordie was ever ready with the wry quip, the cheering word. Young Shacklock quite simply lacked the imagination to appreciate the very real peril in which they stood; as far as he was concerned, his captain was leading them back to their ship, and that was that. If by some unhappy chance the *Daisy* was no longer in being, why – Oakshott would contrive another solution. At the end of their Odyssey, they would see the Solent again, or sail on the flood tide past Plymouth Hoe. Shacklock was essentially the carefree optimist.

150

Pepe Lopez, thought Oakshott, was of an entirely more complex make-up: more than any of them – Oakshott included – their guide and interpreter had been deeply affected by the bloody fray in the shadow of the pyramids. The sight of the victorious French robbing the dead and wounded – and dispatching the latter without mercy – had reduced that essentially ebullient soul to a brooding sadness that had been deepened by the cruel fate of his mount.

An interesting character, Pepe; one must do something to advance his state when the opportunity arose.

Oakshott put aside his deliberations and hauled himself to his feet after a short rest, wiped the sweat from his brow and clapped on his hat, the cocks of which he had taken down to shade his face from the sun.

'Mount up!' he ordered. 'You will take my horse for the next hour, Pepe.'

Squaring his shoulders, he set off again, keeping the afternoon sun on his left cheek. The others followed after.

Nine

Upon Oakshott's departure for Cairo, Thomas A. Brewster, as acting captain of the *Daisy*, had taken a lien on the stern cabin and moved in, bag and baggage. He also posted lookouts on the end of the mole, and these, in addition to those already at the foremast head, were supplied with telescopes and ordered to keep a sharp watch for the French.

On the afternoon of his first day as commander of a ship-of-war, the American's powers of leadership were put sternly to the test – and the opening gambit was not unpropitious. He was seated shirtsleeved in the stern cabin and writing up his diary when his black slave Cuthbert entered and apprised him, by the signs and incoherent mouthings understood only between the two of them, that the purser's mate requested his presence on deck upon an urgent matter.

Brewster, on his arrival up there, found Purser's Mate Butterworth and the ship's cook standing by an opened cask, together with a handful of topmen off watch and with nothing better to do.

'Well?' demanded Brewster. 'What's the trouble?'

'This cask, sir, is part of the consignment which was bought in Naples,' answered Butterworth. 'By *your* authority, sir.' He delivered the last phrase with a fine edge to his voice, as if contriving to convey his resentment at the first lieutenant's interference in the procuring of stores – an activity which he rightly regarded as his own business, together with the perquisites that went with it.

'Ah, yes,' responded Brewster. 'Bought in at a very fine

price, and of excellent quality. I breakfasted off it this morning.'

'Not out of this cask, sir,' was the meaningful response. 'The pork in *this* cask isn't fit for man nor beast, being only the rejected skin, bones and guts!'

'Oh!' was Brewster's response. And, again: 'Oooh ...'

'And it isn't the only one, sir,' added Butterworth, turning the screw. 'This is the third cask we've just opened – and only one of them was filled with salt pork fit to eat.'

The American rubbed his lean jaw. He was silent for a few moments, and then his wide mouth broke into the heartening grin which was his answer to most of the slings and arrows of outrageous fortune.

'It would seem,' he essayed, 'that this gullible former Colonial has been well and truly gulled by a wily Eye-talian!'

'It isn't for me to say, sir,' responded Butterworth stiffly.

'Well, ditch the two foul casks over the side for the gulls, Purser's Mate,' said the acting captain, adding with commendable condescension: 'And let this be a lesson to you not to trust any Eye-talian when it comes to ...'

'*Sails to the eastward ... French!*' came from the masthead – and was swiftly repeated from the end of the mole.

Lieutenant Brewster's expertise at bringing an anchored ship out of harbour and having her fully rigged and ready to fight was amply demonstrated to be well in advance of his talent for procurement. Five minutes after the sighting, the duty watch on deck had the anchor up-and-down, all plain sail was being unfurled, guns were loaded and run out, the lookouts from the mole were tumbling aboard – and the dismayed bumboatmen were presently staring after what they had already come to regard as a sinecure for life, as HM Sloop-of-War *Daisy* glided smoothly out of Alexandria harbour, full-and-by, on a northerly wind, with the bow wave creaming ever more boisterously under and around her stem. It was a good wind, a fair wind in the circumstances, and boisterous enough to take the *Daisy* westwards on the starboard tack, away from the oncoming foe and all his puissance.

'Steady as you go, Bosun.'

'Aye, aye, sir. Due west, sir.'

'Call off the enemy sail!' said Brewster – this to Midshipman Thompson, standing in the mizzen chains, telescope trained.

'Eight – nine – ten – eleven – and more battleships, sir. More transports than I could count – they are massed behind the fleet, sir.'

'Frigates?' Every man aboard knew that this was the nub of the *Daisy*'s problem.

'Four of 'em, sir. And all making ahead of the fleet. They're coming after us, sir!'

'Bosun, steer fine on your best point of sail. We must hold them off till nightfall and then take our chance in the dark.'

Bosun Cox acknowledged the order, whilst privately irritated that it should have been given, since with his long experience of the *Daisy* and all her foibles, he knew to a touch of the helm, a hint of riffling at a jib's leach, how well she was performing, and if at her best.

Brewster took a sight on the frigates. Two of them had shortened sail and were waiting for the rest of the fleet to catch up with them off the harbour mouth, leaving their consorts to continue the pursuit of the British sloop which had so unexpectedly and insolently appeared right under their very bowsprits. Two of them – even one – would be enough, thought the acting captain, if it came to a pounding match; and, given a straight run in daylight, that they would overtake him could never be in doubt.

Only ...

There was not a great deal of daylight left, nor did he intend to bring himself to a pounding match – not if ducking and weaving, feinting and deceiving could carry him through. Mindful of his pioneer ancestry, Thomas A. Brewster squared his bony shoulders, puffed out his chest and grinned backwards at his pursuers. Then he gave his orders:

'Leadsmen to the chains – prepare to commence continuous soundings upon my order!'

'Aye, aye, sir!'

'Bosun, I shall presently be taking her as close inshore as I'm able, and closer than the Frog frigates will care to venture.'

Bosun Cox knuckled his forelock and nodded.

'Cuthbert!'

The little black deaf-mute was all attention to his master's order: watching the formation of the latter's lips like a hawk regarding a rabbit hole from on high.

'Cuthbert, slice me off a piece of salt pork and lay it between two biscuits, if you please. Bring it up straightway, along with a mug of cocoa. I reckon I have a long night ahead of me, and the inner man had best be well fortified.'

The boy understood perfectly. He grinned broadly and disappeared down the companionway.

'Masthead to quarterdeck!' Charteris the senior midshipman was on lookout from on high.

'Speak up!' responded Brewster.

'Sir, the French – fleet and transports – have sailed right past the entrance to Alex harbour and are continuing on this way!'

'Are they, now? Well, it's to be expected, I suppose, that they wouldn't attempt a frontal assault – always assuming Alexandria's their goal.' Brewster was cogitating aloud to himself, as he frequently did. He took another glim at the pursuing frigates and reckoned that they were perhaps one to one and a half cables distant and coming on fast.

'Bosun, bring her two points to port,' he ordered.

'Two points to port, sir!'

The great wheel was turned. The *Daisy*, reacting like a thoroughbred to her rudder's touch, slanted obliquely towards the shore, where the evening sun was already casting long shadows of stunted palms across the sand and rocks.

'Commence continuous soundings!'

The leadsman in the heads threw the bottle-shaped plug of lead as far ahead as he was able; his mate in the mizzen chains held the other end of the line connected to the lead; as the line went aft, he hauled in the slack and held it taut when the lead was directly below him.

He then read off the depth from the mark at the waterline:

'By the mark five!'

'Plenty of water,' commented Oakshott. 'All the water in the world.'

Bosun Cox spat a gobbet of tobacco juice to leeward. With the *Daisy* drawing nine feet – a fathom and a half – 'all the water in the world' was, in his opinion, a slight exaggeration. The next sounding proved him to be right:

'By the mark three!'

Cox threw the acting captain a questioning glance.

'Press on, Bosun,' said the other cheerfully. 'We must proceed' – and here he looked back over his shoulder at the French frigates – "where angels fear to tread".'

'By the mark three!'

Cox closed his eyes for a moment and whispered a prayer of thanks he had learned at his mother's knee.

'The shoal's levelled out,' said *Daisy*'s acting captain. 'It's the luck of the Brewsters, Bosun.'

They were now so close inshore – and still closing – that a good pair of eyes could quite easily discern larger individual pebbles on the beach, the separate leaves on palm trees, the curling lines of tiny wavelets lapping on the strand. The superior pace of the big frigates – who took their speed from the inexorable geometry of length opposed to beam, opposed to sail area – had brought them almost abreast of the *Daisy*'s new track. And the French were also taking constant soundings.

'But they'll not venture much closer in,' mused Brewster, mostly to himself. 'With their draught, not beyond the four-fathom line, I should guess. Resume your original course, Bosun, and keep her parallel to the shoreline.'

'By the mark three!'

'Brewsters' luck holds,' smiled the American. With which comforting thought, he addressed himself to the junk and hard tack which his black boy had brought him, along with a steaming mug of good navy cocoa.

'The Frogs are shooting!'

A fulmination of white gunsmoke centred with a flash of pinkish-orange flame enveloped the waist of the nearest frigate. All eyes scanned the sea between shooter and target. A few seconds later, the ball kicked up a ten-foot-high column of white water fifty yards on the *Daisy*'s starboard quarter.

'That would be at maximum elevation,' said Brewster. 'To have any hope of hitting us, they're going to have to take the bull by the horns and dip their toes in shallower water over here.' The mixed metaphor seemed to please him and he smiled; he was still smiling when it became clear that the enemy ships were maintaining their course outside the four-fathom line.

They continued to dog the English sloop-of-war under reduced sail – keeping strictly abreast of her.

Night. And the moon not up.

Brewster narrowed his eyes. The evidence of the naked eye confirmed again what he espied through his telescope: the visual presence of their menacing shadowers was manifested only by the ghostly pale outlines of their sails. To him, this suggested a stratagem.

'Call all hands to take in sail,' he intoned. 'But quietly – just pass the word.'

There came the patter of bare feet, and the hands clawed their ways up the shrouds, each to his own place on the foot ropes of the sail apportioned to him. Upon the order, Cox spun the wheel and brought the *Daisy* up into the wind; simultaneously, the topmen gathered in the now idly flapping sails. In the time it took to speak of it, the ship ceased to be a living, moving thing and was lying still in the darkness under bare poles.

'Now to see,' said Brewster, levelling his telescope, 'if our sudden – for the want of a better word – disappearance has been observed. Ah, I discern that it has not. Leastways, the Frogs are continuing on their way.'

Five minutes passed, with the *Daisy* as still as a ship in a bottle upon the glassy sea. Every eye, every telescope aboard, was trained on the receding French sails. And a muffled cheer went up as they finally disappeared from view.

'We've given 'em the slip!' cried Brewster. 'Make all sail

again! Set course for the nor'east, Bosun! We'll put some sea room between us and the Frogs before they rumble that we've gone.'

Hearts were high aboard the little sloop-of-war. Even Bosun Cox, doubtful though he had been about the alien former Colonial who had been foisted on to him, could not forbear to nod approval at the success of Brewster's stratagem. The sails drew with a cheerful vigour that echoed the spirits of the crew. Making way full-and-by on the port tack – her very best point of sail – she crossed the four-fathom line, the five-fathom line.

And then . . .

It was as if a giant hand had reached out of the darkness and, placing its open palm against the *Daisy*'s speeding bow, checked her to stillness in a fraction of her length. The men on the quarterdeck were flung into a shocked and cursing heap against the rails. Brewster picked himself up, spat out a broken tooth and, leaning over the side, saw, even in the darkness, that the pellucid waters of the Mediterranean which gently lapped against the ship's side were scummed and swirling murkily with liquid mud. They had struck, and been driven hard on to, an offshore shoal!

How may a captain, even in the moment of his triumph, be laid low! All success in the seafaring trade – dependent upon fairly equal portions of knowledge, experience, bravery, fortitude and style – can so easily be set to naught by the vagaries of nature and the fickle shifting of luck. So it was, that night, with Thomas A, Brewster, scion of the lucky Brewsters of Boston in the Commonwealth of Massachusetts.

What now, Brewster? You are the captain. All eyes are upon you.

'Call away all boats!' ordered he.

Whaleboat, gig and jolly-boat were hauled over the side and crewed. No further orders needed to be given, no starters required to be laid across willing backs. The ship and all on her were lying like one helpless conglomerate sitting duck, clean in the path of the French frigates should they return along their former track in search of their missing quarry. Lines were bent upon the anchors, which were then rowed out into deep water and made fast on the bottom. Then it was all hands to the capstan bars, to haul the ship clear, aided by the three boats pulling away for'ard.

'She's not shifting, sir,' said Bosun Cox at length. 'She's well on the putty and stuck hard abaft. I can't move the wheel.'

With an uneasy glance to westward in anticipation of seeing the two sets of enemy sails coming out at them from the darkness, Brewster gave his next order:

'All hands to the bows.'

The full complement of 130 officers and men who had commissioned the *Daisy* on her departure from home – depleted by three dead from divers diseases and two from drowning as well as the crews of the boats over the side – raced up to the fore end of the ship for makeweight. Though there was a perceptible dip of the bows, the efforts of the burgeoning sails and the hard-pulled boats made no headway against the grip of the shoal.

All eyes were again upon the temporary captain. Think hard, Brewster!

Another glance to the west, and then: 'Shift the waist guns for'ard!'

The manoeuvre of trundling the guns at the centre of the ship – that is to say three, four, five and six of port and starboard: eight pieces and a considerable dead weight in all – to the for'ard end of the main deck under the fo'c'sle, was a simple operation and greatly added to the makeweight in the bows.

Brewster met Cox's eye, as the latter nudged at the wheel, essayed to turn it, one way and the other.

Presently: 'She's shifting, sir!'

And – later: '*She's off!*'

Like a hound unleashed, a hawk unjessed, the *Daisy* spread her canvas wings and won herself free of the sand bar; took courage from the northerly wind upon her best point of sail and glided into deep water that was soon being sounded at eight fathoms and then ten.

Presently, the boats recovered, they were losing themselves in the darkness to the north-east.

The luck of the Brewsters had won through, after all.

*

As *Daisy* scudded through the night there was a council of
war in the stern cabin: Acting Captain Brewster, the officers,
Sail Master Quinch and his mates, the bosun and his.

'My intent, gentlemen,' said Brewster, 'is to be at hand to
take back aboard Commander Oakshott and his party, who
will be returning from Cairo sooner or later.

'Now that the French have arrived, we may expect that the
captain's plans may be somewhat set awry. As to how, it is
idle to speculate. However, I see my task quite plain. It is to
conform to Commander Oakshott's last order, which was to
stand to the east if I have to quit Alexandria. During the
hours of daylight, the *Daisy* will lay out to sea. At night, we
will creep inshore to the east of Alexandria, taking
soundings as we go.' He paused and grinned. 'It has already
been established that we are adept at extricating ourselves
from uncharted shoals.'

This sally won him a concerted gust of laughter of the
mutually-admiring sort.

'Sir,' interposed Quinch, 'how shall we locate Commander Oakshott and his party in all the clatter that's likely
to take place now that the French are here?'

'A good question, Mr Quinch,' replied Brewster, with the
look of a man who has all unexpectedly found himself the
owner of a talking horse. 'And I'm glad you asked it.

'Gentlemen, it hardly seems likely that Alexandria will
long withstand the French assault. As ordered by Commander Oakshott, I will therefore stand off to the eastwards
and approach the coast nightly at eight bells. At that hour
precisely, our captain will cause a fire to be lit on the beach –
but for only a quarter of an hour, no more – every night after
his return. By that we shall know him.'

That the city of Alexander the Great, the Ptolemys,
Cleopatra, Julius Caesar and Mark Antony was incapable of
offering any real resistance to Bonaparte, the conqueror of
northern Italy and scourger of the Austrians, was well
demonstrated next day when, from the decks of the *Daisy*
hull-down on the horizon, the crew saw and heard
something of the taking and sack of Alexandria: the
bombardment by cannon, followed by the mass assault of
infantry (whose concerted musket fire carried quite clearly

160

across the water), the palls of black smoke rising in the still air, and after that – silence.

When, that night, the *Daisy* edged shorewards, as she did on so many successive nights afterwards, Alexandria was still burning. The havoc and horrors wrought within its walls were hidden from the sailors, so also was the knowledge that Bonaparte had already set off on the long march to Cairo – for the cheap victory which his godless hagiographers would accord the preening title of the Battle of the Pyramids.

Ten

He was lying in his parents' canopied four-poster in the great bedchamber whose windows looked out across the Vale of the White Horse, the same in which they had died, and his brother after them – like six generations of noble Oakshotts gone before.

The burden of the inheritance had now fallen upon him; but would not long be an encumbrance, for he, too, was now dying of a malignant fever that racked his weary body and burned into his brain.

God, could not somebody open the damned windows and let in the clean air? Or take off some of the coverlets which they had piled upon him? Was there no one in the place who could be spared to sit and fan his sweating body, lay cool damp cloths upon his brow?

He stirred – opened his eyes – and was dazzled to near-blindness by the sun that burned down at him from directly overhead.

He sat up. A tiny green lizard, alarmed at the sudden movement, skittered away and hid itself in a small mountain of shale nearby.

Oakshott grimaced from the pain of his burnt arms and shoulders that had been uncovered by his torn shirt – his coat he had long abandoned. The movement of his features was a cause of further agony, for the skin of his face, burnt and burnt again, was a mass of sores and suppurating scabs.

Shading his eyes, he looked about him. They were on a tongue of land that pointed out to sea. To the right, one of the wide mouths of the Nile issued from out of the sprawling

162

delta into the Mediterranean, tainting the sea's jewelled blueness with its cocoa-coloured mud. To the left was a wide bay. There was no sign of shelter or habitation: not a single mud hovel, not a solitary stunted palm.

They had arrived there shortly before dawn, having forged ahead through the night, lured by the familiar salt tang of the sea that was borne to them on the northerly breeze. Upon reaching the strand they had fallen and slept where they lay – all four, none of them in very good fettle, Henshawe particularly. And there remained only one of the horses; the two others had simply lain down and died.

Three humped, sleeping forms surrounded him. The hobbled horse, more sprightly now that, like the humans, it had quenched its thirst in the brackish water of the river, gave a small snicker of alarm which drew Oakshott's attention to a mounted figure approaching along the shoreline from the west. Upon closer inspection the newcomer proved to be a man – an Arab – on a small donkey.

Wakening his companions, Oakshott went to meet the rider, who did not slacken his pace, or show any alarm to see the four scarecrows who confronted him. He was an old man, wizened of feature, white of straggly beard, and he watched his challengers with lack-lustre eyes that were encircled with unregarded flies.

'Pepe, find out who he is and what news he has of the French,' ordered Oakshott.

There then followed a protracted dialogue in swift Arabic, with Pepe Lopez making most of the running, and the old man responding with grudging monosyllables, only occasionally breaking into brief, swift diatribes, accompanied by pointings of his withered arm and bony fingers – to the westwards and Alexandria.

Presently, Oakshott said: 'That's enough to be going on with. What do we have thus far?'

'Sir, he is from Alexandria,' said Pepe. 'Or, at least, he used to live there till the French came. He returned home after the city was taken, to find his house burned down and his family all slaughtered.' Lopez' expressive eyes were shadowed with compassion. 'The soldiers had managed to find his small savings and now he has nothing, sir.'

Oakshott nodded. 'And what of the French armada – the war fleet particularly?'

More Arabic. The old man, who by now appeared to appreciate that he was not confronted by friends of the French invader, grew discernibly more cooperative.

'The transports are all in Alexandria harbour, sir,' translated Pepe Lopez. 'And the troops all disembarked.'

'The fleet?'

'They are anchored at the western end of a bay he calls Abou Quir, sir. And he has paid very particular attention to them. Thirteen big ships, he says, and four smaller ones – they would be the frigates, sir. And a few minor vessels.'

Scarcely able to keep the tense excitement from his voice, Oakshott demanded to know if their informant had any news of any other fleet – the British fleet?

The answer was already known to Oakshott and his companions: yes, the British had come days before the French, but they went away.

Yes, yes – but had they been sighted again – had they ever returned?

The bitterly disappointing reply was – no.

'Thank our friend,' said Oakshott. 'And tell him he can have the horse, since we have no further need of it.' So saying, *Daisy*'s captain walked slowly away towards the water's edge, with the glad thanks of the old man drifting after him unheeded.

So that was it – and it was as he had feared: by beating the French to Alexandria, Nelson had missed his chance, and was now searching the entire eastern Mediterranean – perhaps from Sicily to the Holy Land, with the Aegean, the Greek archipelago and Turkey thrown in. Seeking out his enemy on the high seas – while all the time the French lay at anchor a few miles from where he – Oakshott – stood.

Stooping, he picked up a flat pebble and skimmed it across the water; watched it bounce three times and then sink with scarcely a ripple.

Yes, that was it. He must regain the *Daisy*. Seek the seeker ...

Find Nelson and bring him news of the anchored French.

*

It was another day for the tightening of belts. They had not eaten since the last of their supper scraps on the pyramid, nor drunk anything but stagnant water of variable states of filth. The Nile water was distinctly brackish at its mouth, but they went foraging in the cool of the evening and found a sweet-water canal to the south that must have been constructed by Caesar's legionaries: there they recklessly over-gorged, and filled the water-skin. Shacklock chanced to corner a jack rabbit in an angle of the canal bank and must certainly have outrun and killed it in his habitually vigorous condition; enfeebled as he was, the young lieutenant was easily evaded by the rabbit.

That night, they supped off the green leaves of a plant that grew on the banks of the canal in some abundance; though fibrous in texture and almost tasteless, it brought to the half-starved quartette the illusion of nutrition, and certainly filled their bellies.

When the sub-tropical night fell, they sat cross-legged in a line on the beach, looking out to sea for signs of a ship's lights – though it was unlikely that Brewster would venture near the enemy-occupied shore undarkened. They saw nothing; nor any sound but the gentle lapping of the waves and, towards midnight, the distant howl of a wild dog out of the desert.

At midnight by Oakshott's watch, they lit a fire of driftwood and allowed it to burn for a quarter of an hour before dousing the flames with sand. For the next hour, they peered out into the gloom in the hope of having elicited the response of one of the *Daisy*'s boats coming inshore to collect them.

They repeated this regimen for two more days and three more nights. On the third night, their fire was briefly answered by a shielded lantern some distance out at sea, revealed for a half-minute, no more.

Presently, they heard the plash of oars giving way in unison, and from out of the darkness there came a whaleboat, heading straight for them.

'What ship?' called Shacklock.

'*Daisy!*'

They were back home again.

*

Thompson, the smallest and youngest midshipman, was cox'n of the whaler, and proud to bursting that he was the direct instrument of his captain's salvation. A cheerful, promising lad of fourteen with a quite remarkable insight, he prattled away – once he had got his passengers aboard and was heading back the way he had come – without scarcely drawing breath.

'Every night since Lieutenant Brewster gave the Frog frigates the slip and stood out to sea, we have come back inshore to watch for your midnight fire, sir; every night to a different spot betwixt the delta and nigh on Alexandria. Many of us did despair, but Mr Brewster bore us up, saying, "We'll keep at it, gentlemen, and one night I tell you we shall see that fire." And see it we did, sir.

'Sir, we have located the French fleet ...'

'In the bay called Abou Quir,' interposed Oakshott.

The boy seemed somewhat put aback not to be the bearer of pristine news, but he was not out of countenance for long. 'We have only seen them in the dark, of course, sir. By their lights as they lie at anchor. Nor have we ventured close enough to call off their numbers ...'

'Thirteen line-of-battle ships, four frigates and several small vessels,' said Oakshott.

'Oh! So you knew that already, sir? Well, we reckoned something around that number. What are we going to do about them, sir?'

'Mr Thompson,' said Oakshott, who greatly believed in educating the young by the Socratic method, 'you have the facts to hand. Consider – you are the captain of the *Daisy*. Where does your duty now lie?'

'Why, sir,' replied the other without hesitation, 'I must bring this news to Admiral Nelson, wherever he may be.'

'Very good, Mr Thompson. That is your object. How shall you go about it?'

The boy was silent. No sound but the gentle creaking of the oiled rowlocks, the plash of oars, the steady breathing of the rowers.

'Um – well, sir,' said the midshipman at length, 'mindful

166

that the admiral has not watered and provisioned his fleet since – say – Naples ...'

'That would be a reasonable supposition, Mr Thompson. Naples – or Sicily, perhaps.'

'Well, then he will not be in a position to quarter the whole sea in an aimless search for the French, but will assume that his interests and the enemy's interests coincide. And he will look to another neutral port where he may compel the authorities to water and provision him on pain of bombardment. And in doing so, he may also hope to find ...'

'To find the French already there and doing exactly the same thing. Very good, Mr Thompson. Now, tell me – where will you begin this search? – speaking as captain of the *Daisy*.'

'Why, sir, Haifa perhaps. Thence to Cyprus – and Crete.'

'And how shall you occupy yourself on the way?'

'By stopping every ship I encounter and questioning them as to whether they have seen or heard aught of the British fleet.'

'Finally, what shall you avoid most of all?'

'A fight, sir,' replied Thompson without hesitation. 'No matter how advantageous be the odds in my favour – for it can truly be said that the *Daisy* has only one reason for staying afloat, and that's to bring the news to Admiral Nelson.'

With a small lurch of the heart, Oakshott could just discern, in the darkness ahead, the faint smudge that betokened a ship. Soon he would really be home.

'You've answered well, Mr Thompson,' he said. 'At your earliest opportunity, you will make a transcript of our conversation in your log and journal. I will then initial it, and the entry may serve you in good stead when you go to be examined for your lieutenancy.'

'Thank you, sir,' responded the boy.

'What's to eat aboard, snotty?' demanded Shacklock brusquely – he who was of the opinion that things had changed since his young days when ships' captains did not act as snotties' nursemaids; it has to be remembered that Shacklock was rising twenty.

'There was fish burgoo for supper, sir,' responded the other.

'Fish burgoo, by heaven!'

'The waters off the delta are teeming with fish that fairly jump on to your hook,' said Thompson. 'We have had fish for supper ever since you were away, and Mr Brewster has been most particular that ample should always be left for you gentlemen every night.'

'For a basin o' fish burgoo,' mused Henshawe feelingly, 'I reckon as how I would gladly ...'

He did not finish.

'*Oars!*'

The order was rasped out by Oakshott, whose eyes – suddenly widened with shock – were fixed ahead. At his command, the rowers brought their blades out of the water to the horizontal. The whaler lost way and was still.

The ship ahead had manifested itself as being under full sail and in the very act of turning to go obliquely away from them.

Nor was that all ...

'By all that's holy!' breathed Henshawe. '*That ain't the Daisy!*'

'It's a French frigate!'

At that moment, the vessel in question opened fire with a rolling broadside to starboard, lighting up the sea and all about her in a lurid pinkness, soon gone but quite unforgettable in its stark brightness. And the stink of burnt powder wafted down upon the men in the whaler.

'She must be firing on the *Daisy*!'

'Who else?'

'There's the *Daisy*! – there she is, sir!' It was Thompson who pointed. Their ship appeared to the right, coming out of the darkness on a roughly opposing course from that of the Frenchman, and shaping to pass close by the whaler on the starboard tack.

'She's hit – she took that broadside full on!'

Even as they watched, the whole of the *Daisy*'s fore topmast, topgallant and all, came crashing down, carrying with it a cat's cradle of rigging and cordage, sails and yards. And a fire had started for'ard in the heads.

168

The men in the whaler got to their feet and waved, shouting at the top of their lungs as their ship sliced towards them.

'*Daisy ahoy!*'

'*Avast there, lads!*'

Someone saw them from the stricken deck, for the helm was put up and the wounded sloop-of-war was brought up in irons close by. A few frantic strokes of the oars and they were alongside her. Faces stared down on them.

'Up with you lads! Forget the whaler, we've no time to pick her up! Roundly, now – chop-chop!'

They scrambled up the accommodation ladder, Oakshott giving aid to Henshawe, who sagged with sheer weariness in his grasp. Reaching the deck, he was greeted by Tom Brewster. The ship was already under way again.

'Thank God you're back, sir. But this is a bad business. We came inshore once too often and they were waiting for us. Never saw them till they opened fire. And never a chance to reply, though we were at quarters.'

'There'll be chances a-plenty from now on, Number One,' replied Oakshott, pointing. 'Here they come again!'

The Frenchman, having gone about, was racing down upon them on a parallel course to pass close by on the starboard side.

'Starboard battery!' yelled Brewster through a speaking trumpet. 'Stand by to deliver a broadside in succession! Give fire when you bear!'

'Heads down, lads!' called Oakshott to the men grouped about him on the quarterdeck. 'For what we are about to receive . . .'

There was not a split second to spare between both ships opening fire. The foremost gun of the overtaking frigate loosed off as soon as its bows drew abreast of the *Daisy*'s quarterdeck, and the latter's stern guns did likewise. Oakshott heard the humming of countless deadly hornets, as a charge of grapeshot slashed close past him. Somebody fell towards him and he snatched at a slight form that felt pathetically frail in his arms. It was young Thompson, and the boy was horribly dead.

The broadsides rolled on, till the Frenchman was ahead of

them and already making to turn to starboard and come in again.

'Port your helm!' shouted Oakshott, discerning that the manoeuvre would give him a breathing space to take account of damage and casualties before the enemy made his third pass. 'Are you there, Number One?' he cried.

'More or less, sir,' responded the American, getting to his feet and shoving aside the mangled corpse of a quartermaster who had been lending his brawn to the ship's wheel a few instants before.

Two others had perished on the quarterdeck. All four bodies were thrown over the side. Insofar as possible it was done with a certain rough reverence; but obsequies of battle are by necessity exiguous.

Bosun Cox came up the companionway from the gundeck. His right arm hung like a bloody limp rag. He saluted his captain with his left.

'Three hits at the waterline midships, sir,' he said. 'Number four and five guns overturned and the crews dead or wounded, all. As for the foremast ...' he needed only to gesture towards the fo'c'sle, where a party of men had just thrown their dead over the side and were returning to their labour of chopping free the tangle of broken wood, sailcloth and cordage. 'And the fire in the heads has been put out.'

'Is she making much water?' asked Oakshott, mindful of the potentially greatest hurt to his ship.

'Henshawe's down below with the damage repair party, sir.'

'Well, bless him, the stout fellow,' murmured *Daisy*'s captain.

'Here comes the Frog again, sir,' said Brewster.

The enemy frigate, having done a turn, had crossed the *Daisy*'s stern and was making to pass along the sloop's port side. There were men in her tops and they were shortening sail – a clear indication that the French captain, having delivered two stunning blows, was now prepared to sail alongside the smaller ship and slog it out to a finish with his superior armament, or send over a boarding party.

'Get below on the gundeck, Number One,' said Oakshott, 'and if I'm hit, take over command again. Try to get away if

170

you can. Failing that, make it a fight to the finish. Need I say more?'

'King George waters and provisions me, sir,' responded the American. 'While I sup at his table, I'll never strike his ensign.'

They shook hands. 'Good luck to you, Brewster,' said Oakshott.

'And you, sir.'

The moon had risen and by its thin light Oakshott could quite clearly make out the shapes of the men on the French frigate's deck and up in the tops. The enemy had so reduced sail that they were now only creeping up slowly; a bare half-musket length separated the two vessels and the Frenchman was fine on the *Daisy*'s port quarter.

'What fools they are,' mused Oakshott aloud. 'By relinquishing their superior speed, they've tied one arm behind their back!'

He waited a little while – till the frigate's long bowsprit was almost level with his counter – and then ...

'Hard-a-starboard, helmsmen!' he cried.

The two quartermasters – augmented by Oakshott's servant Bantock – hauled upon the wheel and the *Daisy* turned in scarcely more than her own length. Oakshott rushed to the quarterdeck rail and called down to Brewster at the guns:

'Number One – I'm crossing his T! Fire your starboard battery when you bear!'

'Aye, aye, sir!'

Caught entirely by surprise, the Frenchman scarcely knew what was happening until his smaller opponent, turning away and doubling behind his back so to speak, suddenly cut across his stern. The gunners on the depleted starboard battery of the *Daisy* had the fierce pleasure of seeing the glazed and ornamental stern gallery of the frigate pass across their gun ports – and they gave fire with a vengeance. Seven 16-pounder balls, loosed in succession, burst in through the enemy's transom and pounded on through, causing indescribable mayhem during their violent course to the for'ard end of the ship.

The *Daisy* maintained her track, still beyond the bearing

of the Frenchman's guns. There was obviously considerable confusion aboard the latter, for they made no attempt to turn broadside-on and shoot.

In that passage of arms, the score was seven hits and no returns!

Inspired by the same idea that had occurred to Brewster on a previous occasion, Oakshott decided to seek the shelter of the shoaling shore, contingent upon which he turned sharply to starboard and shaped course to circle the Frenchman, cut across his bows (delivering another libation *en passant*), and run due south before the wind.

The enemy frigate which, if its subsequent actions were anything to go by, must have gravely suffered from the *Daisy's* crossing the T, made no move to avoid when the neat little sloop-of-war (which, notwithstanding her slower speed and the damaged foremast, was more spritely in manoeuvre than the larger vessel) cut close across its bows, delivered a broadside into the heads and brought down the long and elegant bowsprit.

'Steer due south!' cried Oakshott. 'Sing out when you sight the shore. No soundings – we'll take her so close that we could get out and walk ...

'*Oh, suffering Jesus!*'

His blasphemy was inspired by the sight of two more frigates appearing ahead on his starboard bow. They were both sailing roughly abreast and shaping course to intercept the *Daisy*; it was out of the question that they could be other than French.

And the first frigate was moving up on his port quarter, making more sail in order to draw abreast of the audacious sloop.

Trapped! ...

In the star-bright night he could see the lines of guns trained upon him, and having no recourse but to give way to the newcomers and steer away from the shore, he was immediately faced with the hazard of being hemmed in on both sides – two to starboard and one to port.

Oakshott leaned over the rail. 'Number One!'

'Sir?'

'Issue cutlasses!'

'Already being issued, sir!'

Oakshott grinned. 'I might have guessed, Number One, that you would have the same – or similar – notion.'

'*Fortis fortuna adiuvat* – I need not translate, sir.'

'Right you are, Number One! One exchange of broadsides with our friend to port, then we grapple and board her. And I hope to see you again in either Portsmouth or Paradise!'

'You shall, sir, you shall!' Cheerfully.

A powder-monkey, one of those told off by Brewster for the task, staggered up to his captain with arms full of heavy-issue cutlasses. He took one from the lad, though without much enthusiasm; his sword play he had greatly neglected, though instructed in his youth by some of the finest of French fencing masters.

The first frigate was jockeying into position on the port hand, obviously with the intent of firing a broadside in concert.

'Give fire, port battery!' shouted Oakshott. And, without pause, to the wheelsmen: 'Close alongside for boarding the enemy!'

Now his whole world was cocooned in fire and sound and stinking gunsmoke. He felt rather than saw the death blows that the two newcomers delivered to his ship as they closed at point-blank range; his own broadsides mingled with the rest, some shots rebounding off wooden walls and careering back, or striking mast-high stalagmites of tortured water. And, over all, the screams and entreaties of hurt men.

The higher side of the first frigate drew close. He saw a massive figure – it was the giant Mudge – poised to throw a grappling iron on the end of a stout line; marked how it landed true and held fast. A fierce dominance surged through the very core of his being, and he gripped the cutlass hilt more tightly.

This was what he had been made for. This was the meaning of his life, what fate had ordained for him, the apogee of his whole being. A wild exultation cleansed him of fear. He leapt for his enemies as a swain to his loved one's couch, with a yell of triumph torn from his throat:

'*At 'em, lads!*'

173

A score of the *Daisy*'s men poured over the side and on to the Frenchman's decks, hacking and slashing as they went. They were met by steel as sharp as their own, and a hail of musketry. Many fell out of the first wave, but others took their place; the cannonade finished, gunners abandoned their pieces and poured up from below, grabbing cutlasses as they came, or bearing ramrods and brass-tipped searchers. Like the first wave, they fell in their dozens, cursing their enemies with dying breaths.

Oakshott won his way to the frigate's quarterdeck, where he witnessed the stark evidence of the *Daisy*'s deadly gunnery that had been honed to perfection in the sweat of long practice: the very planking was scarred in deep furrows, the dead were piled high and the scuppers brimmed.

There was a fellow in the habiliments of an officer: he might have been the frigate's captain, a man of about Oakshott's age. He wielded one of the long, curved sabres much favoured by the French; with this he delivered a slash to the neck that would have cleanly decapitated the Englishman if the latter had not made a high parry, followed by a point to the chest. Oakshott felt the weapon jar against bone and then go on. The Frenchman fell in a torrent of crimson, and the way ahead was clear to Oakshott's next opponent.

The fight – butchery – surged to and fro across the frigate's decks, with the advantage favouring either side at random: here, a particularly outstanding performer – enjoying a brief success by reason of strength, skill, or bravery – or all three – might fire his comrades with his example, only to be cut down in his turn and trampled over in a new tide of brief victory.

With no aim in sight but to fight and to survive, Oakshott presently found himself right by the frigate's shot-scarred stern. A boy officer – a Frenchman – was leaning against the taffrail, supporting some great hurt; livid countenance bowed against his chest, eyes closed. Oakshott had the impulse to dispatch him out of his agony with a clean stroke of the blade, but a gentler instinct prevailed; tucking his cutlass under one arm, he reached out to support the youth when the latter made as if to fall. Upon his touch, the young

174

Frenchman's eyes flashed open and blazed malevolence at the sight of an undoubted enemy. In his glance, Oakshott saw the revolutionary fanaticism that had swept away the Bourbons and put half of Europe to the torch. The vision struck him so forcibly that he did not see the dirk which the youth carried in his right hand – not till it was driven at his chest with a frenzied energy that belied the other's own grave wounds. He parried the thrust with his bare forearm and saw the blade score a scarlet furrow there. Next, a massive hand enveloped his would-be killer's face and turned it round. He heard the neck snap like a carrot – and beheld the grinning countenance of the giant Mudge.

'For that timely service, much thanks, Mudge,' said Oakshott.

'Sir,' said the big man, relaxing his hold and allowing his victim's body to slip to the deck, 'I'm thinking that we be coming to the end on't.'

'I think you're right at that,' conceded Oakshott.

'The old *Daisy*, she be going, sir.'

'By heaven, you're right there, also, Mudge.'

Sure enough, the *Daisy*, holed innumerable times at the waterline on both port and starboard sides, was gently settling in the water. Flanked as she now was by an enemy ship grappled each side of her, more Frenchmen were teeming across her heeling decks to join the fray – which by now had become a mish-mash of sporadic duels raging from one end of the frigate to the other.

Possibly because of the presence of the giant Mudge, not an enemy saw fit to challenge the tall, dark man who stood at the taffrail and gazed at the death of his ship: his first and proud command, his true home and his dearly beloved.

She went with a certain elegance, like a dying swan; not clumsily awry, but with only the merest protest of snapping the lines that held her fast; a dipping at the bows, a sigh as her gundecks filled, and a low moan when the water surged into the quarterdeck screen and the stern cabin – *his* stern cabin – beyond.

'Goodbye, old ship!'

The dark waters closed over her coamings and she made the final plunge with scarcely a ripple to mark her passing.

When she had gone and touched bottom, there still remained the last few feet of her main topgallant mast to mark her grave.

'I fancy it's time for us to go also, Mudge,' said Oakshott.

'Reckon as how you be right, sir.'

'You have the biggest voice around, Mudge. Call upon all hands to save themselves who're able.'

'Aye, aye, sir.' The giant expanded his mighty chest, made a speaking trumpet of his massive fists and gave forth with a bellow that rose above the clashing of steel on steel, the combatants' shouts, screams of the wounded, and all else:

'Over the side with you, lads! – We'll fight another day!'

One by one, as they disengaged themselves, the men of the *Daisy* obeyed his injunction: leaping overboard, to take their chance in the dark waters. Presently, there was only Oakshott and his big companion remaining.

'Over with you, Mudge,' said the former, claiming his captain's privilege of being the last to leave. 'And good luck to you.'

'And you, sir!' Mudge was gone in a trice.

The French, observing that all but one of the crew who had so audaciously boarded them were gone, closed in upon Oakshott as he stood by the taffrail regarding them with his mocking, parti-coloured eyes; yet not one amongst the French could bring himself to strike down the lone figure, nor to put a pistol ball into him.

Oakshott departed with style. A graceful bow, a murmured *'Au revoir, Messieurs'* – and he vaulted over the side.

Once more, he was back in the old four-poster bed at Sennett Palace, with the view of the Iron Age horse carved on the hillside. And still dying, though they had had the thought to open the windows; leastways it was cool to the skin and the intolerable fever had lessened. Someone was lifting him up, supporting his head, murmuring to him ...

'Take a sip, sir, just a mouthful. Help build up your strength.'

Opening his eyes, Oakshott found himself looking up into the face of Pepe Lopez.

'Am I alive – or where?' he asked the apparition.

176

'But for big Mudge, you would be drowned, sir,' replied the other. 'That wound on your arm – you lost more blood than you knew. Mudge seized hold of you just as you were going down for the second time. Come – have a little of this ...' He was holding a crudely-carved wooden bowl, which he placed to Oakshott's lips.

The latter took a sip of the concoction within and, though it tasted like pulverized straw, to his starved palate it was flavoured with overtones of milk and honey, nectar and ambrosia.

He then observed that he was lying under a rough shelter constructed mostly of palm leaves. And he caught the murmur of voices coming from near at hand.

'How many of our fellows survived, Pepe?' he asked.

'We are eight so far, sir,' replied Pepe, 'but our friends are searching the foreshore, and others may be found alive.'

'Who are these friends?'

'Arabs, sir. A small party who have been used by the French like slaves. Set to dig wells to provide water for their fleet. They have escaped and are now with us. This food you eat – unleavened bread soaked in sweet water and flavoured with desert herbs – they are sharing it with us, together with dried dates. They are very hospitable, the Bedouin.'

'Who are the other six survivors?'

'Henshawe, sir. And Lieutenant Shacklock.'

'Good, good.'

'Mudge, of course. And three seamen named Wills, Topley, and Hammond.'

'Good fellows, all,' said Oakshott.

Lopez stared down into the bowl of slops. 'And then, sir – there are the dead who were washed up on the shore,' he said.

'Who?'

'Mr Cox, the bosun.'

'Oh, no ...'

'The sail master, Mr Quinch.'

'Poor old Quinch. He would have been retired on a pension now, but for the war.'

'Three other sailors – I do not know their names.'

'Officers?'

'No officers, sir.'

'No sign of the first lieutenant?'

Lopez shook his head. 'But, like so many of the rest, he may well turn up alive, sir. It is a long coastline, and the Bedouin are still searching. Come, sir – take some more nourishment.'

Oakshott cogitated upon the failure of his self-appointed mission. Not only had his so-called diplomacy failed, but in his proper task of being eyes and ears to the fleet, he had similarly miscarried. It spoke much of Oakshott's character that he never took into account his brilliant handling of the *Daisy*'s last battle against insuperable odds.

At length, Pepe took the empty bowl from Oakshott's lips and nodded approval.

'And now, sir, you will have a little sleep, yes?' he suggested.

Oakshott regarded his companion. It seemed to him that there was something that needed to be settled, and right away.

'Touching upon a conversation we had, Pepe – it was when we were riding towards the pyramids – concerning your future. Have you given it any thought yet?'

Pepe Lopez shook his head. 'Only that the march of events has released me from slavery, sir, and I suppose I could return to Las Palmas and pick up the strands of my old life – except that there are no real strands left.' He looked down at his slender hands, and Oakshott perceived that they were trembling.

'I think that would not be a good idea,' opined Oakshott. 'To try to reassemble your life as it was in Las Palmas could only lead to a kind of despair, for it could never be the same again. However, I have been thinking. You were once a merchant captain's secretary, and you must have been good at it, I should think. How does the notion of returning to the seafaring life strike you?'

The dark eyes regarded him; but they told nothing of what was passing through that guileful, clever mind.

'Opportunities in that line are few, sir,' replied Lopez, 'I am not likely to get an offer of a place.'

Oakshott grinned. 'Don't try to gull me, man,' he said. 'I am getting around to making you an offer – and you know it.

178

What do you think? Captain's secretary aboard a ship of the Royal Navy. Subjected to naval discipline. Dreadful food. Chance of getting your head blown off or drowned.

'Why do you tarry?'

The ex-slave's eyes were brimming, unashamedly, with tears of joy.

'I do not tarry, sir,' he said simply. 'I accept with all my heart.'

Oakshott's excellent constitution swiftly surmounted the hardships he had suffered. By mid-morning fed, rested and refreshed, he essayed to wander through the small encampment that the survivors had built in a shallow fold of ground just back from the shoreline, a place unobserved from the sea. All save Henshawe were on their feet. The ship's carpenter-cum-surgeon was still very weak, but he sat up and knuckled his forelock when his captain stooped to enter his flimsy lean-to of palm leaves.

'A sad day, sir,' said he.

'Yes, Henshawe,' replied the other.

'I never did a happier commission,' observed the older man, 'nor yet served in a sweeter ship. Mind you, sir, I were ever aware that she would not last out this war, on account of the death watch beetle as did inhabit her.'

Masking an impulse to smile, Oakshott responded: 'Yes, Henshawe, I remember you remarking on the fact – often.'

'I mark you did once tell me, sir, that the noise of the death watch beetle was not caused by the little devils acting as Old Nick's clock to mark off the days of they who listened, but was – I think you did say it was – a *mating* call.'

'I was so informed,' conceded Oakshott. 'And he who told me was a man of much learning.'

'Ah, learning, 'tis a wondrous fine thing, sir,' said Henshawe, who was quite clearly still totally unconvinced.

They were silent for a while, since both were essentially very reticent men, though Oakshott was the more complex and, despite his private soul-searching, less given to expressing his feelings openly.

Presently, Henshawe said: 'Permission to speak, sir – touching upon a matter very close to us the both?'

179

'Go ahead, Henshawe,' replied Oakshott.

'Sir, it do seem to me that, the Frenchie fleet being at anchor not so far off, it do offer a great opportunity for us to make a clatter – not a big clatter, mind you, sir, but mebbe only a small clatter – as will go some way towards avenging the *Daisy*.' He looked anxiously towards his captain. 'I trust as I haven't spoken greatly out of turn, sir.'

'By no means, Henshawe,' replied Oakshott, who was experiencing – even before the declaration was out of his companion's mouth – an opening up of the spirit and a wondrous illumination of the mind. 'No, you speak the very truth.

'And I have been a fool not to have realized it earlier.'

'How far is Abou Quir bay – where the French are anchored?'

Pepe Lopez pointed. 'Sir, it lies two or three hours' march to the west,' he replied. 'But, sir, there is danger there. Our friends tell us that the French have working parties ashore, and they have landed cannon to protect their ships form the landward side. With respect, sir, I would suggest you leave it till nightfall if you want to ...'

'We leave at once, and you will guide us, Pepe!'

'Aye, aye, sir,' replied Pepe Lopez, who was fast learning a lot about Charles Oakshott.

There were six men fit to march – and maybe to fight. Henshawe and Able Seaman Topley were incapacitated by general debility and wounds respectively; notwithstanding which, the ship's carpenter begged to be allowed to go; his comrades volunteered to carry him, two-and-two-about, navy fashion. Oakshott had not the heart to refuse the request.

'Off we go,' said Oakshott.

It was not an arduous march along the hard-packed sand behind the sandhills that fronted the beach, for though the noonday sun burned down cruelly, the onshore breeze was blessedly cooling to the skin. From time to time Oakshott himself went to the flank and, peering over the crest of the sandhills, searched for his first glimpse of the enemy fleet. An hour and a half after their departure from camp, he was rewarded by the sight of a line of bare masts strung out at the

180

western end of the wide bay and terminating near an islet lying off a promontory that marked the limit of the gulf.

He counted: thirteen of sail in line, and four frigates closer inshore – just as he had been told.

He returned to his men, and would not be drawn as to what he had seen, though it was obvious from his looks that he had sighted far more than seagulls and spindrift – as the saying went. Pepe Lopez cast him a sidelong glance from time to time, and remarked to himself upon the fighting light in his companion's eyes, how he chawed at his nether lip, bunched his fists, muttered to himself.

There is no telling with such a man, thought Pepe. He could aspire to take on the French fleet – just himself and the five of us!

Presently they came upon a ruined fort that must have dated back to the early days of the Turkish occupation; standing at the entrance to a lake that issued into the bay, it betrayed no sign of occupation when Oakshott and one of the seamen crept forward to make a reconnaissance. The two of them entered the mouldering walls and looked seawards, where the awesome sight of the French fleet was laid out before them in one vast panorama of naval might, and so close that every detail of hulls and rigging, every man on deck and what he was about, the very reek of the galley fires' smoke and the sound of voices was crystal plain to the senses.

'Convey my compliments to Lieutenant Shackleton, Hammond,' said Oakshott to his companion, 'ask him to bring the others forward, and I promise them a sight they will remember if they live to be a hundred!'

Henshawe, predictably, was a storehouse of remembered fact about the fleet displayed before them:

'See at the head of the line,' he said. 'That's *Le Guerrier*, she as we met up with in Biscay. Now, number eleven – no, twelve – she's *Le Mercure*, as put her bow-chasers into us and suffered a smart broadside in return. And I wouldn't go bail, but I've a notion that number eight's the eighty-gunner we sighted a while earlier.

'But see, sir – see – in the centre o' the line ...'

'She'll be *L'Orient*, without a doubt,' said Oakshott. 'A

hundred and twenty guns, and the biggest battleship afloat!'

Four frigates were anchored between them and the main fleet, and one was missing its bowsprit – mute witness to the encounter with the *Daisy* the night before.

'*They'll* not forget us in a hurry,' said Shackleton. 'By heaven, sir, if only there were something we could do to upset the apple cart.'

'We will do something to make a clatter,' declared Oakshott, 'even if it's not more than swimming out tonight and cutting a couple of cables. They haven't heard the last of the *Daisy*!'

It was about two o'clock in the afternoon.

With the heartening prospect of action at nightfall, the men of the *Daisy* settled themselves down for a rest in the cool shade of the fortress walls, leaving one of their number, Able Seaman Wills, to keep a lookout upon the enemy in case a shore party should put out. Wills, eighteen, former fisherman from Mevagissey and a pressed man, accepted his trick with a good grace – and all unknowing earned himself a small, and largely unrecorded, niche in the Royal Navy's annals of fame.

There was no rest for Oakshott; he lay in the shade, arm behind his head, his markedly analytical brain juggling with the possibilities that lay within his power – and he with only himself and four able-bodied men (Henshawe had to be discounted, and Pepe Lopez also), with not so much as a marlin spike between them by way of weaponry – to discomfit the French. And his fine talk about cutting anchor cables! – pah! – were they going to chaw through six-inch hemp rope with their teeth?

A fire-raft, perhaps? Made up of driftwood, piled high with dry shrub and pushed out to the centre of the battleship line? No – it called for more powerful combustibles than a peck of grass to set fire to a wall of matured oak – and they no longer had the means to light a pipe between them! Think again, Oakshott!

'Sir – beg pardon, sir.'

A stalwart young figure loomed above him.

'What is it, Wills?' he asked.

'Sir, there be a haze on the sea to the west, but I've half a mind that I see a sail out there.'

'I will come and have a look,' said Oakshott, getting to his feet.

In later years, when analysing those memorable moments of discovery, Charles Oakshott recalled that his first thought was of a French auxiliary – a brig or schooner, perhaps – bringing dispatches from the transports in Alexandria to the French commander in chief aboard *L'Orient*. On the other hand, whether from the assured wisdom of hindsight or from genuine manifestation of what the savants of the occult called the sixth sense, he seemed distinctly to recall a certain premonition that he was going to experience, that summer's afternoon in Egypt's golden strand, one of the most heart-shaking events of the eighteenth – or, indeed, any – century of the civilized world: a cataclysmic happening to be compared with Salamis, Thermopylae, Cannae, Senlac ...

'There, sir – a shade to the right of the headland,' said young Wills, pointing.

'You're right,' said Oakshott. 'I see it a – a full-rigged ship.

'A line-of-battle ship!'

'And another, sir! Another have growed up since I came to you!'

'Not just two!' cried Oakshott. 'There's a whole mass of sail out there!

'Count, lad – *count!*'

'Four – five – six 'n' seven – I see more than ten, sir!

'And all flying battle ensigns at the mastheads!'

'What ensign? Tell me swiftly, Wills – your eyes are better than mine!'

'The White, sir – *they're flying the White!*'

Captain and boy seaman stared at each other in astounded conjecture.

'*Nelson!*'

Masthead lookouts in the French battle-line had also sighted the oncoming British squadron: from the flagship, and rapidly spreading down the anchored line, there came the stirring sound of the silvery trumpets in which the Gallic soul so rejoiced.

'Aye – blow your trumpets,' said Charles Oakshott. 'But you had best save your breath for what lies before you!'

Eleven

They came in no sort of order, those thirteen of the line, for each captain knew his place, which in Nelson's axiom was to lay himself alongside an enemy; they jostled for places, like eager hounds, to be first at the kill.

'Tell them off, Henshawe!' enjoined Oakshott. 'You, who know the cut of every jib in the fleet. Sing out their names as they appear, do!'

The light airs bore them on slowly: time enough to enjoy a leisurely meal before even beating to quarters. It was coming up to five of the clock before the lead ship rounded the islet that guarded the western end of the bay and came under fire from guns that the French had set up in a ruined fort there. By this time, following a signal from the flagship, the front runners had sorted themselves out into single line, rounding the islet and heading for the van of the anchored enemy.

''Tis *Goliath* in the forefront!' cried Henshawe. 'Cap'n Foley! By all the saints, it were never in doubt but Cap'n Foley would be well in the van. I mind well the time when I served under him ...' He was launched into his reminiscences when Oakshott brought him back to the issue in hand.

'They all be seventy-fours and look much alike,' resumed the ship's carpenter. 'Number two I wouldn't take a wager on, nor yet three. I would half-hazard a guess four is *Audacious*, what had a new bow of astonishing rake after she did collide with the wall in Pompey, do you see it, sir?'

'I see it plain, Henshawe. Continue ...'

'I have me doubts on five.'

'Five,' said Oakshott, 'is *Theseus*. I served as a midshipman in her.'

The gunfire from the island, which had been by no means punishing, ceased as soon as the leading British ships were on the same bearing as the French, so it was in an air of majesterial calm that *Goliath* sailed straight for the head of the enemy line. It was then that Captain Foley's audacious move was made clear to the watchers ashore.

'By all that's holy,' breathed Oakshott. '*Goliath*'s going to place herself *inside* the French line!'

Not only *Goliath*, but the following three seventy-fours cut neatly inside the enemy's bulwark of defence, anchored themselves within pistol shot of the French van and opened fire. Nor were their broadsides immediately returned – for the French, never guessing that they would be taken from the shoreward side, *had not even run out their port-hand guns!*

'There be *Vanguard*!' cried Henshawe.

'*Nelson!*'

'I were at *Vanguard*'s fitting out at Buckler's Hard,' said Henshawe. 'I well remember ...'

Oakshott watched, enrapt, to see Nelson place his flagship on the outside of the French, abreast of the third in line. In swift succession, the following four seventy-fours slid up into places ahead. In the dying light of the evening, the front half of the enemy line was being pulverized from both sides. And there were still three more British ships coming in!

'It will be a massacre!' declared Oakshott, adding, with more truth than he knew: 'In all history of sea warfare there has never been a conquest as we shall see tonight!'

He added: 'And we shall play our part, my lads!'

Night and darkness turned the western end of Abou Quir to the likeness of one of the legendary inner circles of the damned. The thunder of the broadsides was constant and continuous; sometimes a single ship would carry the burden of the hellish dirge alone, next it seemed that every vessel in the bay was thundering in chorus. The dark of the night was lit up all the time – the more so when a ship of the French van suffered a fire which was not effectively quenched till midnight.

And there was much else done before midnight came . . .

Oakshott sized up the progress of the battle and appreciated the unique quality of a night action in an enclosed anchorage. Movement of ships was reduced to a minimum – and that only by the British, who permitted themselves the seamanlike elegance of springing upon their cables to be better positioned for their broadsides, whereas the French were committed to their static line. The death roll was tremendous: by nightfall, the glassy waters of the bay were afloat with corpses admixed with the flotsam of shattered spars and broken bulwarks.

'Amidst such chaos,' declared Oakshott, 'one could pass muster as a dead man in the water, climb aboard an enemy ship posing as a survivor, and – once established – be free to carry out whatever useful work presented itself.'

'Let's go, sir!' cried young Shacklock.

'And go we shall!' said Oakshott. 'Mr Shacklock, you'll take Hammond and Wills.' He turned to the giant at his side: 'You, Mudge, will come with me.'

Preparation for their foray was as exiguous as could be, for they had neither weapons nor equipment – and only rags in the way of clothing. In a pocket of his torn breeches, Oakshott still retained his half-hunter watch: this he gave to Pepe Lopez for safe keeping, privately enjoining him to make sure that, in the event of its owner's death, it was by some means or other to be passed on to his nephew, the young Marquess of Uffingham and Bow. For the rest, he had in the other pocket certain papers wrapped in waterproof oilskin; he toyed with the notion of handing these also to Lopez, but decided on balance to keep them with him come weal or woe.

The water was pleasantly tepid; given the absence of two monolithic fleets intent upon battering each other to perdition in the most frightful ways imaginable, he and Mudge could have been going for a swim in the serene backwaters of the latter's sweet-flowing River Dart.

His goal was the massive flagship in the centre of the French line which, now that its van was crumbling, had become the fulcrum of the shifting fight. As they drew closer

186

to the lurid glare of the battle line, the two Englishmen proceeded more cautiously; coming upon a piece of floating spar entangled with torn sail and cordage, they continued at a slower pace, pushing their screen before them and keeping their heads well down. In this manner they closed with the towering wall of the mighty three-decker which was engaging on her far side, and throwing herself into stark black silhouette with every discharge of her starboard battery. It occurred to Oakshott to pity the ship at the receiving end – whoever she was.

Their makeshift raft gently nudged against the lower strake of L'Orient, close by the ladder of steps set into her lofty side.

'We will split up now, Mudge,' murmured Oakshott in the other's ear. 'For in doing so we double our chances of remaining unobserved and unsuspected. You go first, at the next broadside. I'll follow. Good luck to you. Pick your targets carefully. Cause as much mischief as you are able. And stay alive!'

'Aye, aye, sir.'

The whole of that great ship shook beneath their hands as L'Orient almost immediately fired off a ragged broadside of her starboard guns, contingent upon which Mudge was three parts of the way to the top of the ladder while the choking white smoke of the discharges was blossoming; indeed he disappeared into the cloud and had gone from Oakshott's sight by the time it was dissipated.

Oakshott tensed himself, fingers and toes placed upon the ladder, for the next broadside ...

It may be thought that life aboard a major ship of war is rather like that in a village where everyone knows everyone else and his business; nothing could be further from the truth. In a ship the size and complexity of L'Orient, with a complement of over a thousand men, each confined to a certain mess deck and a specified set of tasks performed with the same group of shipmates; overcrowded, furthermore, and circumscribed to an almost unbelievable degree, with most of the remainder of the ship either inaccessible or prohibited, it was perfectly possible for a man to do, say, a three-year commission in the Red Watch living and fighting on the middle deck and be in total ignorance of his brother carrying on a similar existence in the Blue Watch on the lower deck. There was no shore leave for common seamen, no provision for general association and it was forbidden to hang around doing nothing in the fresh air of the open decks. As may be appreciated, service aboard a minor ship of war like the *Daisy*, with her concomitant freedom, was greatly preferred.

Naturally Oakshott, who had served in ships of every sort and size, knew all this. Furthermore, the navies of both Britain and France had long developed along similar lines as regards ship construction (the classic and much favoured seventy-fours of both countries were substantially identical, and frequently changed sides as prizes of war), while the routines of ship-handling, navigation, general seamanship and administration – not to mention gunnery – had been tried and tested by the two navies to similar conclusions. The language barrier apart, Oakshott knew full well that, no sooner had he thrown his leg over the coaming of *L'Orient*'s open deck, he would be at home, and as familiar as he would have been aboard any battleship flying the White Ensign.

And so it was ...

The next broadside saw him there: standing abreast of the mainmast on the side gangway of the waist that connected quarterdeck with forecastle. Below him, in the open span, he could see the starboard battery of the upper gundeck hauling in their pieces and sponging them out after the broadside. His vantage point, amongst the hammock nettings put there as shield against small-arms fire, was not a battle station and would swiftly draw comment; accordingly, he ducked down a nearby companionway leading to the upper gundeck. He was scarcely half way down into the gloom, acrid stink and smoke, when a British round shot – a 24-pounder – burst in through one of the gun ports on the starboard side, smashed a cannon from off its oak carriage and hurled both appendages, along with a deadly shower of razor-sharp wood splinters, into the men grouped around.

Amidst the screams of the wounded and dying, the turmoil and the hideous mayhem, no one paid the slightest notice to the English aristocrat and ship's captain – dressed as he was like any of them in filthy breeches, naked to the waist, barefoot, with a sweat rag wrapped around his brows – when he slipped past the scene and made his way aft. Nor did they notice when Oakshott stooped to pick up a pair of empty cartridge cases – cylindrical leather containers for the made-up gunpowder charges – which had fallen from the nerveless hands of a mortally wounded powder-monkey; these were to be his *laissez passer* aboard the French flagship.

At the head of the next companionway stood a marine sentry with bayonet fixed. As in capital ships of the Royal Navy, it was standard practice to have marines (acting as ship's policemen and adding not a cubit to their popularity with the seamen branch) thus stationed during battle, to prevent cowards from running to take cover below the waterline; their orders were not to argue the toss, but to kill. Oakshott, hefting his cartridge cases, joined a jostling, busy line of powder-monkeys hastening to descend. All were wild-eyed from their recent experiences, grateful to be going below, fearful of what might be their fate when they returned aloft; none of them was in the mood for conversation, and Oakshott passed muster with all the rest.

When he reached the middle deck the ship gave forth with another broadside, the effect of which in that confined space (there was a shade over six feet of headroom) was to compress the lungs to choking point and nigh split the eardrums. One more guarded companionway and a return broadside came inboard from whatever ship *L'Orient* was engaging. Some of the shots burst in upon this, the lower deck at the line of floatation, which carried the biggest guns in the ship, the 32-pounders. The bustling powder-monkeys, averting their eyes from the butchery thus caused, descended into the submarine orlop deck, where was housed enough black powder to blow up St Paul's Cathedral and a sizeable portion of the city of London.

There was the inevitable marine on sentry in the lamp room adjacent to the magazine. As the name indicated, the lamp room had in it a large lantern which, shining through a transparent screen, provided the magazine workers with enough light in their felt-lined coffin to load up the cartridge cases as they were presented through a trap-door.

The procedure was familiar to Oakshott, differing as it did in no way from that in his own navy: but for the first time he found himself contemplating the possibility of starting a small fire down there ...

On his way back up, he passed many vats of water positioned to deal with that greatest of all perils aboard wooden ships. At the first of these at which he found himself unobserved, he unfastened the leather lids of his cartridge cases and dipped both articles into the water. Regaining the middle deck, he then placed the containers in the centre line, snatched up two empty cases which were lying there and went back down to have them filled.

The puissance of the battleship *L'Orient* would be lessened, in very swift order, by two misfired guns – which could only be cleared by a fairly tedious and time-consuming procedure.

Oakshott took stock after an hour or so of this work.

It was all fine and large; but a dozen or so misfires were scarcely going to affect the issue of the great battle one way or the other; it followed that he must find another, and more rewarding, occupation aboard the enemy flagship.

The upper deck called: that was where the progress of the fight could be observed, and from there also it was directed. He was in ignorance, even, of the French commander in chief's name; but the fellow was up there on his quarterdeck. How to get close to him – influence his judgement, perhaps?

Kill him, perhaps ...?

The cartridge cases served him, as ever, for a passport to the upper decks. He found his way aft to the companionway that actually led up to that holy of holies the quarterdeck, which also accommodated a battery of light 12-pounders in the open. How to find himself the means to remain up there and do whatever mischief presented itself?

Think, Oakshott ... He crouched for a moment at the foot of the companionway, steadying himself against another shuddering broadside. His hand touched dampness on the deck. Blood. There was a lot of blood about, for several shots had come in – as evidenced by the gun flashes appearing through ragged holes in the wooden walls to starboard.

Inspired, he dabbled his bloodied hand against his hip and stomach, befouling his already filthy, torn white breeches that could never have been recognized as the elegantly-cut small-clothes tailored in London's Savile Row – their place of origin.

Still carrying the cartridge cases, but also hugging a simulated wound in the gut, the half-naked, ragged and filthy heir presumptive to the marquisate of Uffingham and Bow emerged on to the hallowed quarterdeck of the French flagship, and pitched onto his face in the scuppers.

So busily engaged were they that no one took the slightest notice of his precipitate arrival.

The battle, which had been joined just after six in the evening, had been raging for over three hours.

'*Est-il mort, celui-là?*'

Oakshott, lying on his belly, half in and half out of the scuppers on the starboard side of the quarterdeck, and so positioned that he could squint out of a drainage port aft at the British ship engaged close by, heard the question. It obviously related to him and was delivered in a mild – even kindly – voice.

In response to the query, a pair of hands reached down and turned him over. Oakshott, who had not the slightest wish to be thrown overboard as a corpse, contrived a muffled groan of agony.

'*Gravement blessé, je crois, mon Amiral!*'

The addressee, as if to assure himself that his aide was not mistaken, leaned over Oakshott, and the latter saw the quality of the French commander in chief: his countenance was cast in a gentle mould, and his eyes were large, dark and melancholy. A gold-embroidered uniform coat sat upon his light frame uneasily, as if it might have been fancy dress.

'*Avez-vous grand mal, mon pauvre ami?*' asked the admiral.

His French being unequal to the task of making a convincing reply to the question of his well-being, Oakshott merely groaned again. He was then left alone.

Alone, though surrounded by the turmoil of battle, with *L'Orient* diligently discharging broadsides every minute on the minute at their nearest opponent, Oakshott was able to size up the state of affairs aboard the flagship. There were significant differences between the manner in which certain matters were conducted in *L'Orient* and in any ship of war in which he had served. To begin: the British considered it inadvisable – putting it in its most practical terms – to allow wounded men to lie around bleeding and groaning on the decks in full view of their comrades; one presumed that the orlop deck of the flagship was too overcrowded to accommodate more casualties, but perhaps one was being over-charitable in that supposition. The French admiral had demonstrated a commendable solicitude, but he was an exception to an Englishman's received notion of the revolutionary French and the ardour with which they sliced off the heads of their own men, women and children for no discernible reason.

One had remarked on many occasions about the slackness of French seamanship in small matters: such things as leaving ropes and fenders trailing over the ship's side, allowing small-clothes to hang on washing lines when entering harbour, and so forth. Across the quarterdeck from where he lay there were large jars of oil and paint, and paint brushes, which had simply been abandoned when the call to action had sounded. Even aboard the old *Daisy*, that would have called for half a dozen strokes of the cat and demotion for some bosun's mate.

Oakshott's meditations were interrupted by another smartly-delivered broadside from *L'Orient*'s principal opponent of the moment: a seventy-four which had had the misfortune, or folly, to anchor herself abreast a ship of twice her tonnage and weight of shot. The seventy-four – unknown to Oakshott by her profile, and the name on her stern counter masked by the tangle of what had once been her mizzen mast and sail – maintained a steady succession of broadsides that out-matched *L'Orient* in both speed and accuracy.

But at what cost!

There was not a mast or a spar left standing on the British seventy-four; like gaps in a mouth of teeth, at least one third of the guns she presented to the enemy were out of action. God knows what horrors existed on her strewn decks. From where he lay in the alien scuppers half a musket range distant, Oakshott could discern two telling factors that spoke of the indomitable valour informing the unknown vessel's actions: regular and telling broadsides – and the battle ensign which streamed in the night air from the shattered stump of her mainmast and was illuminated with every lurid discharge of cannonade.

L'Orient was by now fairly ringed. Two latecomers arrived to challenge the French flagship: one sailed through the line astern of her and engaged her port quarter; the other took station behind the battered and dismasted seventy-four who had played David to Goliath for over an hour, and in doing so had assuredly blunted the sword of the mightiest battleship afloat.

Still firing, that heroic ship, crippled nearly to death, cut her cable and drifted away down the line to lick her wounds. As she passed close by, the wreckage at her stern slipped away – and Oakshott was able to read her name, limned in gold leaf upon her transom:

Bellerophon!*

There is a state in the affairs of men when even the most undiscerning and insensitive will be aware that a climax is approaching, and that nothing can ever be the same after. To Oakshott the Battle of the Nile, such a moment was informed by the departure of the *Bellerophon*, whose Captain Henry Darby had saved his life one long-gone night by bringing the frozen young midshipman down from the masthead of the *Mayfly* frigate.

The *Bellerophon* left with what remained of her guns still firing. Her last libation for *L'Orient* swept the quarterdeck, killing and maiming most of those standing there, including

---

*Though suffering the worst damage and casualties of Nelson's squadron, HMS *Bellerophon* survived to fight at Trafalgar, and received the defeated Emperor Napoleon in 1815.

the commander in chief, Admiral Brueys – he who had shown a moment of tender concern for the supposedly wounded man in the scuppers. For his part, Oakshott was showered by wood splinters where he lay, and also by a sizeable piece of burning wadding (so close was the range). Looking about him, and appreciating that no one was taking the slightest interest in his movements, he snatched up the burning wadding, darted across the deck – and dropped the combustible into one of the large paint jars standing by the mizzen chains. The paint was gratifyingly quick to ignite.

Moments later a party of marines appeared on the scene. They set to at throwing the newly-dead overboard and carrying the wounded officers below – Admiral Brueys included.

'Eh, toi – étiens ce sacré feu!' The order was bellowed at Oakshott by a surly marine sergeant, who also told off one of his own men to assist in dousing the fire.

The party went below, carrying the wounded. Oakshott and the marine were left to carry out an assignment about which it could be said that they had wildly conflicting interests ...

His companion was a big fellow, and capable-looking. Having sized him up, Oakshott, simulating an air of panic, seized a bucket of water and made as if to pour it into the blazing paint – while knowing full well that such a move could only scatter the oil-based conflagration over the deck. The marine was equally prescient: snatching the water from Oakshott and throwing it aside, he next took up a bucket of sand that had been placed for the like purpose and prepared to pour it on to the flames and douse them. It was an enterprise that faltered and died in the execution: as soon as his back was turned to Oakshott, the latter delivered what, in his midshipman days of roystering and dirty fighting with dockyard mateys in the wharfside taverns of Pompey and Devonport, had come to be known as a 'rabbit chop' to the back of the neck. The French marine went down – and there remained.

Triumphantly, Oakshott then overturned the blazing paint jar over the deck, noting with high satisfaction that the mizzen chains were already well ignited and that the flames were enveloping the rigging and ratlines as far up as the mizzen gaff.

Well satisfied, he picked up his cartridge cases and made himself scarce below.

The paint fire aboard the French flagship was noted by her nearest opponents, His Majesty's Ships *Alexander* and *Swiftsure*, anchored inside and outside the enemy's line respectively. Upon sighting the fire, both British captains predictably concentrated their attentions upon the source, rendering *L'Orient*'s quarterdeck totally untenable to her fire-fighting parties.

By half-past nine of the clock, the biggest battleship afloat was a blazing inferno abaft, and the encroaching fingers of destruction were probing their way downwards, through the decks.*

Lit by the flashes of the guns, the combatants continued with their bloody work through the night. By the time *L'Orient* was fairly ablaze, the van of the French fleet was overpowered. The ship at the head of the line, *Le Guerrier*, kept fighting for three hours, despite a total dismasting and repeated requests for her to surrender. At last, tired of the fruitless killing, Captain Hood of the *Zealous* sent one of his lieutenants over by boat to persuade the French to haul down their colours, and their single gun – the last aboard *Le Guerrier* – fell silent. Those astern of her: *Le Conquérant, Le Spartiate, L'Aquilon, Le Peuple Souverain*, were all taken and, renamed, spent many useful years sailing under the White Ensign.

But it was in the centre of the line, aboard *L'Orient*, that the high drama of the night – and the eventual outcome of the battle – was played out.

Near-panic reigned aboard the French flagship. Raked by leaden death from both sides, the upper decks – particularly

---

*The fire aboard *L'Orient*,which led to her destruction, was rightly attributed to the painting materials which had been left lying by the mizzen chains on the quarterdeck. The means by which they became ignited have never been satisfactorily explained – until now.

the quarterdeck where the British fire was purposely aimed – were virtually abandoned. The commander in chief mortally wounded and her captain killed, it fell to Brueys' chief of staff to make the decisions. His proposal to cut the ship's cable and allow her to drift away down the battle line (like the *Bellerophon*), was strongly opposed by the other officers on the ground that *L'Orient* would then become a fire-ship and a fatal menace to the remainder of the French fleet. A heated argument followed, during which time nothing was done.

And *L'Orient* continued to burn.

Admiral Brueys was dying.

The surgeon had amputated both of his legs and applied tourniquets. Brueys sent for an armchair from his day cabin, and caused them to carry him in it to the forecastle and set him by the foremast facing the enemy so that he could make some imaginary shift of directing the outcome of a battle which had long since passed out of his hands – if, indeed, with his inadequate preparations, there had ever been a chance of a French victory after Nelson took the decision to sail on to the attack in the gathering darkness, where a more prudent – and less successful – admiral would have anchored to await daylight.

So poor Brueys sat back in his armchair and awaited the end which had had the inevitability of a Greek tragedy from the moment that Captain Foley, by taking the *Goliath* inshore of the French line, had demonstrated the inspired intellectual vigour of Nelson's Band of Brothers and pre-determined the outcome.

Brueys contemplated all this in his armchair, with the grapeshot splattering into the foremast above his head, showering him with splinters. His aides now dead, or prudently departed below, the admiral was alone with his thoughts; half-fearing, half-longing for the clean hit that would end his agony.

But he was not quite alone. Something stirred at the corner of his vision. Painfully craning his neck, he espied a tall figure of a man who, having emerged from the companionway, was standing by the rail, as if gathering himself to jump overboard.

'*Eh, toi là bas – viens ici!*' ordered the admiral.

The man obeyed. Naked to the waist, his dark hair bound by a filthy sweat rag, he loomed over the doomed figure in the armchair, and in doing so presented his profile to the lurid glare of the fire that raged in the after part of the ship. Brueys recognized him at once – for it was not a face that one would easily forget.

'*Eh bien, tu n'est pas blessé du tout!*

'*Qui es-tu? Quel est ton nom?*

'*Réponds-moi!*'

'*Je – je m'appelle Oakshott.*'

The bland acceptance of the dying overcame Brueys' brief moment of incredulity upon hearing his mother tongue so unexpectedly delivered in the alien accents of Perfidious Albion.

'You are – English?' he asked mildly.

'Yes.'

'Officer?'

'Ship's captain, sir.'

Brueys winced – as a round shot came inboard, smashed through the elaborately-carved balustrading, tore a furrow along the foredeck and vanished over the far side in a fresh hail of matchwood.

'Is there anything I can do for you, Admiral?' Oakshott touched the other's shoulder. Brueys' head was bowed on his chest, his breath was laboured.

'There is nothing anyone can do for me, *mon ami*,' responded the admiral. He looked up at Oakshott, and those melancholy eyes were darkly shaded with a strange longing.

'A ship's captain, hein?' he repeated. 'I would die happy, Englishman, to have been just a ship's captain. To have had the responsibility for only my own ship – that would have been sufficient.

'But to have been the cause of – *all this* ...' He gestured for'ard, where the van of his fleet was by then largely overcome; he then pointed aft, past the blazing sternquarters of his flagship, to the rest of the battle line that had not a hope of escaping a like fate.

Oakshott regarded the hunched figure in the armchair with the shattered stumps of his legs stuck out before him, the slender shoulders which now bore the blame of certain defeat; and he speculated upon the quality of the man within, who had accepted that blame without complaint or self-exculpation, and awaited his end with gentle Stoicism.

'Admiral, I think that you are a brave man,' said Oakshott.

The pain-racked eyes closed. Brueys gave a tired smile. 'It is not enough, Englishman,' he murmured, 'being sufficient only for me.' Again he looked back at the flames, which were now mast high and had spread to the waist, from which men were already leaping overboard.

'Save yourself, my friend,' he said. '*L'Orient*, like her admiral, is almost done for.

'Shake my hand, Englishman.'

Their hands met in the fiery glare; Brueys' was like the delicately-boned corpse of a small bird.

Oakshott then turned and walked towards the heads; as he did so, the vessel on the starboard bow, HMS *Swiftsure*, with the deliberate intent of hastening the process of the flagship's abandonment, fired a broadside of grape and langridge across the Frenchman's decks. Oakshott felt the hem of Death's garment passing him close; when the smoke had cleared, he turned to see that Brueys no longer existed.

Plunging over the bow and hitting the water cleanly, he emerged and set off to swim to the *Swiftsure*; but had not covered two thirds of the distance before the night was rent by a cataclysmic explosion which reddened the sky from horizon to horizon and to the zenith all around.

Oakshott dived low and in doing so undoubtedly saved his hearing, if not his life: the shock wave of the explosion, and its thunderous reverberations, carried quite clearly through the water – though mercifully muffled.

When the clatter had ceased, he came to the surface. Debris of all sorts and sizes was raining down about him.

Of the French flagship, largest vessel afloat, there remained nothing but a hulk which, having in that brief while burnt right down to the waterline, overturned and sank with sullen slowness.

It was ten o'clock – perhaps a little later.

Envoi

The destruction of *L'Orient* was both the climax of the battle and the beginning of its end. So great was the horror that the mighty ship's terrible annihilation inspired among the men of both fleets that by a mutal consent the gunfire slacked and then died, and the gunners fell asleep, lying or standing about their weapons, worn out with their killing work – till their officers and petty officers moved among them, shouting and wielding their starters, and the firing recommenced; but it was never so intense again.

Nevertheless, when the sub-tropical daylight dawned, only two French ships of the line and two frigates still flew their colours and were able to slip away (the battleships and one of the frigates were later captured; one frigate, only, survived the holocaust of the Nile). The Royal Navy had taken eight capital ships; the rest were destroyed. The cost in blood amounted to 895 British killed or wounded; of the French, 5,225 in addition to 3,105 sent ashore on parole.

It was more than a victory; it was a conquest – Nelson's own words.

'Sir Horatio will see you presently, Commander,' said the young flag lieutenant with the self-importance of the young, handsome and well advanced. 'The surgeon is dressing his wound again at the moment. He thanks you, by the way, for delivering the letter.'

'Is the admiral greatly hurt?' asked Oakshott. They had lent him a threadbare undress coat aboard the *Swiftsure* where he had taken refuge and made himself known. This young sprig was eyeing him as if he were a rag-and-bone man come to the door; it rankled in his mind to feel irritation over something so trivial at such a momentous occasion; he put it down to tiredness.

'Sir Horatio was hit on the brow by a piece of flying shot, sir,' said the young man. 'We thought they had done for him, but the hurt is less grave than it looks. Do you mind waiting here for a few minutes? I'll be back.'

Left cooling his heels in the upper deck lobby leading to the admiral's quarters, Oakshott was interested to see that, though only mid-morning, the approach to the holy of holies no longer bore any signs of the battle save two neat holes punched in the side and a scarring of the deck. The light panelling was already back in place, and a ship's carpenter and his mate were busily letting in a piece of fresh teak where a French 12-pounder had scored a long groove.

'Oakshott! By all that's holy!' The speaker wore the braid and facings of a captain, and Oakshott knew him to be Berry, Nelson's flag captain. Only a couple of years older than he, this former shipmate was clearly destined for high advancement.

They fell to discussing the momentous events of the night; Berry was charitable enough to inquire of his companion's doings and expressed his condolences at the loss of his ship; while unconsciously conveying the message that the loss of one small sloop was picayune compared with the total destruction of the French; a pity – no more.

Whilst Berry enthused over the many individual triumphs of the ships of the squadron, Oakshott let his mind wander to the one great joy of his morning: when from out of the dawn there had appeared a small Arab dhow packed to the gunwales with waving, cheering ragamuffins. Standing in the stern, his hand on the tiller, was a tall, skinny vision clad with the utmost elegance in a brocaded khaftan, with a turban wrapped about his head and surmounted by a peacock's tail feather. By his side was a grinning black boy not dissimilarly dressed in high oriental finery. Tom Brewster had come back from the dead, along with a score of other *Daisy* survivors who had put ashore much further to the east of the delta; had been feasted to stupefaction by a band of anti-French Levantine fishermen and brought back to join their comrades. As an added bonus, Mudge also escaped from the doomed *L'Orient* in good time; he turned up aboard the *Swiftsure* in the uniform of a French marine corporal – but was characteristically reticent as to how he came by that attire. Young Shacklock and his seamen also survived their boarding of the second ship in the French line, *Le Conquérant*, and had witnessed the striking of her colours – after assisting in her defeat by sundry acts of surreptitious mayhem.

Oakshott smiled to himself ...

Berry took his expression for a token of his appreciation. 'Yes, last night's work puts paid to Bonaparte's ambitions in the eastern Mediterranean and any march to India,' he said. 'We've done well – and you not the least, my dear fellow. Ah, here come the other captains ...'

They had been summoned to the *Vanguard*, the victorious ships' captains, the Band of Brothers: Saumarez, Troubridge, Louis, Peyton, Ball and the rest; not Westcott of the *Majestic*, who had been killed; not Darby of the *Bellerophon*, wounded in the night's bloody shambles.

Oakshott inquired anxiously of Henry Darby – the man to whom he stood in debt, a long-standing debt, of his own life. Darby would survive for an admiralcy and a knighthood, they jested. And they were right.

'Gentlemen, will you please step this way.' The exquisite flag lieutenant stood aside to let them pass on through to the admiral's day cabin.

'Gentlemen, gentlemen – this has been a night – such a night!'

The victor of Abou Quir was seated in an armchiar in his day cabin; he rose upon their entrance and held out his left hand for them to take. Coatless, the stump of his right arm gathered in a pouch of the linen shirt, and with a bandage wrapped about his head and almost covering the almost sightless right eye that he suffered at Calvi, Nelson would have presented a pathetic spectacle had it not been for the almost iridescent fervour of energy with which he greeted the captains: wringing their hands, kissing one or other of his oldest comrades on the cheeks, talking incessantly:

'My dear Louis, what a support you were to me ... I marked you well, Payton ... Tom, Tom, my dearest Tom, how my heart grieved for you upon that unhappy shoal ... and Foley, what words could express the joy I had in your enterprise ...'

It was then, in the midst of his congratulations, that his glance lit upon Oakshott, and their eyes met across the sea of blue-clad, gold-braided forms between them.

'Lord Charles!' exclaimed Nelson. 'It has been a long time.' And he extended his hand.

'Sir Horatio,' said Oakshott, stepping forward to take it, 'may I subscribe my own congratulations upon your resounding victory.'

Nelson bowed acknowledgement and smiled brilliantly round his circle of captains.

'Gentlemen,' he said, 'some of you may know Commander Lord Charles Oakshott, with whom I have long been acquainted. He it was who bore certain secret dispatches to the court at Naples which led to our being allowed to water and provision in Syracuse.' His commanding grey eyes – even the near-sightless one held the attention – flashed with a sudden inspiration as, producing a letter from his shirt breast, he held it aloft. 'And this great service was performed, gentlemen – this stumbling block to our enterprise – was successfully overcome through the influence of Lady Hamilton, consort of our Ambassador in Naples. I have her promise here, in a letter she wrote brought to me by Commander Oakshott, that she would arrange it.'

Murmurs of appreciation followed this revelation. Oakshott thought back to the impressive woman who had descended to making something of an exhibition of herself with her 'attitudes', but then recalled the fervour of her apparent devotion to Nelson and the Navy in general, and all one had heard of her influence with the Queen. Yes, on balance, it seemed possible that Lady Hamilton might, indeed, have been the prime architect for bringing Nelson to Abou Quir bay at the eleventh hour.

'And Darby?' demanded Nelson, his quicksilver mind extending to details of the present. 'How is gallant Darby, and how the *Bellerophon*? I see you are representing your captain here this wonderful morning – er – is it Tew?'

'Tew indeed, Sir Horatio,' responded a youngish fellow close by Oakshott's elbow. Like Nelson, his head was also bandaged and there were lines of strain about his tired eyes. 'Acting First Lieutenant, sir. Yesterday, I was third ...' his voice faded away, and he looked down.

'Yes, you suffered greatly, Tew,' said Nelson gently, stepping forward and laying a hand on the young officer's shoulder. 'Two hundred killed and wounded. But, oh, my dear Tew, it was during the long hour of *Bellerophon*'s agony that the sword of *L'Orient* was broken – and the battle truly won.'

There were murmurs of accord from all round, in which Oakshott joined – for it was in that moment that he had formed a certain firm resolve ...

His name was again on Nelson's lips; he looked up from his reverie.

'Sir, I beg your pardon ...'

'I was saying, Oakshott, that I have decided to have the *Vanguard*'s repairs effected in Naples. You shall accompany us.' The admiral smiled. 'I expect you will be pleased to see that fascinating city again. And during the voyage, you must tell me something of your exploits. How, for instance, you came to be here in Abou Quir ...'

Alone on the *Vanguard*'s poop deck, Oakshott looked out across the anchorage. White Ensigns now fluttered bravely from the captured prizes; the survivors of the *Daisy* had been remustered aboard these vessels to help bring them to Naples and elsewhere. Tom Brewster had been appointed senior Royal Naval officer aboard *Le Peuple Souverain*, with the commission to sail that ship with a mixed French and prize crew to Syracuse.

It was over – the long, hard trick was finished.

Two issues were now settled in his mind. First, the matter of settling his score with Henry Darby of the *Bellerophon*. To Darby, his men and his ship should have every credit they deserved for the sinking of *L'Orient* – and to hell with the handful of burning wadding that he – Oakshott – had dropped into that paint jar. No word of that would ever pass his lips, to lessen the glory due to Darby and the *Bellerophon*.

Secondly, he had not given Nelson the details of his self-appointed 'diplomacy' in Egypt, nor ever would. So far as Nelson was concerned, he had transported Gisborne upon a certain mission, and the envoy had died of natural causes in the commission of the same.

Put it this way, he told himself: in the face of Nelson's staggering victory – which would assuredly win him immortal fame and a peerage – it would cause Pitt the greatest public embarrassment – not to say obloquy – if it became generally known that, doubting the admiral's likelihood of catching the French, he had (what was the horse-racing term?) hedged his bet by dispatching Gisborne to intrigue with the Mamelukes.

'You are not without a touch of the diplomat, after all, Charlie,' he said to himself aloud.

In his pocket, still wrapped in the oilskin, he had Gisborne's letter of appointment and the accompanying memoranda which he had kept with him, together with Lady Hamilton's letter which he had delivered to Nelson. Taking them out, he shredded them into small pieces and threw them over the side into the Mediterranean ...

The sea that Nelson had won for England.